DIARY

of

LIES

There are lies.
There are truths.
In between is life.

BARBARA GURNEY

"A fellow who says he has never told a lie
has just told one."

\- unknown

Kate's Diary

1968

25 October: ...and the lies—tremendous scenarios—I've had to be totally creative. Even Stan wouldn't believe some of them.

Raconteur

A diary records the truth of a moment, usually emotional jottings, often cryptic, rarely revealing the full details.

Adaptations of the truth sneak into Kate Wallace's young life, where hints of her character hide. Can you spot them?

Chapter One
1955

Seven-year-old Kate pulled Benji into her chest. The teddy bear's tummy squashed against her pyjama top, a button caught on his thinning fur. She remained motionless, rebelling against her mother's insistent cajoling.

'We have to make the most of it, child. We're lucky to have been offered this job. And a room, of sorts.' Nora sighed, tossing her cardigan onto a camp stretcher pretending to be a luxurious bed. 'Better than being homeless—out on the streets. There are people with nowhere to go. Some even look like the *real* bogeyman.'

'But Mum, it's nearly Christmas. What if Santa doesn't know we're here, not at our proper home?'

Nora thought of the gifts she should have bought, the gifts she couldn't afford due to her husband's complete lack of awareness of the plight he'd created. Nora didn't know how one was supposed to fully explain finances to a child who, in the past, had received an excess of gifts from Santa and her parents. Not without bursting the illusion of Christmas.

'Of course he will. Santa's got lots of elves who keep track. Don't worry, he'll find you. Although... things are tough even for Santa.

1

You can't expect...' Nora shook her head at the vagaries of life, where a husband could disappear overnight, and a comfortable home became an asset for the bank almost as quickly. 'Things are different this year,' she said.

'But Mum, I've asked him for a walkie-talkie doll. All the girls at school have one.'

Keeping her rising anger at bay, Nora said, 'You'll just have to wait and see. But don't go counting chickens before they hatch. Even Santa can run out of money.'

Nora Wallace and her daughter Kate had moved to an empty room at the back of Chidley House, a lodging house owned by sisters Alice and Clare Chidley. The room, previously a laundry in the days when the weekly wash was done in a separate outbuilding, had a small window and a recently repaired wooden door. The internal fireplace and copper, once used to boil the clothes free of dirt and germs, had been removed. The remaining outer structure of the chimney could only be observed by standing hard up against the fence and on tiptoes if you were of a shorter stature. Fortunately, this particular laundry had a toilet attached. However, occupancy could be easily noted as only one door hinge still worked. A concrete wash trough, previously used to rinse the clothes, was now used for bathing.

Kate had to bend her knees so she could fit in the trough for her perfunctory daily bath while Nora managed with a bucket wash. Alice Chidley permitted them to use the facilities in the main house twice a week. Their two camp stretchers filled the space at the far side of the ten-by-twelve-foot room. After they had been there for about a month, Clare Chidley offered them two kitchen chairs and a wooden box, which, turned on its end, made do as a table.

Santa only brought a skipping rope, coloured pencils, a toothbrush, and an orange. Nora bought her daughter an almost-new Barbie doll and three books from the Cantonment Street Op Shop, promising to take Kate to the beach on Boxing Day as she had Christmas lunch to help prepare.

Christmas Day arrived. After a meagre breakfast and the disappointment of Santa's efforts, Kate lingered outside the kitchen door as lunch preparations continued.

Then, with Miss Chidley overseeing the proceedings, lunch began with grace, followed by a toast to the Queen, and with Kate being reminded to watch her manners, they all tucked into the luxury of roast turkey, ham, crunchy potatoes and beans. After plum pudding and creamy custard, the adults retired to the sitting room with a small sherry or a beer.

Kate refused to play with Barbie, shoving the doll into the bottom of the only wardrobe in the washhouse. The books kept her amused until Nora demanded she help by putting the clean dishes away.

Christmas soon became an unremarkable memory and Kate slept through the distant celebrations of New Year, waking each following morning hoping *something* would be different.

It was the same most mornings. Nora would prod her forefinger into the thin arm of her daughter and yell like a drill sergeant, 'Katie, get out of your bed. It's time to go to the kitchen. Come on, child, hurry up. There'll be no breakfast if you don't get there before they finish up.'

Kate usually endured this first issue of commandments, longing for a few more minutes under the bedcovers.

'Look here, get up at once. Katie, for God's sake. Hurry up, child. I'm starving. Katie, get a move on. Do you want to get the strap?'

Waking up to the raucous voice of an angry parent didn't make for a good start to any day. Kate put her skirt and blouse over her pyjamas and hurried after the bulky frame of her mother.

Despite wobbling against the narrow passageway between the walls of the outer buildings, Nora could move quickly when she wanted to.

Leaving the confines of the room she had to call home for a second time each morning, Nora would arrive in the boarding house kitchen out of breath but eager to find a plate that she would overfill with sizzling strips of bacon and creamy scrambled eggs.

There was no welcoming chatter from Nora Wallace as she plonked her ample bottom down on a kitchen chair. Only after a mouthful or two would she look at the other occupants of the room.

'Good tucker,' she would acknowledge to Doris, who was standing by the stove as if she couldn't move until she'd received the daily compliment.

'Good tucker,' Nora repeated as she nodded to all those at the table one at a time—between mouthfuls that weren't fully digested.

This morning, Kate nibbled on cold toast made enjoyable by a generous portion of homemade marmalade.

'Katie, don't take so much. Katie, sit up straight.'

'Leave the blighter alone, Nora, she's hungry too.' Doris plopped a fresh piece of toast on the child's plate.

'Don't you go giving her ideas. She's got to do as she's told. Katie, for Christ's sake, stop dripping the marmalade down your front. Who do you think will have to wash the blessed thing?'

Kate hunched her shoulders and dropped her head into her chest. She looked at Doris for support, which wasn't forthcoming. Nora Wallace scared everyone at least a little.

The boarding house had three regular occupants. Miss Beryl Tillman, a recently retired schoolteacher, told anyone who cared to listen that she came from wonderful English parents who had the misfortune to die young but fortunately well off enough to leave their daughter sufficient money to start a new life in Australia. Her teaching had provided her with the only satisfaction to be gained in the country she considered backward. Now she was deciding if she should spend her savings on returning to Manchester to live near her cousin or investing in a small house in one of the newer suburbs near Perth. At this point of Miss Tillman's repetitive dialogue, most people scraped their plates clean and voiced an urgent need to return to whatever they'd been doing before the meal.

Kate cringed as her mum tapped the table with the end of a knife. She'd listened to her mum speak her mind often—and wished she wouldn't.

Miss Tillman paused mid-sentence.

Kate wanted to slip under the table, but that would only cause another barrage of demands from her mum.

Before Miss Tillman could continue, Nora sighed unduly loudly.

Kate knew her mum regularly complained about the repetitive stories of England versus Australia and would say so without beating around the bush.

'Bloody hell, Beryl. Surely you've decided by now. Return to the snow and bloody freezing winters, will you? You don't know when you're well off. For Christ's sake, stop complaining.'

Miss Tillman looked at the flushing face of the cleaning lady and spoke with an accent not used so strongly for some time, 'I'd prefer you to call me Miss Tillman, Mrs Wallace. And without the use of vulgar words.'

'Go on! It's not the eighteen hundreds. You're in bloody Australia. It's 1955. I'll call you Beryl, and you'll have to like it or lump it.'

Kate looked at her mother and wondered why she always made people frown and why this house never felt like a home. She didn't remember feeling like that when they lived with her father. When they had a little house in Bassendean near the train line. When Daddy came home every day. Although she did seem to remember that Daddy and Mummy only smiled at her, never at each other. Seven-year-old Kate couldn't work it out.

Boarders number two and three were brothers.

'Brothers! I bet me last pair of knickers that they're not bloody brothers,' Nora said to Doris during a gossip session when they were supposed to be finishing off the weekly cleaning of the men's bedsitter.

The two men, one tall and rangy and one of medium height with thick arms to match his waistline, had been living in Chidley House for nearly two years and they enjoyed the convenience of having much of their chores done for them.

Doris returned to the bed-making, shaking out the blankets

before replacing them over clean sheets. She giggled at Nora's choice of words. She still hadn't decided if she liked this woman who was employed to do the cleaning of the boarding house and help in the kitchen, in return for lodgings. *Calling a spade a spade is all right for some,* Doris thought uncharitably, *but I always prefer to give people the benefit of the doubt.*

'Don't see that it matters,' Doris said.

'Of course it matters. I'll not have a child of mine being brought up around *that* sort.'

'See here, Nora, *they* told me they're brothers, and I'm sure Miss Chidley would have asked them before she agreed to have them stay here.'

'Alice wouldn't know if her bleached curls were on fire.'

'Now that's going a bit far. Miss Chidley has been good to you. Look at you and the little one. Where would you be if you had to fend for yourself?'

Nora ceased sweeping and leant heavily on the broom. She frowned as she spoke, 'Haven't a clue where I'd be if I wasn't here. Couldn't afford rent without the job. And Kate, what'd I do about her if I did have another job? After school, like?' She pushed the broom forward. 'You're right, Doris. Time I bit me tongue and got on with this here sweeping. But I still can't help but think they're not brothers.'

'Well then, you'll be safe without your knickers!'

Nora struck Doris playfully on her shoulder, and the work seemed easier as they giggled each time they caught each other's eye.

The two men *were* brothers, but the family resemblance ended with their names. Stanley Blennerhasset looked like his father and maintained his athletic build by disliking anything sweet. To make up for the refusal of his brother to try any of Doris's puddings, Syd would often volunteer to enjoy second helpings.

Stan walked a couple of miles to the office where he worked as a clerk in a furniture warehouse, while Syd managed to toddle out the front door and catch the bus to the factory where he candled eggs. He was proud of every day his supervisor didn't have to discard any inferior egg missed by the eagle-eyed Sydney Blennerhasset.

Most days after work, he would get off the bus a few stops early and down a pint of Guinness at the Freemason's Hotel before catching another bus home. 'Can't wear out the shoe leather,' he would say, echoing his Irish mother's catchcry. No wonder he took after her generously proportioned side of the family.

Within a few days of arriving at Chidley House, Kate decided both Mr Blennerhassets were not at all too bad.

No matter how many questions Kate asked about why she and her mother couldn't go home to their real house, why she couldn't have a room of her own, why they didn't have a bathroom, but most of all, why her dad no longer lived with them, Kate couldn't comprehend the reluctant and insufficient explanations given by her mum.

Kate missed her dad's teasing, the occasional treats he brought home, and the trips to the beach. Most of all, she missed the bedtime stories he read, even though he sometimes slurred some words— usually the times he came home when she was almost asleep.

And now Syd and Stan filled a corner, a tiny corner, of her longing.

She had difficulty saying their name and as it was too confusing to have two men being called the same anyway, they told her she could be all grown up and call them by their first name. Nora scolded her for her insolence, so Kate stopped calling them by any name in her mother's presence.

'Mum, the tall man said I could have this marble.'

'Mr Blennerhasset. It shouldn't be difficult, child. Say blenner.'

'Blenner.'

'Say hasset.'

'Hasset.'

'There see, it's easy. Say Blennerhasset.'

'Bledderhasset.'

'Blenner Hasset!'

'Beller Hasset. Sorry, Mummy. Bledderhasset.'

'Stone the crows. An idiot, I have. Blenner, blenner, say blenner, Katie.'

They both gave up.

Kate realised her mother's plump shape echoed Syd's body type, and there'd be hell to play if she described the brothers as the skinny one and the fat one. So, they became "the tall man" and "the short man" when she spoke about them to Nora.

Kate wasn't sure about Miss Chidley, who demanded courtesy from all her boarders, insisted they remember who owned the establishment, and never left her *boudoir* without donning substantial quantities of cosmetics. Some days, Miss Chidley, who seemed old to Kate, would be pleasant enough but other times, she would treat Kate as a nuisance.

One time, Kate was sitting on the floor in the front room, looking at a book full of pictures from the other side of the world. Kate loved the ancient buildings of Rome and the blue seas of Spain that lapped against squat brown cliffs. It didn't feel like geography homework when Syd and she poured over the white cliffs of Dover or the plains of the Serengeti.

Syd took time to find an atlas and point out the "boot" of Italy and how many tiny countries of Europe fitted into the equivalent expanse of Australia. Fascinated by the comparison, she declared nothing could take much longer than the train trip from Bassendean to Fremantle.

When Syd explained how long it would take from Perth to the town that had been named after him, she insisted on proof. Patiently, and with the aid of a map with dicey fold marks and a ruler, Sydney Blennerhasset proved travelling time could be endless.

Absorbed by the beauty of a glossy page full of cherry blossoms, Kate's hand jerked when Miss Chidley entered the room with her voice in full throttle.

'What have you got that child learning now,' Miss Chidley said, indicating displeasure. As she passed, she clipped Kate ever so slightly on the side of her head. 'You should be in your room doing your homework.'

Kate looked at Syd, frowned in question. She was allowed in the main house, but her mum constantly used a confusing phrase that slightly worried Kate. 'Don't abuse the privilege, child. You don't want to overstay your welcome.'

Miss Tillman, Syd and Stan always made her feel welcome. The dictionary had shown her what privilege and abuse meant but the descriptions were hard to relate to their situation. She continued to opt for silence rather than say the wrong thing and tried hard to go unnoticed, returning to her stretcher bed only when Nora yelled a third time.

There was no homework to be done. Kate gripped the edge of the book cover and looked up at Syd, silently asking for direction.

'Don't worry, young'un, you stay as long as you like.' Syd glared at the disappearing Miss Chidley.

Kate returned to the pages of the book on her knee. When Miss Chidley walked back into the lounge, Kate sat perfectly still. She imagined a lack of movement would make her a statue that could be ignored. It was a practised art of a child who sensed attitudes before they were voiced. However, Miss Chidley stepped around Syd's feet and leaned over Kate. Kate held her breath.

'Here you go. Straight out of the oven. Don't burn your mouth.'

Kate put the book aside, took the warm rock cake with her fingertips and then dropped it into her lap. 'Thanks, Miss Chidley.'

Alice Chidley paused as she pushed open the ornate glass door of the room; she turned and said, 'Don't forget to pick up any crumbs.'

Kate offered to share with Syd, but he was already on his way to the kitchen to badger Doris for one of his own. Kate looked at the small sugar-topped cake and then toward the ceiling. Miss Chidley's footsteps could be heard clearly as she climbed the uncarpeted stairs.

'There you go, young'un,' Syd said as he devoured his second rock cake. 'She's a conundrum that one.'

Kate nodded but didn't really understand what Syd meant.

Kate liked Miss Tillman.

When Kate returned home from school, she would change out of her school uniform and go into the kitchen for something to eat and drink. Sometimes, Miss Tillman would invite Kate to join her in the small sitting room next to the dining room, encouraging her to talk about her day at school.

'What did you learn today, Katherine.'

Kate liked being called Katherine by Miss Tillman. No one else called her that.

Nora had complained to Miss Tillman, 'Now see here, Beryl, I named her. You can't go calling her whatever you like. Kate's her name. You should call her by her rightful name.'

'Mrs Wallace, Kate is a derivative of Katherine. It's an old English name. Katherine means pure.'

'Well, big deal. Her name's Kate. Just Kate—no fancy highfaluting name. Now it's just Kate, or I'll be not letting her come in to talk to you again.'

The two ladies stared at each other before Miss Tillman dropped her eyes to glance at the child scrunched up in a lounge chair with her arms tightly wrapped around her legs.

'Nora, it's all right for you to call *me* a name I have asked you not to, but I can't have the same liberty with this child who will blossom with the correct nurturing.'

The pause as the two women glared at each other, had Kate

holding her breath. Then, with a humph of insolence, Nora stormed off, dragging a reluctant but silent Kate with her.

I'd like to be Katherine, thought Kate as she slumped over the rickety wooden box substituting for a desk. *It sounds like a name for a lady. A lady who has servants and a great big palace.*

As "Just Kate" did her homework, she wished she could be Katherine Rebecca or maybe Katherine Suzanna. *"Just Kate"! How horrible.* After eating a cold meat sandwich and drinking a glass of milk alone, she went to bed. She dreamed of staircases with gold steps, long dresses, and people calling her Miss Katherine.

Chapter 2

Two days later, Miss Tillman put down her knitting as Kate entered the room rubbing her too-full belly.

'Well, "Just Kate". Can you keep secrets?' Miss Tillman patted the seat next to her. 'Come. Sit.' She nodded. 'Yes, I suppose you can. You probably have many secrets. Now, what do you think? Can you... can you keep a secret?'

Kate sat, swivelled sideways so as not to miss any part of a grown up's secret. 'Yes, Miss Tillman. Mummy says I must keep lots of things to myself.'

'Really, child. And you don't tell anyone?'

'No, I wouldn't.' Kate fiddled with her skirt's hem. 'Mummy would use the strap.'

Miss Tillman drew in her breath. It was true many parents used a strap or wooden spoon as punishment, and several of her fellow teachers had used a cane on wayward boys in the past, but this tall child of seven didn't seem capable of doing anything worthy of a strapping. *Secrets... well that's a different story*, she thought as she patted Kate's knee.

'This secret is just for us. Now come closer. A secret has to be whispered.'

Kate wriggled along the couch but didn't dare sit too close.

'Would you like to be called Katherine?'

Kate's eyes opened widely as she looked at Miss Tillman. 'Did Mummy say it's okay now?'

Miss Tillman put her arm around the child's shoulder and whispered, 'No, she didn't, but that's the secret. I will call you Katherine when we are alone. Would you like that?'

Kate slipped from the chair and stood facing Miss Tillman, her eyes full of disbelief. She wriggled her fingers against her legs. 'It's a secret... from Mummy?'

'Yes, but only if you would like to be called Katherine.'

Kate held out her skirt, twirled twice, then skipped across the room. 'Katherine, Katherine,' she sang softly.

She ran over to the chair and threw her arms around a startled Miss Tillman. 'Yes, please. Oh! Yes, please. I don't want to be "Just Kate". I want to be Katherine.'

'Well, my dear, maybe you will be a famous Katherine one day. In the meantime, perhaps we can read about your famous namesakes. Let's see, who do I remember? Ah, yes. King Henry's first wife, Katherine of Aragon, and the gorgeous Miss Katherine Hepburn. I'm sure we can find something at the library. Now come here, bring your book. Read your homework to me.'

A tiny smile emerged with the turning of each page as Miss Tillman listened to the story in The Happy Venture Reader. But as they headed into the dining room for dinner, the newly appointed Katherine worried her mother would know she had a secret. Keeping her head down and eating quickly, she couldn't help sneaking a look at Miss Tillman every so often.

'Just what are you up to, Kate?' Nora asked as she took the empty soup bowl from her daughter.

'Nothing, Mummy.'

'Mm, you seem a little quiet. If it's not mischief brewing, I hope it's not a cold.'

'No, Mummy.'

'Well, you had better eat your fish fingers and get away to your bed. You can read for a while if you're quick.'

After Kate had washed her face, hands and feet and cleaned her teeth, she flicked through a National Geographic. After absorbing the intriguing habits of a giraffe, only being caught out by the scientific data, she snuggled down into her bedclothes. 'Benji, say "goodnight, Katherine",' she instructed. She didn't think Miss Tillman would mind her teddy knowing about their secret. After all, Benji knew all her other secrets.

Stan Blennerhasset kept mostly to himself. No storytelling of younger days like Syd, no bearer of an insight into his past, and certainly no unnecessary dialogue. He didn't indulge in the after-dinner chatter, which often led to a friendly disagreement between Miss Tillman and his younger brother.

One evening, Syd had come home a little light-headed from having downed one extra pint of Guinness.

Doris's crusty beef and kidney pie had been to everyone's liking. However, Syd pointed out that the Freemason Hotel served bigger portions.

While everyone considered the size of the pie on their plate, Doris and Nora exchanged glances, rolled their eyes, and went back to finishing their dinner.

Minutes later, Doris stood, shoved her chair in and clunked her knife and fork on the empty plate. 'Bigger is not necessarily better,' she flung over her shoulder as she headed to the kitchen.

Chuckling softly, Nora rose. 'You'll be getting the smallest piece next time.' She knocked Syd with her elbow. 'You see if you don't,' Nora chuckled when Syd's fork missed his mouth and dabbed pie on his chin. 'Just finish whatever size you've got. I don't want to spend all night in that damn kitchen.'

Miss Tillman patted her mouth with the linen serviette while deciding if it was necessary to rise to Sydney's bait. Did the size of a slice of pie really warrant discussion? Stan, refusing to be involved, put his knife and fork down with a clatter, rose from his seat, and walked out of the dining room.

'I'm just saying one likes a good piece of pie. That's all,' Syd reiterated.

After folding the used serviette and dusting off imaginary crumbs from her navy-blue skirt, Miss Tillman placed her cutlery neatly across the empty plate, pushed her chair back slowly, and followed Stan into the sitting room.

Syd poked his finger at the last drop of tomato sauce on his plate, licked the spot from his finger, and noisily left the table.

Stan sat in his favourite spot—a well-used armchair next to the window where he could watch the passing parade. He never voiced his opinion about any of the people who distracted his mellow mood but often would grunt in seeming disapproval or chuckle without explanation. In the late evenings, he peered into the darkness as if imagining what could be happening outside his warm cocoon. With a shrug, he'd turn from the window, select a book and read until bedtime.

An observer might notice he returned the book to the overcrowded bookcase the same evening without a bookmark and replaced it with a different book the next night. One could never be sure if he lost interest in the book, or if he liked the variety of reading the opening chapters and then imagining the rest.

This particular night, Syd was still needling no one in particular about the size of his pie. Miss Tillman sat on the couch nearest to the front door. She, too, liked the options presented by the reading matter, which grew weekly after Miss Chidley's trips to a second-hand shop in Fremantle. Having read many of the books, Miss Tillman could discuss the plot, the characters, and the relationship the story had to herself in great depth with anyone who cared to listen—or even those who didn't. However, the couch by the door had poor light for reading and was not her usual choice. She anticipated Syd's need for a discussion over the pie and knew she wouldn't be able to concentrate on either her knitting or her reading until he had adequately presented his point of view.

Miss Tillman waited patiently. Syd would niggle away without encouragement from her.

'It's alright for you, Miss Tillman. Your frame doesn't demand a generous portion,' started Syd as he sat down on the other end of the couch, patting his girth that pushed against his shirt.

'If you say so.' Miss Tillman entwined her fingers, her eyes darting between them and Syd's mouth.

'I do say so. I do indeed. I'm not saying it was a mean serving, but the chef at Freemason's knows a chap my size needs a relative portion.'

Miss Tillman added she had more than enough pie and Syd should be content with the portion offered. Syd then huffed and puffed about the lumpy mashed potato while Miss Tillman moved her slight frame an inch to the left and back to the right again with every one of her counteracting comments. The two combatants nodded vigorously or shook their heads slowly to emphasise their remark. They never argued with any vitriol but jousted until one got tired of the game.

Miss Tillman was the one to finalise this squabble. She moved seats and took her diary from her large tapestry bag, which homed her knitting. Syd recognised the conclusion and said, 'All right, I give in, the pie was big enough.'

Stan remained silent and motionless throughout this light-hearted domestic tiff. He had certainly been witness to the regular banter between the two boarders many times.

Once Syd had removed his shoes and propped his size 10 feet where Beryl had been sitting, Stan rose from his armchair and stood next to the window. He leaned closer to the glass to see further up the street. 'Not much happening out there tonight.'

He didn't expect or receive a response. Miss Tillman was recording the day's monotonous events, and Syd's head lolled sideways towards a nap. Stan walked to the bookcase and chose a history book.

'Ah, yes, Prague. Let's see what it's all about back then.'

Kate was overawed with Stanley Blennerhasset. He towered over her, making her feel like an ant that could disappear beneath him and hide.

His silence also bothered Kate without her knowing why. Silence was a rare commodity in her life. Nora was always shouting something. 'Get out of bed. Hurry up, you'll be late. Come for tea. Now! Get into bed.'

Even when alone in their small room, Kate could hear the noises of the boarding house. She often had to pull the bedclothes over her ears to try and block out the traffic sounds. At school, the playground was a cacophony of children's sounds. In the classroom, the teacher's pleading for total silence was invariably interrupted by directions or sounds from other classrooms.

Yes, Stan was about the only silent person she knew.

Not long after she and her mother had arrived at Chidley House, he'd handed her a scruffy tennis ball and apologised for its age.

She rolled it against her chest, flattening the fluff. 'Ta. I don't mind. My blocks are old.'

'Goodo. Would you like to play catch?'

Remembering her mother's constant demand for politeness, she half-heartedly nodded and stepped back, tentatively tossing the ball to Stan. He bounced the ball towards her. It hit her palm and tumbled under some wooden crates. Her second attempt at catching proved equally disastrous. On the third attempt, the ball hit her knee and rolled back to Stan.

After two fumbling catches, she held the ball behind her back and stared at her feet, hoping the game was over.

'Perhaps you could practice by throwing it against the wall,' Stan suggested before he walked away without any further conversation.

Being allowed to keep the ball proved to Kate that Stan wasn't mean, so Kate felt guilty about not liking him as much as she liked the other Mr Blennerhasset.

One evening when she had been allowed to join the adults in the sitting room, Kate had asked Stan what he was looking at. He moved the footstool and lifted her onto it. No longer feeling like an ant, she smiled and asked again, 'What do you see?'

Stan placed his hand on the top of her head then, as if burnt, quickly removed his hand and placed it in his pocket.

'Life. It's happening to all those who are scurrying somewhere.'

'But I can only see one man.' Kate pointed to a young man striding past their picket fence.

'Ah, yes. You should ask yourself who is he, and why is he in a hurry?'

'How do I know?' She looked up at Stan.

'Perhaps he is rushing home to his wife. Maybe he is going to meet a man about a dog.'

'A dog. I don't see any dog,' Kate said, trying to stand on her toes.

'Well, if he is going to see a man about a dog, he wouldn't have one yet, would he?' Stan said.

Kate wobbled on the footstool and Stan reacted by making a shield with both hands.

'Steady on,' he said. 'Don't go falling.'

Regaining her balance, Kate turned her head to get a better look at an elderly couple who came into view.

'Do you know them, Stan?' Kate asked.

'No.'

'What do you think they are doing out after dinner?'

'Maybe they haven't had dinner and are going out to get it.'

Kate watched the pair disappear around the corner. With Stan's help, she climbed down. Stan retreated to his chair. Kate sat on the floor and ran her fingers along the carpet pattern. After a few minutes, she said, 'I think they are going to see their grandchild.'

Stan smiled. He tapped his long finger on his forehead. 'I think it must be their grandchild's birthday and they are taking him a present.'

Kate wriggled across the floor until the leg of Stan's chair bumped her shoulder. 'It's a granddaughter!'

'Oh, so you reckon it's a girl.'

'Yes. She is probably turning six today.'

'Six! Then she is quite grown up.'

'Not as big as me.' Kate jumped up and leaned on the arm of Stan's chair.

'No, not as old as you. What do you think she is called?'

'Elizabeth.'

'Is that so?'

'Yes, like the Queen.'

'And what are they taking her?'

'Shoes. Pretty red shoes. Shoes with a bow.'

Kate could almost see the little girl waiting at the door for her grandparents. Red shoes were something Kate constantly requested but her mother had said they were a wasteful item. Black shoes were necessary for school.

Kate knew all little girls wanted red shoes for their birthday.

Stan watched the young face closely. He liked how her tiny eyebrows moved. When Kate was concentrating, they would crease together, then when she had decided on the next part of the make-believe, her eyebrows would separate and lift above wide eyes.

She reminded him of a little girl he had known many years ago. Ruthie had been four when she died in a catastrophic flu epidemic. His wife Sally couldn't cope with the loss and spent time in

Graylands Mental Hospital, passing away six years later. Now, all he had were long-ago memories and make-believe.

Alice Chidley, the more agile and determined sister, ran Chidley House. Clare, not caring for the company of others, lived around the corner in a two-bed dwelling. She preferred books to people and spent temperate days in her minuscule garden. A weekly lunch at Culley's Tea Rooms with Alice, where the latest gossip and a brief financial discussion, was sufficient for Clare.

When their father died and the property passed to the sisters, Clare wanted to sell, move from their cottages to somewhere grand.

'No,' Alice said. 'This is all the grandeur we need. We'll live upstairs and rent the ground floor. I've always wanted to live here.'

'It wouldn't work.' Clare slapped the tabletop. 'I'm not becoming a slave to others.'

'I'm not about to cook and clean for people I don't know either,' Alice quipped. 'We'll employ someone. Then neither of us will need to cook, even for our own dinner. What could be better?'

They argued passionately for several weeks until Alice presented a solution. 'We can sell both our current homes. The money will be enough to renovate Chidley House and put the rest into an account for hiring a cook.'

'And where will *I* live?'

'We'll both live at Chidley House.'

'Now see here, I'm not living there. I hate the noisy stairs, the old-fashioned furniture, and the curtains! No. If you want to keep it, you can, but there has to be enough for me to buy a nice modern place.' Clare stood, walked to the window, held up the patterned curtain. 'Smell this horrid thing. And there's no privacy. You can see up and down the street. That means people going by can see in.' She turned around. 'Don't you get it, Alice? All this is your dream, not mine.'

After many prickly discussions, they agreed to sell their suburban homes. Within two weeks, they solved their differing preferences amicably. Clare purchased a two-bedroom unit with an upgraded kitchen and bathroom in a South Fremantle triplex. Alice remained dogmatic about retaining the family home, so Clare facilitated joint ownership of both properties to balance out the inheritance. After carefully managing finances, they renovated the stately looking Chidley House and prepared advertisements for "quality lodgers".

The expected income would cover running costs and, more importantly to Alice, allow her to live "in grandeur". New voile curtains hindered the view from passing pedestrians, while the heavy royal blue velvet curtains smelt satisfactorily new.

With amenable boarders and a reliable housekeeper who lived in a neighbouring suburb, Alice enjoyed playing the lady of the house. The first floor oozed with chintz and flowery wallpaper. The double bed draped with expensive linens, highlighted the fuss Alice had made over the room. A two-seater buttoned-back couch sat near the window. Alice took all her meals at the petite mahogany table, where the elaborate fabric covering the two chairs echoed her outdated tastes. The newly tiled bathroom sparkled under Doris's attention and, later, Nora's.

Despite the overindulgence of her private upstairs rooms, Alice used a sitting room on the ground floor. The large room, at the end of a long hallway, was renovated after an elderly boarder died in her sleep. Alice said it would be bad luck to have another boarder accommodate the room, although no one believed that explanation.

At the time of this newer renovation and with the delivery of a television set, Alice turned the space into an evening room. Five eclectic lounge chairs faced the television. She bought a jarrah sideboard and coffee table from a second-hand shop in Cantonment Street and had a local tradesman sand and polish them to a high shine. Each week, she had Doris handwash and starch a different set of embroidered doilies to sit under elaborate knickknacks, dusted every second day by Nora.

However, the pride of Alice's heart was the new television set. The music, which played along with the test pattern, competed with the radio blaring in the kitchen. Alice believed she was sharing this new-fangled toy with her boarders. but *sharing* was not quite how it came across to the others.

After eating her meal in her private rooms upstairs, Alice would poke her head into the dining room and announce, 'Coronation Street tonight' or some other program she intended to watch. The men and women, amid their evening meal, would nod politely but resume eating without comment.

TV Week lived on the top of the television cabinet, and anyone was welcome to peruse the pages. However, it was almost impossible for anyone else to view a program of their choice. Syd liked sport; Miss Tillman enjoyed musical or historical movies, while Stan would rather sit by his window, with or without a book, than contemplate watching the Bobby Limb Show.

If someone did decide to join Alice for a night of television, they would be regaled with a running commentary of the characters on the screen. She delighted in giving the full background of who and what had gone before. Even the advertisements were given the Alice Chidley interpretation.

Kate wanted to watch the children's shows after school but her mother had other ideas. It was either time for homework or Kate would be assigned chores. These tasks invariably took the exact time between her afternoon snack and dinnertime. However, Nora let Kate watch *Skippy, The Bush Kangaroo* once a week.

'It's Australian,' Nora said. 'Guess Miss Chidley will let you watch that.'

Sometimes when Syd had nodded off, Miss Tillman was engrossed in her knitting with an open book balanced on the arm of the chair, and Stan staring into the darkness, Kate would venture down the unlit passage to Miss Chidley's sitting room. The blaring TV sounds covered any squeaks from the polished floorboards, so the inquisitive child would go unnoticed.

Kate would usually stand at the doorway watching the black and white figures on the screen. One evening, Miss Chidley spied the child leaning against the doorframe, entranced with the performance of dancers accompanying the internationally renowned Frank Sinatra.

'Quickly, child. Come in and watch.'

Kate scurried in and sat on the floor. She pulled her skirt over her folded knees without her eyes leaving the screen.

'"Ol' Blue Eyes" they call him,' Miss Chidley said. 'Obviously, he has blue eyes. Lucky thing.'

Kate flicked her brown eyes at Miss Chidley, then back to the dancers gathered around the singer in their final gesture of indulgence.

'He's very good. Made lots of records.'

Kate applauded along with the TV audience.

'Sammy Davis Jr. as well.'

Kate stood, disappointed the sparkling girls had danced off the screen.

'Dean Martin, that's the other bloke linked with Sammy and Ol' Blue Eyes.'

Kate waited to see if the dancers would return.

'They're American. New York, I think.'

Kate went and poked Syd and woke him up. Together, they found the big atlas and located New York, Los Angeles and Seattle.

Miss Chidley never tired of the repetitive nature of television in its infancy, but it quickly lost its appeal to Miss Tillman and the Blennerhasset brothers. Nora and Doris were mostly too tired to bother as they had to be up early to start their daily work, while Kate loved to see the glamour and excitement of other people's lives.

Within the first month of Nora and Kate arriving at the boarding house, Miss Chidley and Miss Tillman encouraged them to attend the local church. Nora had no time for all the "fuss and nonsense" of Sunday church. After six days of constant work, she was not moving her large frame anywhere in a hurry. She would tell everyone, 'If the Lord rested on the seventh day, then it's good enough for Nora Wallace to have a day off.'

After Nora had firmly refused to accompany Miss Chidley and Miss Tillman to the morning service at the Scots Presbyterian Church, the two ladies turned their attention to Kate.

'Now see here, Nora, a child must be guided in this matter. It's your duty to show the child the Christian way,' Miss Chidley said as she and Miss Tillman stood facing Nora after repeated knocking at eight-thirty on a Sunday morning.

Kate held onto her mother's dressing gown with one hand and a half-eaten slice of toast with the other. Nora flapped at her daughter with her free hand while swallowing the last piece of her toast.

'I'll not see anything, Alice. Today is my day off. You can't go bossing me around today. If you two want to go wafting into town to say prayers that could be said in your own house, then you go on, but don't come bothering me.'

Alice was used to having her way and was shocked into silence. Miss Tillman quickly took up their cause. 'What about young Kate? Wouldn't you like to come with us, dear?'

Kate turned her face to her mother and nodded. 'Please, Mummy, can I go? I'll be good.'

'She's not dressed,' Nora said then turned to Kate. 'You'll be late. Perhaps next week.'

'I can dress quickly.' Kate dropped the handful of pink robe, placed the toast on the corner of the washstand and started to remove her pyjama top.

'Then you two can wait outside,' Nora instructed as she closed the door.

Alice patted the folds of her floral blouse and moved back from the doorway, almost stepping on the other woman's foot.

'I do hope she doesn't take long. I don't want to have to rush to the bus. One doesn't like to arrive all hot and bothered,' Alice said.

'I'm sure the child won't be too long. Did you see how eager she was? Shame Mrs Wallace won't come with us,' Miss Tillman countered.

'I don't think we'll have too much luck there, I'm afraid.'

'Well, the child's coming, and that's a blessing.'

Meanwhile, Kate scurried around trying to fend off her mother's attempt to wipe her face and bring some semblance of order to her disobeying hair. There was no mirror in their small abode and Kate was more eager to be away from the Sunday morning demands of her mother than care how she looked. Her yellow-spotted dress had been her best dress for two years and was a little short but, in a few minutes, Kate was presentable enough to be taken to church for the first time.

The high ceiling and the stained-glass windows fascinated Kate. The music made her think churchgoers must be happy people. Not used to the sustained formalities, she wriggled on the hard, polished seat during the sermon. When Miss Tillman gently took her hand and told her to sit still, Kate had second thoughts about being there instead of at home throwing her ball against the wall. She filled in the monotonous minutes by counting how many ladies weren't wearing hats and how many men seemed to be dozing. *Six and three.* Another young girl caught her eye, and they smiled at each other. Kate leaned sideways, watching the other child fiddling with something on her knee. Alice tapped Kate on the arm and, in an agitated whisper, said, 'Kate! Sit up straight. Listen.'

The last hymn sounded like a marching tune, and Kate happily made up some silly words to join in with the enthusiastic singing.

'Read the words, Kate.' Miss Tillman pointed to her hymn book. 'We're up to the chorus. Onward Christian Soldiers...'

Kate had to stretch onto her toes to see the small, printed words but joined in tunelessly.

The congregation filed out into the sunshine, shaking the minister's hand as he thanked them for coming. After a few words with Miss Tillman, he bent down to Kate's level. 'First time we've had the pleasure, young lady.'

Kate put her hands behind her back and stepped back between the two women. The portly minister leaned over her and gave a practised smile. 'You're with Miss Chidley then?'

Kate shrugged, stepped further back.

'Yes,' Alice said. 'Her mother works for me. They're boarding at Chidley House.'

'Good child. Eager to learn.' Miss Tillman nodded at the minister. 'You like books, don't you, Kate?'

Kate shuffled, didn't answer.

'Come child, say good morning to Mister Penworthy.' Alice pushed Kate closer to the outstretched hand.

'Good morning,' Kate said without looking up. She kept her fingers tightly entwined behind her back.

'Like to read, eh? That's a worthy habit. You should start with the New Testament. Will we see you again, young lady?'

Alice poked Kate's shoulder and whispered demandingly, 'Answer, child.'

'I have to get my mum's breaky on Sundays, but I might come if you sing the marching song.' Kate peeked up through her eyelashes at the smiling man, who suppressed a laugh.

'The marching song, eh? Can't promise to sing Onward Christian Soldiers each week, young lady, but I'm sure you will like some of the others just as well.'

'No, it's going to be my favourite, always.' Kate moved away.

The adults, who had been close, either chuckled openly or smiled at each other, acknowledging the innocent response.

Within days, Kate struggled to remember more than the title and a few lines of the chorus of her "favourite always" hymn as she sat in the sitting room swinging her legs in time to resolute humming.

'What's that, young'un ?' Syd asked.

'The marching song.'

Syd demanded an explanation. 'Who is marching, and to where?'

'If you went to church, you could ask them to sing it. It's about soldiers. It's called Onward Christian Soldiers.' Kate stood and saluted as she loudly hummed the first line again.

Syd laughed. 'I don't think it is those sorts of soldiers.'

Not liking being laughed at, she stopped humming and folded her arms. 'It's from the Bible.'

'Well, there you go. Who knows what that'll tell you?'

Kate turned away from Syd and moved towards Stan, who had remained motionless during the conversation.

'Do you read the Bible, Stan?' Kate asked.

Stan turned from the darkened window and grimaced. 'No, child. The Bible isn't for me.'

'But the man at the church said that Jesus died for everyone. That must mean you too, Stan.'

Stan flopped into the chair and seemed to shrink into the padding. It was a while before he made an odd noise, making Kate think of the last drop of bathwater disappearing down the plughole.

'I can't understand it,' Kate said as she sat beside Stan's feet. 'The Bible. It's got funny words.'

'It's old archaic English. And codswallop as well,' Stan said.

'Ar-cay-ic?'

Stan remained lost in his thoughts, and Kate tried again, 'What's that mean?'

When Stan ignored the tugging on his trouser leg, Kate wriggled across the floor to Syd. Although giving the impression of being asleep, he was listening intently to the conversation between his brother and the inquisitive child.

'Syd,' whispered Kate. 'Syd, I know you're not asleep.'

One eye opened, followed by a smile. 'How about half asleep.'

Kate jumped up and ran her fingers along the arm of the chair. 'What's ar-cay-ic, Syd?'

'Pass me the dictionary, Kate. Let's see what *that* says. More facts than the Bible will give you.'

Syd covered the word with his plump finger, pretending he couldn't find it.

'Ar... arc... no, it isn't there. No such word, young'un.'

'Move your finger. Arch... Look, there it is,' she shouted.

Stan returned to his spot by the window and muttered something inaudible.

'Archaic—old fashioned,' read Syd. 'Like the Town Hall.'

'When was it built, Stan?'

'I don't know, but I was looking at a book on old buildings the other night. Let me see if I can find it again.'

Kate forgot about the Bible as they poured over the colourful pages of grand buildings.

Chapter 3

After the following Saturday's lunch, with Nora being allowed a few hours to herself, she and Kate set off for a walk towards town to browse the city's shop windows. Since her arrival at Chidley House, window shopping was Nora's distraction.

'I can dream, can't I?' she often told Doris before repeating how Derek Frederick Wallace had left her homeless *and* poor. 'That bugger of a husband left me with no option but window shopping. Used to be that I could indulge a little. Now and then like. Then, those bastards of friends—huh, some friends—taught him how to gamble away everything. Yeah, window shopping is all that's left.'

As Nora tugged her daughter's hand, warning her to keep up or there'd be no ice cream for the walk home, Kate asked, 'Mum, do you have a diary?'

'A diary? What prompted that silly question?'

'Miss Tillman has a diary. I've seen Miss Chidley writing in a little book. Maybe it's a diary.' Kate pulled her hand from her mother's hand. 'Is the Bible a diary?'

'Questions. Always questions. Do you have a brain full of questions?'

Kate stopped, poked her finger at her temple. 'The short man says you should always ask questions.'

'Mr Blennerhasset?'

'He says it's the way you learn.'

'Well, how then can you not say Blennerhasset? Short man! Indeed. And hurry up. We've not got all day. We have to be home to help Doris with dinner.'

'Mum, why does Miss Tillman have a diary?'

'So she can write down all the stories of long, long ago and bore us with them.'

'Are they true stories?'

Nora had her eyes firmly on the window display of shoes, deciding which would make her legs look longer.

'What?'

'Are they true stories?'

A pair of navy-blue sandals on an elevated shelf caught Nora's eye. 'Lovely. What I wouldn't give for those.'

'Mum?'

'Not now, Kate.'

'Mum, can I have a pair of red shoes?'

With her shoe-owning illusion shattered, Nora gripped her daughter's arm. 'No. You. Can't. Have. Red. Shoes.' She sighed. 'You can't, I can't. That's what it's come to.' She glanced back at the display of sandals. 'I can't have new sandals, new anything! The bastard. I'd like to tell him a few true stories. The only trouble with that is he doesn't know anything about truth.' She released Kate's arm. 'Come on, let's forget about lies and truths and get that ice cream. I think I might have a double.'

'But Mum—'

'No more questions, Kate.'

Stan refused to be drawn into the conversation after Kate asked Syd and Miss Tillman if the Bible was a diary.

Kate continued her rapid-fire questions: 'It must be a diary if someone has written about things that happened long ago, isn't it? Who wrote it? Does a diary have only true stories? Does everyone have a diary? Should I write a diary? What would I write in my diary? Is it a special sort of book? Do they cost a lot? How do you keep it a secret, and is it—'

'Whoa, slow down, young'un,' Syd said. 'One question at a time.'

Miss Tillman pulled her diary from the huge knitting bag on the seat beside her. 'This was a gift to me from a very dear friend. Let's see. Over twenty years ago, when I left to come to Australia. Laura Stenhouse. Yes, Laura. Ah, she was my best friend.'

'Can I read it?' Kate extended her hand.

'No. Diaries aren't to be shared.'

'Why not?' Kate asked. 'Aren't stories written so someone can read them?'

Stan cleared his throat, lifted his hand and pointed at Kate. 'Ah... maybe not. You see, Kate, folks like to put their own slant on life.' He tucked both hands in his pockets, shook his head and added, 'Diaries have a way of only telling one side of the story.'

'That's not true, Stanley Blennerhasset, and you know it,' Miss Tillman said. 'Diaries are for the facts, but with the heart and soul of the writer.'

Syd laughed. 'Got you on that one, brother. And, Kate, let's just say diaries are about memories. Just so you don't get your facts wrong. So you know it was Vera *Linton* you asked to the school dance and not Vera *Jones*.'

Stan whispered, 'Memories don't need to be written in a book.' Then he returned to his spot near the window.

Before Miss Tillman could reply, Nora entered the room demanding Kate get ready for bed.

Complaining that she still hadn't found out everything she wanted to know about a diary, Kate stomped into their room and ignored her mother's request to "stop with the questions".

With a mouth full of foaming toothpaste, Kate told Teddy a secret, 'I'm going to write a diary.'

After Nora returned to the house to help Doris prepare for tomorrow's breakfast, Kate tore the middle two pages out of her school maths book and wrote "Kate Isobel Wallace—Diary" across the top of the first page. With her best running writing, she added "Strawberry ice cream and red shoes" confident she'd remember having the shop-bought ice cream and not getting red shoes.

By Wednesday, Kate had enough of diary writing, thinking it felt too much like homework and so very dull. She scrunched up the pages and pushed them into the kitchen's rubbish bin, under eggshells and bacon rind.

One evening, Miss Chidley called Doris and Nora into the sitting room despite the dinner dishes still not put away.

'Leave them a moment, would you?' Miss Chidley said. 'I have an important announcement that will affect you all.'

Doris frowned and Nora's eyebrows shot up, acknowledging the unusual interruption.

'Bloody hell, maybe she's selling,' Nora whispered as they removed their aprons and headed for the sitting room.

'Good God, I hope not. Better the devil you know...' Doris whispered back.

They pushed open the sitting room door, and Nora beckoned her daughter. 'Take your book into the kitchen.'

'Kate should stay. She needs to hear this.' Miss Chidley motioned for the child to sit back down. Kate shrivelled against the wall hoping she wasn't about to be punished for a wrongdoing.

'Bunch up,' Syd said to Miss Tillman. 'Stan, sit here.'

'I'm fine. I can hear anything that's going to be said.'

Miss Tillman moved further away from Syd and re-arranged her skirt, her head tipping back as she straightened.

Doris and Nora stood by the door, looking for any hint of Miss Chidley's announcement from the other faces. Miss Tillman smirked, Syd's face contorted in time with the thoughts going through his mind, only Stan's face remained static, but none revealed any clues.

At Miss Tillman's request, Miss Chidley announced that Miss Tillman would be leaving Chidley House in four weeks.

Miss Tillman stood, gave a minute bow of her head, pausing for maximum effect before adding that there would be no need for cajoling or commiserations; the decision was final.

No one could believe Miss Tillman had actually made a decision, that she'd bought a ticket for a flight home to England. She'd been convinced by her sister in Essex that now was the perfect time to purchase a cottage in the English countryside.

With dozens of questions being flung at her, Miss Tillman did her best not to sound ungrateful. However, she left no doubt Australia had the better deal with her forty-five-year endeavours.

'There's one other thing,' Miss Chidley said loudly.

The room quietened. 'This is important. Especially for you, young Kate.'

Kate had been standing next to Stan with her hands over her ears, wishing the adults wouldn't all talk at once and in such loud and excited voices. Now, she pushed back against Stan's legs. He held his hand in the middle of her back. 'It's okay, Kate, it'll be okay.'

Kate wasn't sure it would be but folded her arms and listened closely.

'I've decided,' Miss Chidley said, 'that once Miss Tillman has gone, Nora and Kate can have her room.'

Nora's eyes widened.

Doris slapped Nora on the arm. 'Bloody hell, Nora. Good for you.'

Nora attempted to speak; the words not decipherable as she struggled to put her emotions into words.

Miss Chidley hushed her. 'You've been a good worker, Nora. Consider this a raise. A substantial one. I'll talk to you privately, but we'll need to come to some arrangement. We have four weeks.' Miss Chidley smiled. 'Now, Doris, I think we could do with a hot drink. I'm sure Miss Tillman wants to tell you all about it.'

Doris lingered with her hand on the doorknob. 'I'm sure she will. Rushing back to England, not a thought about all the benefits she's taken from Australia.' She shook her head slowly. 'However, be that as may, I know we all wish Miss Tillman the very best.'

Kate had a thousand questions bouncing around in her head. Wasn't this the perfect time to have questions? Nora flapped her hand in front of her face, trying not to shed tears of blessings. Doris gave Nora a quick hug before forcing her towards the doorway. 'Come on, let's get that cuppa. Maybe Syd will find us some brandy to add. Might even sneak some of the cooking sherry. Come on, girl, look lively. Didn't you hear what she said? You're going to get a decent bed at last.'

The sentiments moved from expressing sorrow that their fellow boarder would be leaving, pleased they wouldn't have to listen to Miss Tillman's soliloquy on the benefits of leaving Australia and watching Nora's face light up.

It was Stan who answered Kate's questions as she struggled with the loss of Miss Tillman, and therefore Katherine, but with the excitement of having a real bed to sleep in.

Chapter 4

A month is a long time for a nearly-eight-year-old to understand why time goes so slowly when you want it to rush by. Kate had been ticking off the twenty-three days before Miss Tillman's farewell party but had missed several. She decided days went quicker if they weren't crossed off a calendar.

'Mum, when do we get the proper room?'

'I've answered that four times today already. It's the same five days it was this morning. I can't stand here forever. Just you get finished washing those feet. How on earth you get them so dirty I'll never understand.'

'Will I be able to have a bath every day?'

'Now look here, you don't need one *every* day.' Nora held the towel towards Kate, then in a playful mood, moved her vast body in a prolonged shimmy as she wiggled the towel and grinned broadly. 'But we will have an option of a shower or a bath. It's so long since I had my own shower.'

'I wish Miss Tillman wasn't going.'

'What?!' Nora tossed the towel across Kate's knees. With her arms folded and a frown covering most of her eyes, Nora stood over her daughter. Kate pulled the towel across her chest.

'Don't you dare wish that,' Nora yelled. 'Here's our chance to get out of this... this hole of a place, and you are wishing... don't you dare go wishing our chance away.'

'But Mum. I want a nice room, but I like Miss Tillman.'

'Yeah, yeah. I guess she's not a bad stick.' Nora wriggled her hips again. 'But, if I have to choose between Miss Tillman and having our own room... well, Kate Isobel Wallace, I'm sorry but I'll dance at Miss Tillman's leaving party with great enthusiasm.'

Miss Tillman had invited Nora and Kate to inspect the room they would inherit on her departure. What was once a dingy back veranda used as a dumping ground by the previous owners was now a skilfully converted, cosy bedroom. There was plenty of room for several pieces of bedroom furniture, a desk, and a pillowy lounge chair that Miss Tillman used when she grew tired of Syd's company. The renovation included a bathroom with a shower over a deep bath, a hand-basin and a toilet tucked away beside a huge built-in wardrobe.

'It's so lovely.' Nora ran her hand over the top of the chest of drawers. 'Are you taking this with you? Won't it be expensive to ship?'

'Far too costly. I'll only be taking my personal effects.' Miss Tillman picked up a small vase, smelled the rose, putting it down as she added, 'I'm only allowed a certain allocation on the flight, other items will have to be shipped. But my sister is rounding up furniture, so, no—I'm not taking it.'

'All the same, I can't afford to pay you for any furniture.' Nora looked longingly at the bed with its floral linen. 'I might be able to give you something for the quilt.'

Miss Tillman put her hand on Nora's shoulder. 'I knew you wouldn't be able to pay for all this, so I spoke with Miss Chidley. She's agreed to buy the large pieces. She'll negotiate the rent to include the furniture.'

Nora stood silently, shook her head slowly. 'I don't believe it,' she said. 'Oh, Miss Tillman, I could hug you.'

Miss Tillman stepped back. 'No need for that. It's best all round. And I'm guessing you'll have to work hard for this room. Just see that you are kind to young Katherine.'

'Katherine? Oh, Kate, yes, of course. And... I'll forgive you this once.'

'Mum, where will you sleep?'

The two women turned to see an exuberant Kate rolling across the large single bed, tucking the bedspread over her as she rolled.

'Kate! Stop that at once. Get off the bed.'

Kate stopped rolling and peeked out from the bedspread, her eyes changing from glee to distress at the sight of her mother, hands on hips, glaring at her.

'Um... sorry, Miss Tillman.' Kate scrambled to her feet, smoothing out the bedclothes, expecting a slap. She clutched the pillow, hoping her mother wouldn't continue to scold her in front of Miss Tillman.

'Go on, child. It's okay, this time,' Miss Tillman said kindly.

'Anyway, Kate, this will be *my* bed,' Nora said. 'You'll have to do with the camp stretcher.'

The joy of moving from the washhouse to this lovely room shattered instantly. Kate glowered at her mother and scuffed her feet as she left the room.

Nora apologised to Miss Tillman for her daughter's lack of respect and, after a final look around the room, declared she'd be forever grateful.

On the day of Miss Tillman's farewell party, everyone had an allocated task in the preparations. Syd, Stan and Kate were in charge of turning the comfortable but formal sitting room into a room where guests might be encouraged to dance. The men shifted the chairs to the edge of the room, carefully removing the knickknacks from danger, reluctant to drape crepe streamers and inappropriate Christmas baubles on the picture rail.

'Come on, Kate. Stop daydreaming and pass me some of those streamers,' Stan said.

Kate lifted her unsmiling face and held out a roll of blue streamer to Stan.

'Hey young'un, what's with the happy face?' Syd asked.

Stan placed the rolled-up mat against the wall and waited for Kate's answer.

'Cat got Kate's tongue?' Syd teased. 'It's party time. You can't come to any party without a smile.'

Stan kneeled beside Kate but she turned away from him. He placed his hand on her shoulder. 'What's up?' he asked.

Kate burst into tears. The two brothers glanced at each other. Syd raised his eyebrows and dropped the streamer and Stan stood stock-still, shrugging.

'Come here, young'un. Tell Sydney what's up.' Syd opened his arms.

'It's terrible,' Kate said between sobs.

'Are you that sad because Miss Tillman is leaving?' Stan asked. 'We are too. But she's happy about going. We should be happy for her.'

With another downpour of tears, Kate ran from the room. Stan followed her, while Syd, dumbfounded, decided he could at least be successful at gathering the streamer from under the chair.

Stan found Kate standing soldier-straight between the fence and the washhouse. He wriggled his skinny frame into the tiny space and stood silently near Kate. Her uneven breath and intermittent gasps were daunting for a man of many thoughts but few words. When Kate reached out and took his hand, Stan hoped she hadn't felt him wince. It was a long time since he'd been given such a connection from a child.

'What's up, Kate?' He softly squeezed her hand. 'Can I help?'

'But Stan, I want a proper bed.'

It took Stan a while to hear the whispered words, even longer to understand what they meant. 'Oh, I see.'

The fence palings dug into Stan's back. Kate dropped his hand and rubbed her eyes. He said, 'Perhaps we should get out of here.'

She pushed up against him and nodded.

Side-stepping from the confined space, Stan held his hand out. Kate took it but kept her eyes on her feet.

'Come on,' Stan said, 'let's see if there are any of Mrs Baird's biscuits left in the jar.'

'I don't feel like any.'

'I thought little girls liked biscuits.' He grinned. 'Especially if—'

'No,' interrupted Kate. 'I'm too sad.'

'Even for a biscuit?' Stan couldn't remember how to treat a child who was clearly upset. It'd been too long, and his memories were as sad as Kate.

Now free of their confinement, Kate sat down on the step of the washhouse. Stan leaned against the door frame, wishing Nora would appear. Or Doris. Or even Alice Chidley.

Nora did appear and Kate jumped to her feet, opened the door and disappeared inside.

'What are you doing, Stanley?' Nora growled.

'Just on my way.'

Nora glared at him and then glanced through the doorway. 'You haven't been upsetting her, have you?'

He shook his head, whispered, 'No,' and strode away. He had plans to complete.

The party went well. Two teachers who had worked with Miss Tillman, and five of the members of the Ladies Guild, along with their husbands, turned up. Dressed in their Sunday best they chatted with the occupants of Chidley House, refused to be encouraged to dance, but heartily sang along with Elvis Presley's Blue Suede Shoes from one of the records Miss Tillman's friends had brought along.

Doris proudly brought through a generously sliced three-tiered cake, which Kate—even though it was past her bedtime—was tasked with handing out. They drank a toast of whisky, or sherry to Miss Tillman, with Miss Chidley offering up kind praise for her longest boarder.

After promising she'd clean her teeth with extra care, Kate took her piece of cake to bed and offered a nibble to Benji.

With the cake rumbling in her tummy and her mouth now only tasting of toothpaste, Kate slid under the bedclothes and cuddled her teddy. She wiped away a dribble of tears before falling asleep, dreaming of putting her feet into giant bowls of icing before dancing on a bed that crashed to the floor.

On the final day, when helping Miss Tillman to take her suitcase to the taxi, Nora deliberately pulled aside the curtains so she could peek into *her* room whenever the coast was clear. Syd caught her, a glass of orange juice in her hand, nose almost through the glass. His teasing heightened her delight.

Nora had taken care not to look like the cat that got the cream for the two days after Miss Tillman's departure. When the maintenance inspection confirmed the room could now be occupied, she sang—occasionally whistling—while she did a final clean and re-arranged the furniture.

Eager to have a decent amount of comfort again, it didn't matter her spare time would be halved or she'd be working longer hours, she was moving up in the world.

Saturday shone, literarily and metaphorically, for Nora as she hummed while sweeping, dusting, and tidying the already tidy room now to be her home.

'Bloody lovely,' Doris said, bringing two hot drinks from the kitchen. 'It's nicer than my place.'

'Maybe, but skerrick of the size. At least, from what you've told me. Don't you have three bedrooms?'

Doris sighed. 'Yeah, and lots of space now the kids have left. But I can't get Dick to buy any new furniture.'

'This isn't new either.'

'But it's of value.' Doris put the cups and saucers on the chest of drawers and opened a drawer. 'Dovetail joints, and all. And what are you going to do with all this cupboard space? You have so few things.' She sighed loudly. 'Didn't mean to rub it in, but it's true. Perhaps we could go to a church bazaar or the like. Find something to make it look a bit more homely. A doily or two. Some jugs or vases. I might even have something I can pass on.'

'Just stop!' Nora pointed the duster at Doris. 'I don't need your charity. I have it all worked out. I've rung Janice, my sister, and her husband has offered to bring my stuff around on the weekend.'

Doris gripped the feathers of the duster. 'Your stuff? What stuff?'

'My things.' She pulled the duster away. 'When I had to leave our beautiful home in Bassendean, I packed some things into a couple of tea chests and stored them in Janice's shed. I just hope the linen isn't mouldy.' Her voice rose a decibel. 'I wasn't going to let that bastard of a husband sell everything to pay the bailiffs. Not my crystal dressing table set. It was my twenty-first present from Mum and Dad.' She took Doris's hand and attempted to twirl her around. 'Oh, Doris, it'll be like Christmas.'

Doris ducked under Nora's arm, playfully twisting the other woman into a jive. As they caught their breath, Nora explained that Janice and Barry would arrive mid-morning, and tonight she'd be sleeping in her new bed, complete with the bedclothes from the disastrous marital bed of her past.

'What about Kate? Are you getting her a new bed? Where will you put it?'

'There's room against that wall. Stan and Syd have offered to shift the chest of drawers for me. Her stretcher bed will have to do. I can't afford a proper bed for her. Not even a second-hand one.' Nora kept talking as Doris opened her mouth to speak. 'And, no, you can't give me one. We'll be standing on our own two feet. Just you wait and see. I'm off the bottom rung at last, and I'll not have you looking down at me anymore.'

Doris tipped her chin up, looked to the heavens. 'I do not! And, anyway, what about young Kate? She deserves to be off that bottom rung too. Have you thought of that?'

'I know. It's a shame but she's just a kid. She'll cope. I'll get her a new pillowcase for her birthday. I've seen one with a ballerina. She'll like that.'

Doris was unusually quiet but Nora was too excited to notice any lack of chatter.

'When's her birthday?' Doris said as they wiped down the hand-basin and put a new toilet roll in its holder.

'In two weeks. Could you put some candles on your weekly cake? I think I have candles in a tin. In the tea chest.'

'Mm. It's the least I can do for Kate. She's a good kid.'

While they worked, Nora heard every vehicle driving down the back street. At two-thirty, Kate wandered in with the news the anticipated vehicle had arrived.

By offering to work on Sunday morning, Nora had been given Saturday afternoon off. Transferring their few belongings, mostly clothing, and Kate's stretcher bed from the washhouse to the veranda room wouldn't take long, and Kate wasn't as enthusiastic as everyone thought she should be.

'Come on, Kate,' Syd said. 'Surely the veranda room is prettier. You won't have to go outside for the toilet.'

Stan stood against the back door of Chidley House, his eye on the street.

'What are you looking for?' Kate asked, avoiding Syd's comments. 'Aunt Janice has already come. Mum is unpacking. I might ask Uncle Barry for sixpence. Will you take me to the shop for ice cream?'

'Ice cream? That'd spoil your appetite. Dinner is just around the corner.'

Syd slapped his brother's arm. 'Don't you know anything?' He winked at Kate. 'Ice cream slips down between the cracks.'

'Don't you want to see what's in the tea chests? Didn't your mum say there're things of yours in there?'

Kate's face shrivelled with distaste. She folded her arms. 'I don't care.'

Syd took his brother's arm and whispered, 'Look, I'll go for the ice cream.' He dropped Stan's arm and lowered his voice, 'With any luck, the you-know-what will arrive while we're away.'

Stan nodded slowly, realising the inference in Syd's words. 'That might work exceptionally well. We could set it up before Kate gets back. Be a better surprise.'

Syd said, 'Kate, I'll go with you to the shop if your mum says it's okay. I'll even shout you. I can always do with some exercise.' He chuckled and patted his girth.

With an ice cream each and some Liquorice Allsorts to share, Syd and Kate ambled back from the shop, with Syd pointing out so many delaying distractions but Kate said she was in no mood to be educated.

'No mood? Where did you get that from?'

'Mrs Baird. She told Mum she was in no mood for hearing about fuss and nonsense.'

'Doris? And you're in no mood because...?'

'Just because.'

'No one can be in a mood because of nothing. Now see hear, young'un, everyone gets in a mood, but you should have a reason.'

Kate considered this. 'My reason is that I have to keep sleeping in that rotten stretcher. My neck gets crinkled. Sometimes the edge sticks into my shoulder. And Benji hates it. He's in no mood too. So there.'

Syd had trouble stopping a burst of laughter. 'Poor Benji. Now finish the ice cream and let's get back. Even if you're not interested in what's in the tea chests, Benji might be.'

Syd asked Kate if she could skip. Astounded at his question and determined to show off her talent, she quickly forgot about being downhearted. She couldn't stop giggling at the sight of Syd's ample body bouncing haphazardly beside her.

When they reached the back gate, Stan rushed up to them whispering quickly to Syd, encouraging Kate to go see her mum.

'I don't want to,' Kate said.

'She's asking about where to put your bed.'

'I don't care where it goes.' The joy of ice cream had melted, and a *no mood* had descended again.

Stan took her hand and led her past the washhouse, through the back door and into the veranda room.

'Kate! At last. What took you so long?' Nora put her hand on her daughter's shoulder. Kate dropped Stan's hand and reluctantly responded to being eased forward. 'Come and look at our room. It's ever so lovely.'

With a glance at the chest of drawers, her eyes took in the tea chest in the middle of the room, newspapers spread across the floor, and landing on a bed, a single bed, where she expected her camp stretcher to be.

'Is... is it... is it for me?' She stared at her mother and then looked back at the line of adults cramming around the doorway she'd just come through.

'Happy Birthday,' Syd said.

Kate frowned. 'It's not my birthday.' After looking at Miss Tillman's bed, which was now her mother's, she stepped slowly towards the other bed. 'Is it for me?'

'Not entirely, you'll have to share with Benji.'

Kate flopped down on the bed, careful not to smother Benji, who was grinning as best he could. She grabbed him, squeezed him as she rocked back and forward. 'I love it.'

She looked at her mum, then at Auntie Janice. 'Did you buy it?'

Nora sat next to her daughter, slipped her hand around small fingers. 'No. I would have if we had the money, but these wonderful people did.'

Kate scanned the grinning faces.

'I didn't know about it. I swear, love. I didn't...' Nora's eyes watered.

'Everyone?' Kate asked.

'Mr Blennerhasset and, oh, *both* Mr Blennerhassets, and Mrs

Baird. Even Miss Chidley chipped in. All the time they were hiding the truth from me.'

'Did they lie?'

'No, my love, they didn't. Well, not really. A secret isn't the same thing.'

Arranging Benji on the pillow, Kate wondered how she could save this bouncy, creamy, excitement feeling forever. She turned and ran to Stan, hugged his legs. He ruffled her hair briefly.

Syd squatted down as best he could and accepted her hug. He kissed her forehead and said, 'Happy Birthday for whenever it is.'

Doris had to wipe away tears as she waited for her turn, then she picked up Kate and twirled her around, laughing and singing a toneless "Happy Birthday".

The mess from unpacking remained over part of the floor for a few days as Nora now also worked for Miss Chidley's sister Clare, ironing on Tuesdays and vacuuming on Thursdays. With Clare recovering from a recent stroke, Nora's availability could, in the sisters' eyes at least, kill two birds with one stone.

Doris teased her that with all this extra work, Nora would be a bean pole in no time. 'I don't intend to stop eating,' Nora said, before laughing. 'With all this extra work, I'll be expecting an extra serve.'

After Nora finished helping Doris clear away the empty lunch dishes and made a blackcurrant jelly for dinner, she returned to the veranda room hoping Kate had done as asked and folded all the newspapers into a neat pile. Then she could put the last few items away and enjoy sitting in Miss Tillman's comfy chair (now *her* comfy chair) and while away the afternoon with a Barbara Cartland novel.

'What are you doing?' she snapped as she entered the room to see her daughter on the floor unwrapping items from the tea chest.

Kate fumbled a round parcel and looked at her mother. 'Just taking these out. For you.'

'I hope you haven't broken anything?' Nora's voice softened. 'And look at your face. You've got newspaper print all over it.'

When she returned from the bathroom having washed her face with one of the new cakes of soap Auntie Janice had given them as a house-warming gift, Kate said, 'I found a diary. Is it yours?'

'Where? What did you do with it?'

The severity of the questions wasn't lost on Kate. 'I... I didn't look. I didn't read it. Honest, Mum.'

'Where is it?' Nora's eyes scanned the room then glared at her daughter. 'Where did you put it?'

'In the drawer by your bed.'

Nora kicked aside the newspaper as she rushed across the room and opened the drawer so aggressively it came all the way out. The drawer fell, landing on her foot. She yelped, pushed the drawer aside, and grabbed the diary. She sat on the bed and pinged the elastic band around the book. 'I should have thrown the stupid thing out.'

Kate picked up the drawer and attempted to slide it back.

'Here, let me,' Nora said.

Once she'd managed to realign the drawer, she shoved it back, flopped onto the bed, and let the diary fall from her armpit. She picked it up from the floor and removed the elastic band.

'Load of rubbish,' she whispered.

Kate had sidled up to her mother. 'I've never read a diary.'

'Of course not. A diary is for the writer. Not anyone else.'

'That's a silly thing. Why write something you don't want anyone to know.'

'I guess...' Nora ran her hand around her chins. 'I don't know...' She opened the diary and read, 'Wednesday 12th. Had to have sausages AGAIN. Seems the good crockery has to go.' Slamming the book shut, she turned to Kate. 'Well, that's over now. We don't have to eat sausages unless we want to.'

'I like sausages.'

'It's okay to *like* them. But when that's all you can afford, when you *have* to have them four times a week because *someone* doesn't hand over enough money...' She tucked the diary under her leg and patted Kate's knee. 'Anyway, enough of that. Why don't you go and get a biscuit? Doris would have left the biscuit tin on the kitchen table. Take your time. I've got something better to read than this load of rubbish.'

'But Mum, couldn't I read it? I'll read it quietly. I won't ask you. Even for the big words.'

'Child, go get a biscuit and get a book from the sitting room. You're not going to read my diary.'

Chapter 5
1960

Kate's early years with the people of Chidley House set her up to be interested in the colouring of stories, imagination in all its imagining, and an idea of diaries. By the time her twelfth birthday came around, her life had changed dramatically.

After Clare Chidley's death, Alice Chidley announced she would be selling Chidley House and moving to her late sister's small unit in South Fremantle.

Kate experienced total grief when Syd Blennerhasset died. His brother Stan moved to a Fremantle men's home and, without the brotherly prodding, disappeared into his shell a little more.

With the notice of the sale of Chidley House, Nora had applied and, after several months, was granted a State Housing Commission home in Beaconsfield. Her sisters, Janice and Jennifer, gave cast-offs. Doris offered curtains and cushions, which Nora recovered.

After Chidley House sold, Miss Chidley let Nora have many kitchen items far more than the value of the holiday pay she was due. Kate's bed took place of honour in a small second bedroom at the back of the newly painted house. Nora continued to work at Chidley House until the sale went through. Then afterwards, for

Alice at the South Fremantle unit. She wheedled her way into jobs at the local collection of shops, intimidating those who brought their washing into the laundromat, and accepting under-the-counter payment for the ironing she did for her favourites. After-hours cleaning for Yeo & Co Grocers meant she, most days, sat on her ever-broadening backside reading magazines and devouring lollies she'd bought with her staff discount from Lance Yeo.

An often-present scowl hindered Kate from making close friends at her new school. She excelled in the classroom. Her imagination astounded the teachers—no doubt a result of Stan's sharing of his window to the world.

She visited Stan six months after the move, but he'd changed in ways she didn't understand. After a warm but formal greeting, he led her through to the communal sitting room and organised tea and biscuits from the small kitchen. He remained silent throughout the afternoon tea, nodding occasionally at Kate's questions, restlessly playing with the hem of his cardigan. He wasn't interested in what the gentleman chattering to himself on the other side of the room might have on his mind.

On the bus trip home, Kate imagined Stan saying how proud he was of her Top of the Class certificate because she couldn't bear he'd not even read it properly.

He continued to live a solitary life and died a few days after presenting Kate with a diary, the dedication stating, "Shine as best you can". Kate's life tipped completely upside down and she refused to smile, even as things improved.

She fathomed a diary—even a blank one—should be kept hidden, so tucked her diary under a loose board in the bottom of her second-hand wardrobe. The pages remained pristine—she didn't want to write just anything in such a classic book. Benji still shared her secrets, her heartache, but scribbling them into permanency was something else entirely. Many times, she'd turned the key, turned the key, turned the key, turned the key, but slipped it back into its hidey-hole unopened.

Nora, tired by her long day at the beck-and-call of lazy customers, expected a lot from her almost-teenage daughter, and their relationship became fractious.

Arguments often started over the jobs Kate hadn't done to Nora's satisfaction, the tardiness of Kate in preparing dinner, or her reluctance to make another cup of coffee for an "exhausted-from-working-so-hard" Nora. Kate often threatened to leave. Nora saying she'd help pack her bags.

After finishing school at fifteen and being employed at Culley's Tea Rooms in Fremantle, Kate knew she wasn't as bad off as those bundles of homelessness she'd seen curled up in alleyways and hotel doorways when she raced from evening classes to the bus. She also knew smiling sweetly at the elderly when they came for a Toad-in-the-Hole lunch, or jollying along the ladies with grizzly toddlers, wouldn't achieve self-sufficiency.

After a mother and daughter yelling session, Nora had screamed, 'And I guess that'll be another bloody chapter for your diary.'

'No way. Wouldn't put your stupid rantings in *my* diary. Not that I'm writing in it anyway. Fill yours with it!'

'Huh, Miss Hoity-Toity. Too good for us, are you?'

Kate slammed her door shut, flung herself onto her bed. She listened to her mother expanding on how ungrateful a daughter Kate was. As Nora's voice faded and the fridge door opened, Kate rolled onto her back and hugged her teddy.

'She can put it in *her* stupid diary.'

Kate thought back to the day in the veranda room when she'd found her mother's diary. 'Mm, I should find it again. Maybe it'll explain why she's in a permanently bad mood with me.'

With Nora sweeping Yeo & Co's floor, Kate had plenty of time to search for Nora's diary.

Nora's Diary
1956

1 July: The bastard. I'm sick of him coming home drunk. I'll not have him in my bed like that. Hope the couch is uncomfortable. Kate doesn't seem to notice. Fortunately, she's in bed when he staggers in. He's mildly sober in the morning. Remembers to whisk the blanket from the couch. Kate's oblivious.

2 July: No money! The bastard. He gambled my housekeeping. Again. Bastard. Bastard. Bloody Bastard.

3 July: I hate using credit. Only way to have something to eat. Thank God for Wilma. I'll pay her back next week. He'll not use my money again.

22 July: Lasted a while. He's at it again. Spending everything on the horses or at the bloody pub.

23 July: K asked why we had sausages again. She thinks he's a flaming wonder. Brings her lollies. Would be better if he sucked them instead of all the booze!

31 July: Friggin' hell! Now we are going to lose the house. I tell you. I could murder him. Then I'd have a roof over my head. Hah! Not worth the trouble. It's so hard to be cheerful. Little Miss Happy doesn't help. She thinks the sun shines out of her father's bloody backside. But I won't be the one to tell her. He *was* a decent father.

And husband. It's those mates of his. Taught him to bet. One small win and he's off again, bigger and bigger. He just can't drink like they can. That's him coming in now. It's after midnight.

3 September: By God, I've had enough. Lost his job. Because of the drink.

10 September: He's not been paying the mortgage. The car is on hock. Probably lose that soon. If tears could help, we'd be millionaires. Poor K. I'm the bad guy. More sausages.

9 October: K couldn't understand why I couldn't buy her a new dress for Milly's party. Had to buy a second-hand gift. I tell you, I was mortified. Jennifer and Janice could tell. Damn. Blast. At least we got to have a decent feed at the party. Janice can afford to have a caterer. Her husband earns money that actually goes in the bank. K had a stomach ache afterward.

14 October: It's her birthday today. Can't believe she got so tall. Janice came good with a loan—have a feeling she'll have to wait a bit. Money doesn't go far. Even had to say no to a school trip. I want to smash that no-good husband's face in.

15 October: He suggested we apply for State Housing. Ugh. He can. I won't. The stigma. Honestly. That's other people. Not me. Anyway, it's a bit late now, we've already received the eviction notice. Got a month to find somewhere.

20 October: He suggests a lot of things. I suggested he gets a job. All he does is get drunk and stagger into the TAB. Who would employ such a person? No one, that's who.

16 November: Not going to put up with the hopeless bugger any longer. I'll get Wilma to help put my stuff in some tea chests. Send them to Janice's. He won't be any the wiser.

17 November: Not putting up with it any longer. He's a bastard. That's what he is.

18 November: Started looking. Too many forms for a state house. They want to know everything. I'll find somewhere without him suggesting where I can go. Just for the record, I know where he can go. He can go to hell. Probably with a carton of beer and betting dockets in his pocket. Damn him.

22 November: Found somewhere. Hardly perfect. I'll manage. Short term. Kate will be fine. She's a kid. She'll be okay. Food and lodgings. I'll apply for government assistance. Thank God.

8 December: Bloody hell. Tomorrow's the day. Even booked a taxi. Bugger him. Have to use some housekeeping I've saved, but I can't go by bus. He thinks that measly amount of money he's given me will help. All the rest he's spent on booze or bloody nags that never win. Now to tell Kate.

Chapter 6

1956

Kate had come home after a perfectly normal day of school to be told she had to pack her things as they were going to a new home.

'Why, Mummy? I like it here.'

'Do as I say, child. And hurry up.'

Kate placed her doll, Judy, and her well-loved teddy, Benji, on her bed. Next came three books which had been birthday gifts from Aunt Jen, Aunt Jan, and Daddy. She guessed she would have to take her school bag, so stuffed her pencils and other items from her desk in between the empty lunch box and the exercise book. The last page of the brown-papered covered book showed she had earned nine out of ten for her maths test earlier in the day. Perhaps Daddy would give her a lolly from the jar on the sideboard when he got home. He was sure to be pleased with her test result.

'Come on. Hurry up. Get your things together.'

'Where are we going, Mummy?'

'Never you mind for now, just hurry up. You can take whatever you can fit in that bag by the door. I've already packed your clothes. Don't stand there, get a move along.'

Kate stuffed the books into the large bag and contemplated on the need for her pillow. No, wherever they were going they would have a bed and pillow. Judy and a few other toys filled a smaller bag. She put her school case in one hand, tucked Benji under her arm, and dragged the bags behind her as she left her mauve-curtained bedroom where she'd always felt safe.

'For goodness' sake, what have you got in those bags? Come on, let's have a look.'

Kate unwillingly pulled the bags over to her mother. She stood with them leaning against her leg, squeezed Benji to her chest, and waited.

'You won't need those,' shouted Nora as she tossed aside two stuffed toys. 'No room for that either.' A colouring book flew across the room. Nora straightened and glared down at her daughter. 'Now look here. We'll have to start basic. There won't be a lot of room for just anything.'

Tears welled. Kate couldn't understand why they had to go anywhere. Kate hugged Benji tighter. She shrugged off her school bag and looked up at her mother. 'But Daddy can carry it for me. It will fit in the car. Daddy won't mind.'

Nora walked away from Kate and stood looking out into the backyard. She could see the sandpit with a red bucket and blue spade. They'd been left after a brief cooler day but now the tiny items waited forlornly. The plumbago displayed an abundant number of bright blue flowers on its excessive growth but the gerbera's, which were Nora's favourites, were wilted due to the last three waterless days.

'It's too much, child. We have to go now, and your father won't be coming with us.'

Nora turned and her shoulders slumped with pity for herself. 'All this! All this should have been my home. Should have been our home forever.' Nora's hand spread through the air pointing to the leather Chesterfield. 'Can't take that. I'll kill him, I will.' She ran her hand over the laminate bench. 'Was mine, now what? It'll be someone else's, along with the furniture. To pay his stupid debts, and *he* doesn't give a damn.'

Kate couldn't work out why her mother was talking this way. 'Mummy, I have to go to the toilet.'

'For God's sake, go on. The taxi will be here soon. At least we can go in some style.'

KATE'S DIARY
1964

14 May: I miss my dad. I know he loved me. I can't believe Mum. Perhaps she's making it up. I wonder where he is. If it's not the truth, then why did we have to leave our home? I remember Dad coming home in a funny mood a lot. Now I realise—unmistakably drunk. Did he gamble that much?!

22 May: Of all the first things I could write in my lovely diary I wrote THAT! I guess it's because I miss Dad so much. He might still love me. And I'm so mad at Mum. She's never told me the whole truth, that's for sure.

23 May: This diary thingy works. Looks like it did for Mum. Sort of! And I don't have to write EVERYTHING.

24 May: Good job I'm working at Culley's. Pay is a bit stingy but at least it's something.

25 May: Those stuck-up bitches at typing. If their noses were any higher, they'd snap their pretty little necks. I'm as good as them. I could do these classes with my eyes shut. Ha! We actually might as well. Those boxes are the pits. But I can, even without anything to practice on. Lola—oh my god, that giggle. And that freak Wanda— six foot five if she's an inch. Fiona. She's almost nice. At least she says hello. Not like those others. I'll be glad when I get a certificate to wave in the faces of the disbelieving—and get a decent job.

28 May: Mrs Fothergill caught me out. But she laughed. The next time she came in, she brought me a fab gift. Wow! Note recorded: Smiling at old biddies works.

Chapter 7

Each Thursday evening, Kate ate something from the reject pile in the kitchen of Culley's Tea Rooms—often a slightly burnt pie or the drying edge of an undecorated slab of orange cake. She would gulp down the last mouthful as she hurried up the street to the first floor of a Bannister Street building where Mrs Trantor intimidated various teenagers into "being one" with a typewriter. Most of the young women arrived after a fifteen-minute wander from the train station, while a few, including Kate, left their low-paid jobs and with minutes to spare, slid breathless onto a chair, just in time to stand and say good evening to Mrs Trantor.

They had twelve weeks to master the *qwerty* keyboard enough to be awarded a certificate signed with a flourish by their teacher who started every lesson with words of wisdom.

'All young ladies have to be able to interpret the often-illegible script of a man who pays their wages, present a letter without error, and smile while he insists you retype it because he needs to change a sentence.'

Kate huffed.

Mrs Trantor glared. 'You won't get to be a personal secretary with that attitude, young lady. Now let's get those fingers dancing.

Here's this evening's lesson.'

For Kate, this weekly lesson was a means to an end. She didn't want to be like her mother—sweeping floors, at people's beck and call, never achieving anything. Kate wanted to live like those in Cottesloe or Peppermint Grove. Like those customers with an account who swanned into Culley's for lunch, loaded with bags containing their retail shopping. Kate longed to snuggle her face in a gorgeous silk blouse, caress stunning leather shoes, or simply feel the soft embroidered towels of the bejewelled customers as they bragged over their latest whim with their equally glamorous companions.

'That's so gorgeous,' Kate oozed, as she placed a plate with Mrs Fothergill's weekly treat onto the table.

'This? Yes, it is. It's for my granddaughter. She's off to a friend's party on the weekend.'

'How old?'

'Let's see. Pauline was ten in August. Yes.'

Kate wanted to smash her fist into the vanilla slice. Instead, she bit her lip and folded her arms. 'Ten, eh? Gosh, I've never had something as nice as that.'

Mrs Fothergill's eyebrows arched skywards. 'Well, maybe you will one day.'

Watching as Mrs Fothergill returned the silky blouse into a labelled bag, Kate said, 'One day.'

'Well, dear, if you work hard enough your dreams can come true.'

Imagining the vanilla slice hitting the wall, Kate said, 'Oh, yeah. That's all it takes, isn't it? Dreams and time.' She calmed her voice.

'I mean medical school is hard enough but having to work here six days a week so I can afford it—well, I've no time, but I do have plenty of dreams.'

About to walk off in a controlled huff, Kate was surprised when Mrs Fothergill laughed and waggled her forefinger at Kate.

Kate paused, not used to being caught out. 'Um...'

'It's okay, my dear. My grandson is a first-year medical student.' She laughed again. 'All of us do it at some time. I remember telling an over-eager salesman that I was the daughter of the Premier and wouldn't be talked to like an idiot. He went a great shade of red. I giggled all the way to the bus. I was seventeen at the time. And Dad, well, he was a lawyer. Not nearly as important as the *Premier*.'

'Sorry about that. It mightn't be medical school, but I—'

'What is it you want to do, Kate? Eh? Are you a budding nurse in a waitress uniform?'

Kate glanced back at the kitchen. 'Um, I'm learning to type. You know, get out of here and into an office at least. Just for starters.'

'Good for you. Practice hard. I'm sure you'll get on.' She ran her finger over the pink icing of the vanilla slice. 'I rather think you're a bit like this icing, covering the real good stuff. Yes?'

Straightening the cutlery on the opposite side of the table, Kate said, 'Perhaps. I mean, I would practice if I could, but there's no typewriter at home. I just cross my fingers I can remember the keys from one week to the next.'

Mrs Fothergill picked up her cup. 'I'm sure you will. You always remember my vanilla slice and exactly how I like my tea.'

Aware of the possibility of being scolded for taking too long with one customer, Kate thanked Mrs Fothergill and slipped back into the kitchen for the next order.

After a long day at Culley's, Kate found it difficult to fall asleep. Mrs Fothergill's tale of pretence bounced around her mind.

Does everyone do it?

Images of viewing the world with Stan made her grin involuntarily. A little girl wanting red shoes flashed into memory.

What was wrong with a little made-up scenario?

Pulling the blanket over her shoulder, she considered if creating a better background to one's life constituted lying.

It doesn't actually hurt anyone.

Whether Mrs Fothergill was the daughter of the Premier or a lawyer didn't matter. This white lie didn't harm the salesman.

'It's not like it was a *real* lie!'

Benji wasn't sure. She moved her teddy and rolled into a more comfortable spot.

Life was hard. Life needed to be *less* hard. Maybe life just needed assistance sometimes. 'Yep, Benji, I reckon I'm up for helping life be a bit more agreeable.'

As Kate pummelled her pillow and snuggled down again, she recalled her sudden medical vocation.

The thrill of pretence against the annoyance of disclosure sat in her chest.

'I mean, why couldn't I be a medical student?' Visions of vomit and blood instead of gravy and tomato sauce made her cringe.

Maybe I should find more realistic career.

During the next battle with the typewriter and with Mrs Trantor hovering, Kate made several mistakes on one line of typing.

'Holy shit,' Kate whispered.

'Miss Wallace. Please, if you're going to be seen as a product of my academy, then I suggest you refrain from such abhorrent language.' Mrs Trantor pulled the page from the typewriter. 'And it seems you have a long way to go before I'll be giving you a pass mark.' Turning the page over and flapping it at Kate, she added, 'Type it again. And this time, correctly.' Mrs Trantor continued down the aisle, peering at the other student's attempts.

As Kate took the page, she heard a snigger from across the aisle. She turned sharply. 'Yeah, what?'

Lola smirked. 'Huh! Seems you have a long way to go,' she repeated Mrs Trantor's words, adding sarcastically, 'Long, long way.'

'Shut up. I'll get somewhere faster than you, you rotten—'

'Please, girls. Stop that whispering. You can talk all you want after class. Now, for the next exercise you must still keep the boxes over your keys, and this time we'll be timing you.' With a flourish, she pulled a stopwatch from her pocket and stared at the disbelieving students. 'If you keep practicing you should reach sixty words a minute before the twelve weeks is up.'

As the girls scurried down the steps and out into the street, Kate confronted Lola. 'Why are you so concerned with my progress? Shouldn't you be worrying about your own pretty little, scarlet-tipped fingers? Or are you scared of competition, eh?'

'No competition that I can see.'

Wanda leaned her arm on Lola's shoulder, scowled at Kate. 'Yeah, none that I can see, either.'

'Well, come back in a couple of years. You'll see a lot from up there,' Kate retorted.

'Now look here.' Wanda took a step towards Kate. Lola took a step forward. Fiona pulled her satchel across her chest.

Kate folded her arms, held Wanda's stare. 'Yes?'

Fiona's satchel now hung from her shoulder as she tapped Lola's back and gripped Wanda's arm. 'Come on, we'll be late for the train. And I want to get a Fanta on the way.'

Wanda blinked, shook Fiona's hand free, and stepped sideways. 'Yeah, let's go. Nothing to see here.'

Lola linked her arm through Fiona's. 'See you next week, *Miss* Wallace.'

'Yeah,' Wanda copied, 'See you next week, *Miss* Wallace.'

'For God's sake, will you just come on. I'll buy you both a Fanta.'

Kate watched them saunter away. When they reached the corner, Lola turned back and waved theatrically. Her high-pitched giggles disappeared slower than those of the three girls.

Kate strode along Banister Street determined to put the altercation from her mind. During the long bus ride, she typed on her knee: The quick brown fox jumps over the lazy dog. The quick brown fox jumps over the lazy dog. *I've got to remember this. I mustn't fail.* The quick brown fox jumps over the lazy dog. *I wonder if I can get a second-hand typewriter at an op shop.* The quick brown fox jumps over the lazy dog. *I'll look during my lunch break tomorrow.* The quick brown fox jumps over the lazy dog. *Huh, if only Mrs Trantor's typewriter was as accommodating as my knee.* The quick brown fox jumps over the lazy dog. *Yep, then I'll beat that stuck-up Lola.* The quick brown fox jumps over the lazy dog. *I wonder who made this sentence up.* The quick brown fox jumps over the lazy dog. *There has to be another sentence with all the letters of the alphabet.* The quick brown fox jumps over the lazy dog. *Sixty words a minute! Not possible.*

The next day, Kate was surprised to see Mrs Fothergill in her usual spot in Culley's Tea Rooms.

'My goodness, two days in a row.' Kate pretended to check her watch. 'A bit late for morning tea. Can I get you the usual, Mrs Fothergill?'

'No. And I do know it's nearly two o'clock. I'll just have a cup of tea. I can't linger. Have other things to do.'

'Sure. Won't be long.'

When Kate returned with the tea, Mrs Fothergill strained to lift a large parcel onto the table.

'Here, let me. Are you taking it to the Post Office?' Kate took the parcel and placed it on a chair. 'It's a bit heavy. Should you be carrying it so far?'

Mrs Fothergill flexed her arm, giving an impression of a weightlifter showing off their muscles. 'I'm not a weakling. I've carried it from the train station.'

'You should have stopped at the Post Office before coming here.'

'I'm not posting it,' Mrs Fothergill said. 'It's for you.'

'What?' Kate glanced around the room. 'I'm not allowed to take gifts.'

'Come now. Surely you can accept something from *me*.'

Kate whispered, 'Well, I'd like to. But the rules.'

'Oh, tush! Rules are meant to be broken. Haven't you learned that yet?'

'Um, yes. But I don't want to lose my job. Not yet. Not until I can—'

Edith, the other waitress glared as she walked past. 'Kate, stop yakking and get back to the kitchen.'

'I'm sorry, Mrs Fothergill. Really sorry you've lugged that parcel so far. But I can't take it.' Kate ran her finger over the cardboard parcel. 'What's in it? I mean...'

Mrs Fothergill stood. 'Who is the manager? I'll speak to him. Make him see sense.'

With her eyes flicking to every corner of the establishment, Kate took a deep breath and let it out slowly. 'I don't want to get into trouble.'

'Nonsense, I make sure it doesn't come to that.' Mrs Fothergill stepped in front of Edith, who was on her way to the front counter. 'May I speak with the manager, please?'

Edith paused, then glared at Kate before speaking to Mrs Fothergill. 'Is everything alright? Can *I* help with something?'

'No. And Kate has done nothing wrong. I just would like to speak to the manager. If it isn't too much trouble.'

'Alright. I'll get her. Just one moment, please.'

Kate didn't know if she should stay. In the minutes before Edith and Sarah Bell returned, Kate took two orders to the kitchen and, deciding to stay out of sight, stood next to the doorway folding napkins, hoping she could hear what Mrs Fothergill had to say.

Sarah and Mrs Fothergill used their hands to emphasise their words, both of them glancing towards the kitchen on several occasions. The clattering of kitchen utensils, the squeaking of the door, and the general busyness of the tea rooms meant Kate had no idea what passed between the two women.

Mrs Fothergill left—without her parcel. Sarah carried the parcel into the kitchen, placed it on a benchtop, and spoke to Kate.

'Now, see here, Kate, you know the rules. No gifts from the customers.'

'Yes, I know. I told her that.'

'She was most insistent, so I've decided to let it go. This time only.'

'Thanks, Sarah.'

'You'd better find somewhere else to store it. I can't have it taking up space on the workbench.'

'No, Sarah.'

Kate lifted the parcel and looked around for a likely spot.

'Don't take all day,' Edith snapped. 'Customers are waiting. And you should be helping.'

Curiosity tempted Kate, but she knew she couldn't take any more time away from her duties. The rectangular shape of the box gave no clues to its interior. A slight metallic click and clang, along with its weight meant it was unlikely to be a silk blouse.

Fifteen minutes before closing time, Sarah came through from the front counter checking on the cleanliness of every surface in the kitchen. After spying Kate's parcel tucked under the stack of chairs, she asked, 'And what did you get?'

Kate closed the dishwasher. 'I honestly have no idea. She didn't say. Or rather, she didn't tell me when I asked. I wasn't expecting anything.'

'Well then, I think we've seen the last of the customers for today. Why don't you open it? It's heavy, so see if it's worth taking on the bus.'

'Can I?' Kate's eyes darted to the package. 'I guess it's not a handbag.'

Tossing another tea towel into the washing basket, Edith folded her arms, pursed her lips, and waited. 'Got to see this.'

With a mixture of nervousness and excitement, Kate tugged at the string and opened the box revealing a portable typewriter.

Flabbergasted by such an expensive gift, she picked up the typewriter. Her mouth stayed open as she placed it on the counter and pushed the return arm. Grinning at the familiar sound, she whispered, 'Holy shit!'

Even Edith was silent for a moment. 'Wow,' she finally said.

Tucked under the portable typewriter's plate was a handwritten note:

> *I happened to have this typewriter. No sense in it gathering dust, so I thought you should have it. Practice hard. Reach the stars. But don't forget how to make a proper cup of tea. Flora Fothergill—Premier's daughter.*

Kate read it twice, chuckling through the second reading. She passed the perfumed card around.

'I didn't know she was the Premier's daughter,' Sarah said, surprise evident in her voice.

'Mm.' Kate pointed to the note. 'Yep, seems so.'

'No way,' Edith said.

'Well, why couldn't she be?' Kate took the card from Edith. 'Now to get this home and start practising.'

'Just a minute,' Sarah said. 'Are you leaving us?'

A warning stabbed at Kate. 'No. Why?'

'I thought you were a long termer. The owners wouldn't be too happy if you're wasting our time. If you're just here until you get something else.'

'Ah, no, but...'

'Think about it, Kate. You have a future here. The customers like you. Look at Mrs Fothergill. Her account is valuable.'

With no idea what to say, Kate mumbled, 'Yes, um... no. Yeah. I mean, I could... type, um... I could always type up the menus.'

'We'll see.' Sarah turned to Edith. 'Is the washing ready? Laundry vehicle is due soon.'

'Yes, it's ready. I've finished them earlier.'

'Thanks, Edith. I know I can rely on you.'

Edith's lips twitched in a condescending smile as she looked at Kate. Ignoring the inference, Kate slid the typewriter back in the cardboard box and pushed on the masking tape, hoping it would hold.

'You going for the bus?' Edith asked Kate.

'No, I'm ringing for the chauffeur.' Kate laughed.

Edith, with a change of heart, chuckled. 'Well, tell him to bring champagne and I'll ride with you.'

On the way to the bus stop, Edith took a turn carrying the parcel.

'Thanks, Edith. Sarah does rely on you. I bet you'll be manager one day.'

'Do you think so?' Edith narrowed her stare, trying to see the truth in Kate.

'Sure. She trusts you. She obviously doesn't trust me.'

'Go on. Why would you say that?'

Lowering the parcel and standing it against the bus stop post,

Kate said, 'I can tell some people don't like me. The girls at typing are awful to me. They constantly badger me. I mean, you're not always...'

'Sorry.'

'It's okay. For some reason I—'

'Kate. You bring it on yourself. You don't give out much. People probably think you have tickets on yourself. You know, a snob.'

Kate laughed. 'What? A snob. How can I be a bloody snob? I live in a housing commission house. Catch a bus! Have to work in a cake shop. Oh, so sorry, a bloody *tea house*, and buy my clothes from op shops. A snob! You must be joking.'

Opening her purse, fiddling to find her bus fare, Edith spoke softly, 'Anyone can be a snob, Kate. You talk differently when talking to the likes of Mrs Fothergill and Mr Nelson, the bank manager. Posh like. Then you make comments about Rome and France, and stuff very few of us know about. It's as if you're someone else half the time.'

Kate's eyes widened. 'I honestly didn't know that. I thought everyone knew about... well, the stuff I know. For heaven's sake, Edith. You've got it all wrong.'

'No, I haven't. You're educated in a way most of us aren't. I'm not quite sure what it is, but I bet you're not still with Culley's say, in two years. But, in the meantime, I'll see you tomorrow. My bus is coming. Got to go.'

Watching Edith cross the road for her bus, butterflies circled in Kate's chest. The excitement of being somewhere exciting in two years swirled around her thoughts—two years—she couldn't wait that long. She'd have to start tonight. Typing would be the way to her future.

KATE'S DIARY

1964

5 July: Can't have them coming to the house. That giant Wanda asked. They teased me about state housing. I told them we'd be moving once Mum cashed in her shares and Dad sold the house in Cottesloe.

6 July: Mum can stick her complaints. I need to get my typing certificate. Maybe then I can get a decent job.

10 July: Mrs Trantor said I need to spruce up if I'm to be a secretary. SPRUCE. What! I'll not SPRUCE up for anyone. If my skills aren't enough for some boring old git of a boss... then I'll do something else.

11 July: Ha! Changed their tune, didn't they? Told them Dad had a new house in South Perth and I'd probably be able to get a job in the diplomatic corps with his influence.

15 July: A homeless man said he was my dad. Can't believe that. He stank! Ugh!

16 July: I have no idea what that was all about. Who was he?

17 July: Hope he wasn't my dad.

Chapter 8

Nora complained about the clacking of the typewriter keys, how the "damn thing" took up space on the kitchen table, and Kate's colourful expletives when things went wrong.

Kate reshaped the cardboard box into a cover over the keys, typed most evenings, and several sessions during the weekend. Her fingers ached from the constant pressure required. The ribbon jammed several times and her forefinger became black from constantly unsticking the keys.

When Mrs Trantor expressed her pleasure at Kate's improvement, Kate beamed, glad the compliment had been loud enough for others to hear. When the keys jammed again, she flicked the "S" key, separating it from its mates.

'We all have to stand alone, not be a mass. Don't we, S?'

At the end of class, Fiona hung back behind Wanda and Lola as they reached the bottom of the stairs.

'Did you get a typewriter?' Fiona asked.

'Yeah. I did.'

Lola, then Wanda turned.

'Op shop trash, eh?' Lola smirked.

'Yeah,' Wanda said. 'Op shop trash.'

Kate's anger tickled the back of her throat. 'If you must know, my father brought one home from Singapore.'

'What?' Lola's face showed disbelief. 'Singapore?'

'Singapore?' Wanda echoed.

Kate stifled a laugh at the blatant copying. 'Yeah, Singapore. Dad has just returned from a stint at the embassy over there. They were updating.'

'I'm glad,' Fiona said. 'It must have been difficult without one.'

Lola scowled. 'How come you live in a state house if your father is a diplomat?'

'Well, Mum and Dad are separated. Mum got the state house when Dad was overseas. He's coming back and going to sell the Cottesloe house, probably kick the people out of his house in… ah, South Perth, and move in. Mum might buy something in Floreat Park.' Kate tugged at the neck of her blouse. 'Not sure where I'll live. It'll work out somehow.'

Fiona glanced at the others with a spasmodic grin throughout Kate's explanation. Wanda continually looked for a response from Lola who pulled a face of disbelief as she said, 'Still don't believe it. No one can just get a state house if they already have a house. I don't believe you.'

'Don't care if you do or you don't,' Kate said.

Lola leaned forward, peering closely at Kate. 'What if we come to your place? You know, speak to your soon-to-be-Floreat-Park mother.'

Stepping away from the scrutiny, Kate asked, 'Speak about what? How long does it take to fly to Paris?' Kate paused, watching Wanda waiting for Lola to speak first. 'And why do you think my mum would want to chat to the likes of you, eh?' She paused, smirking, as if interested in a reply. 'Anyway, Mum's too busy packing. Now that she's sold her shares... And, dear non-believers, I've gotta go. See you next week.'

She smiled throughout the bus journey as she recalled her creative stories. Who knew where her father was? And her mother? Well, Nora probably didn't even know what a stock market was.

As she spotted a neat brick house complete with a rendered veranda and a circular driveway, Kate sighed. If only *that* was the house she was going home to.

One day. One day I'll have a house I can be proud of.

At the final typing class, Mrs Trantor explained, 'One can't expect to work in a high-class office if one's attire is inappropriate.'

A couple of students giggled. Someone said a mite too loudly, 'One can't!'

'Now, girls, it's all well and good to snigger but let me tell you, no boss wants a dowdy secretary. It wouldn't do. A few of you need to spruce yourself up before you go for an interview.'

Lola's head swung to the side, directing her comments at Kate. '*Some* more than others.'

Kate stuck out her tongue.

'That is exactly the childish behaviour that will have you left behind,' Mrs Trantor snapped. 'Now, let's see how you've all done. Joy, you've topped the class. Nina, your marks are impressive. And

Kate, such an improvement. Now, one-by-one in an orderly fashion, please come up and get your certificate.'

As she pushed the chair back, Kate wanted to stick out her tongue at Lola again.

All sixteen of the young women received their certificates, Kate rating third with speed and fifth in accuracy.

She made sure she was first out the door and didn't stop to exchange farewells to any of the people she hoped she'd never need to see again. Typing was going to be the passport to another world.

However, Lola, arm-in-arm with Fiona, yelled at Kate as she reached the street. 'Hey, what's the hurry?'

When Kate didn't stop, Wanda raced ahead of her friends and caught up with Kate. 'What's the hurry,' she said as she whacked Kate on the arm. 'Too stuck up for a goodbye, are you?'

Kate spun around and glared at Wanda. 'A sentence of your own? Surprises will never cease. Now, if you don't mind, I'll just disappear into the sunset and never see you lot again.'

'Don't be like that,' Lola said. 'I was going to ask you to my party. You know, celebrate.'

'Celebrate,' Wanda repeated.

'What a shame, I'm doing something that night.' Kate forced an over-the-top smile.

Fiona chuckled. Wanda's eyes flicked from Kate to Lola.

'I didn't even tell you when it was.'

Kate shrugged. 'Yeah, but I'll still be busy.'

'Be like that, then. I don't care. You're too stupid to realise I could be a step towards—'

Kate interrupted, 'No, you're the one who's not realising who you're talking to. Next time you see me, I'll be working at the French embassy, dining with the who's who of the international fraternity, and being able to give a party like you've never attended in your narrow, boring life.'

Lola's eyes widened. 'As if. How's that going to happen?'

'Hah! See you don't know anything. My dad is on every guest list for every embassy. I just have to ask.' Kate fiddled with the strap on her bag. 'Now if you don't mind, I have a bus to catch.'

Wanda looked to Lola for the next retort but it never came.

Fiona said, 'Good luck. We should catch up sometime. After we've all got jobs.'

'Yeah, sometime,' Wanda said.

As Kate walked away, Wanda poked Lola in the ribs. 'Say something.'

Lola slapped away Wanda's hand. 'Go to hell.'

Kate wasn't sure if destination hell was meant for her or Wanda. She didn't care.

Hurrying up Bannister Street, a little wary of the winter's early darkness, Kate turned into High Street towards the bus stop.

'Hey, spare a pound or two?'

Kate grimaced at the sight of a man leaning on the inset doorway of a closed tobacconist. Ignoring his request, she stepped into a small spot of light near the bus stop and pulled her bag tightly against her chest.

'You!' he called. 'Hey, I know you.'

Looking around to see who the homeless character could be addressing, Kate suddenly realised he was speaking to her. 'No, you don't. I certainly don't know you.'

'Yeah, Katie. Katie love.'

'Leave me alone.'

'Do you have a quid or two? Come on, Katie. Anything?'

'No. And, anyway, how do you know my name?' As he came closer, she shuddered at his odour. The dankness of his overcoat repelled her. 'Piss off.'

He held out his hand. 'It's me, Katie love. Your dad. See here. Derek Frederick Wallace. It's me. Come on give your old dad a hug.' He stepped within arm's length.

'Don't you dare come near me. You're not my dad. My dad would never look like that!'

'Katie. Katie love. Remember I bought you a teddy. Do you still have Benji? Your birthday is on the fourteenth of October. See it's me. Come on, love. Do you have any money? I could do with a bob or two.'

Not able to comprehend whether this bundle of awfulness might have any connection to her, Kate held up her palm. 'Don't!' she said. 'I don't know how you know that stuff, but just don't come near me.'

He shook his head; tears filled his eyes.

Kate waivered, but just then the bus arrived. 'If you're my dad, you'd better spruce yourself up before you talk to me again.' She hurried onto the bus. When the bus driver asked if she was okay, she paid her fare and nodded, not convinced she could form words.

As the bus pulled away, the man on the pavement waved. She instinctually lifted her hand from her knee but refused to complete the wave.

At the dinner table, Nora accused Kate of being sullen,

ungrateful, and most definitely a worry for a poor mother who had just cooked dinner after a long day in a suffocating laundromat.

'What's with the long face?'

'Mum, what happened to Dad? Where's he living?'

Nora stopped spooning a portion of steam pudding into her mouth and scowled before asking, 'What's this then? Asking about him after all this time.' She licked a smear of jam from the spoon. 'He's a no-good bastard. That's what he is. So, I don't know, and I don't care where he's living. Now eat up and forget about him.'

'But Mum... What if he's homeless?'

With a plonk of the spoon on the table, Nora glared at her daughter. 'Look here, your dad, bless his bloody rotten cotton socks and smelly undies, got us into this situation. We had a lovely home. Nice furniture. Pretty garden. And he, yes, he alone, lost it. So why, now, should we care where he lives? He didn't care enough about where we would be living. Just cared about where the next throatful of alcohol or another nag to bet on might come from.'

Kate left the table. Tears threatened, but instead she cuddled Benji, told him stories about having a dad who read nursery rhymes and tickled her feet.

'Benji,' she whispered, 'I hope that man wasn't my dad. But how could he know about you if he wasn't my dad? Maybe he knows my dad and heard stories about us. Yes, that's what it is.' She rolled over. 'Don't you reckon it's sometimes better not to know the truth?'

KATE'S DIARY
1964

2 August: Thank goodness I don't have to see that lot again. Although, I think Fiona would be okay if she didn't hang around with Wanda and that jealous bitch Lola. I definitely won't be catching up with them. EVER! In fact, it just might be interesting to see where they are in five years. Pity I can't get a job at an embassy. Maybe I should try.

4 August: Went to an agency. Honestly. They advertise that they can get you a job. Boy, the tests I had to do. Shorthand! Failed it. Don't have a clue. Surely, they can take your word. Ha—maybe not. She didn't believe a thing I said about my experience either, and some of it was even true.

17 August: Got a letter from Leighton's Agency. About time. Three interviews next week. Phillip & Co Engineering Consultants in Mouatt Street, near Culley's. I could go there for lunch. Doctors in Subi— bit difficult to get to. Baker and Woods Accountancy in Perth. Would mean a bus trip to the train. Like to work in the city. More shops.

Which one should I choose? Not the doctor's job—sick people. Ugh! Ordinary people don't use accountants—that's a positive. Engineering—depends. Consultant? Let's see what they have to offer. I'll not just pick the first one.

29 August: Mum's a pain. Wish I was old enough, RICH enough, to get a place of my own. First a job. Then a flat. Edith said she knows of one in Applecross. Depends on where I'm working.

Chapter 9

On her way to an interview at Rokeby Health Clinic, Kate decided this first interview would be a learning experience—she didn't like the idea of having to be pleasant to a bunch of sick people every working day.

She'd made an effort to "spruce up", wearing a navy-blue skirt, over new stockings, and low-heel shoes she'd borrowed from her mother.

'Not much else I can borrow. Maybe gloves if I ever need them,' Kate quipped.

Nora ignored the insult and tutted repeatedly as she checked for stray hairs on Kate's floral blouse.

'You did remember to ask for a late start at Culley's, didn't you?'

'Yeah, Mum. They were pretty good about it.'

'Thought they mightn't like you trying to get another job.'

Kate spoke quietly. 'They didn't mind at all that I had to go with you to the doctors. Said I was a good daughter.'

Shaking her head with disbelief, Nora said, 'You'll tell one lie too many, one day.'

'Forget the lecture, Mum. I'm off.'

'Well, remember your manners; no swearing.' Nora held out some coins. 'And, here, treat yourself in one of those smart cafes.' She patted down the front of Kate's cardigan. 'My goodness! My little girl getting her first proper-like job.'

'Bloody hell, Mum. Stop fussing.' Kate took the money. 'I don't think I'll accept *this* job. Can you imagine having to deal with snotty-nosed brats?'

'Huh! Why bother going then? All that way to Subi. You could be at Culley's instead. Earning some honest money.'

'I have to start the interview process somewhere. Don't worry, I'll be polite. I'll say I have to think about it.'

'Good plan. Then you can pick the one you like best.'

'The one with the most pay,' Kate chuckled. 'Or the one with the cutest boss.'

With another shake of her head, Nora sighed, 'The cute ones aren't always the keeping sort.'

'What would you know? Anyway, I'm off. Wish me luck.'

Nora stood near the letterbox watching Kate walk towards the bus and her future. Nora remembered when she'd been young, slim, and eager to make her mark in the business world. She walked back into the house, slammed the front door shut, and headed for the fridge and the chocolate bar hidden behind a jar of pickles.

'Luck! Bloody luck!' She snapped the chocolate in half and ripped the paper off.'

If luck comes knocking, you should grab it by the shoulders and make it stay. Planning never worked for me.

Kate fidgeted as Susan Whitmore read her meagre resume sent by Leighton's Agency. Susan wrote a comment on the page, then looked up. 'Seems in order.'

Kate held back her sarcastic reply. 'That's good.'

'It's your first full-time job?'

Yeah, it says on the report in front of you.

'Yes. I worked part-time. Just while I got through high school. Now they've given me more hours. Almost full-time.'

'And why do you want to work in our particular office?'

I don't.

'It would give me experience with so many people. All the patients.'

Susan tapped the pen on the file as she spoke. 'You wouldn't see many patients. You'd be doing general office tasks, making the tea, mailing out referrals.'

Holy crap, making the bloody morning tea.

Kate quickly turned the automatic grimace into a smile. 'That's fine, but I thought it was the receptionist's position.'

'Not as such, as I'm sure the agency would have explained. You will need to manage a bit of everything, including relief reception. We require a person who can think on their feet.'

Why would you not?

'Sure. I've had to help my mum. She works, so I manage when she's not home.'

After Susan explained the office tasks in more detail, she shut the file and said, 'Good. I have other girls to interview, so Leighton's will be in touch. Now, any other questions?'

Money.

'Did you say how much I'd get?'

'We'd start you on sixty pounds. There'd be a probation period, and if you work out, we'll make you permanent, and an increase in wages after six months.'

Holy crap. That's a lot more than I thought.

'That's generous. Sixty a week. Good.'

Susan tapped her pen on the desk again. 'No, as we outlined through Leighton's, it's sixty pounds a fortnight.'

Nup. Not doing it for that. Might ask for full-time at Culley's. Stick with vanilla slices and Mrs Fothergill.

'Oh, okay. Well, I'll think about it.'

With a hint of a smile, Susan Whitmore said, 'We have five other applicants. We'll advise Leighton's by the end of the week. They'll advise if you've been successful.'

Kate stood, straightened her skirt, and held out her hand. 'Thank you. I'll wait for Leighton's to advise me.'

She scowled at the receptionist, shuddered at a crying baby being rocked in its mother's arms, and sighed several times as she headed for the bus.

Two days later, Kate stood at the entrance to Phillip's & Co in Mouatt Street finger-combing her hair. Deciding "sprucing up" probably required tied-back hair, she tucked her long curls behind her ears, pushed open the heavy door and entered a wood-panelled foyer.

After perching on the leather couch for nearly fifteen minutes, Kate approached the receptionist for the second time, touching the wooden block showing Trudy's name.

'I don't mean to be a nuisance, Trudy, but should I come back another day?' she asked, hoping the inference would create action.

Trudy stopped typing, replied, 'Sorry, Miss Wallace, Mr Creighton had an overseas call he had to take. If you could just be patient just a little longer. I could get you a cup of tea.'

Now embarrassed, Kate shook her head. 'No. Sorry. I... just thought perhaps if he's busy... I could—'

The phone on Trudy's desk tinkled. 'That's probably him now. Just one moment, please.'

She murmured into the phone, placed it back on the cradle, and nodded at Kate. 'Yes, I'll take you through.'

More wood-panelling covered the walls of Mr Creighton's office. Venetian blinds slanted beams of the sun across his paper-strewn desk. As Kate entered, he stood and extended his hand. 'Sorry for the wait. Miss Wallace, isn't it?'

Kate's knees threatened to defy gravity as she took his hand. Holding his eyes for longer than his hand, she swallowed hard and after a slight nod, turned away.

The interview was a disaster. Kate stuttered and stammered when answering every question. She resisted the urge to stare at his chiselled chin and his illuminating green eyes. When he explained the job entailed going to the bank and, therefore, she might need a raincoat and umbrella in case she got washed away, his smile strangled her next breath.

'Any questions?' he asked.

'No. Ah, yes. I mean, when would I start?'

He ran his hand across his oh-so-wonderful chin. 'The third of next month, Marcia is leaving the week after, that would give you that week to see what's what.'

'Good. The third. Okay.'

'Well, the agency will be in touch. Confirm the details.' He stood, held out his hand again. 'Thank you, Miss Wallace.'

Kate wiped her hand down her skirt before shaking his hand. 'Thanks. Um... I'll go.'

She almost forgot to speak with the receptionist and doubled back from the main door. 'Sorry. Thanks, Trudy. I... I'm just going.'

Trudy looked up, said with an all-knowing giggle, 'That's fine. Don't worry, he has that effect on all of us.'

'Oh! No, it's fine.'

With a quick shake of her head, Trudy spoke softly, 'Of course. And thank you for coming in. No doubt the agency will contact you.'

Wondering how different the final interview would be, Kate caught the train into Perth the next morning. Woods and Baker's newly renovated office impressed her. The crisp white floor tiles would have had Nora throwing her hands up in horror at the cleaning requirements. However, behind the reception area, the glass interior walls revealed many young women with eyes down either typing or writing in a large well-lit area. Senior personnel worked in glass-walled offices. A row of solid-walled offices painted a light blue with closed navy-blue doors embellished with golden names ran along the back wall. A surge of excitement struck Kate. Here was a situation with enough variables for promotion. There was no way she would be doing the lesser jobs for long.

'Miss Wallace?'

Kate ignored the glares of the other girls waiting in the reception area. With only two minutes to spare before her appointment time, they apparently thought she should still have to wait in line.

Once seated in front of a bird-like woman who seemed at least as old as her mother, Kate relaxed.

This might be exactly what I'm looking for.

'We take in three girls every year,' Miss Atkins said. 'One in each department: Typing, Filing and Scheduling. We don't have many resignations, some retirements, so these spots are usually because of promotion. We always promote from within.'

'Excellent,' Kate said. 'I'm keen to progress quickly.'

Miss Atkins's eye twitched. 'I see. But your resume doesn't list any office experience.'

'No, not in an office. I have a certificate for typing. I'm looking for a job I can learn and grow with.' She paused for effect. 'But I've worked part-time. I'm reliable. Very rarely sick.'

'Good. We don't tolerate tardiness.'

The explanation of the job in the typing department seemed straightforward, and Kate's mind wandered as she took in the activity in the large outside office. A bell rang. Kate turned towards the sound.

'Ah, that's morning tea,' Miss Atkins announced.

Chatter quickly filled the spaces outside Miss Atkins's glass box. The young women stood around in groups as a woman with a stainless-steel trolley full of cups, saucers, a jar of biscuits, and a large urn, clattered between them.

'We all take our breaks at the same time.' Miss Atkins stood, opened the door. 'Perhaps you'd like to go and join them. I think we've covered the important aspects of the position. The agency will be in touch.' Miss Atkins watched as the tea lady brought in a cup of tea and two plain biscuits on a plate, leaving them on the desk. 'Thanks, Nancy.'

Kate was unsure of the protocol. Did having morning tea indicate she had the job? Was it a final test?

'Come with me.' Miss Atkins led her to a group of girls. 'Beth, would you be so good as to look after Kate?'

After drinking the tea and being told that biscuits were only for the managers, Kate lingered on the edge of the chattering group. When her patience ran out—inanely nodding with the pretence of being spellbound by the chatter—she made an awkward goodbye and left them to it. Another candidate sat on the edge of the chair in front of Miss Atkins as Kate hurried past.

'How'd it go?' asked one of the girls in reception.

'Good. Very good. Seems positive.'

'Lucky you.'

Unsure if her luck would hold, and even more unsure where she wanted that luck to land, Kate wandered through Piccadilly Arcade into Hay Street, avoiding the traffic on her way to London Court where she ogled the fine jewellery and opulent millenary. Returning to the train station via William Street, she grimaced at the smell of alcohol coming from the Palace Hotel. Her thoughts turned to the homeless man who reckoned he was her father. She trembled. How could anyone drink their life away?

Snippets of questions followed by vague answers, didn't satisfy

Nora. She wanted every detail of all three interviews, but her paths and Kate's hadn't crossed much in the past weeks. Either she or Kate was at work, getting ready for work, or in Kate's case—for another interview, or they were preparing for bed.

After coming home from her shift at the laundry, she leaned against the doorjamb of Kate's room, not waiting until her daughter responded to her presence. 'I've made us a cuppa. Sliced some of that orange cake you brought home. So, come and tell me about the jobs.'

Kate closed the book, pulled her feet from under the bedcovers, and followed her mum into the kitchen. 'I think they all went well. Unsure how I'm going to choose. They all have something going for them.'

'Tell me about the one in Fremantle. That'd be closer. You might even be able to work on the weekends at Culley's.'

Kate rolled her eyes. 'No way, Mum. When I accept one of these jobs, I'm not going to keep working *there*. It's been embarrassing enough.'

'Now, Kate. That's not nice. You know we wouldn't have survived as well if you hadn't had that job. And they've been good to you.'

'Yeah, but—'

'Mrs Fothergill; remember her generosity? I reckon you won't get that sort of thing from your posh establishments. They'll make you pay for everything.'

'I suppose.'

'And if you work on Saturday, think of the extra money we'd have. We could get a new couch. Or maybe pay Bill to do more than mow the grass. We could save for a little holiday down south. We'd do so much better with both of our wages.'

Kate plopped down on the couch—the one Nora would like to replace—and closed her eyes while Nora continued to devise a wish list as she cut the cake in two uneven slices.

'Maybe a telephone. You'd like that. And I could chat with Doris and Janice. Ring Jennifer, sometimes.' With Nora's final comment, 'We could have a nice meal out at the pub,' Kate opened her eyes, fisted the arm of the couch, and yelled, 'Stop. Just stop.'

Nora jumped. 'Shit! What's wrong now?'

'If... no, *when* I get a job, the money I earn is all mine. I'm not going to be giving you any. I've supported myself for ages. When was the last time you bought anything for me?'

'Well... what about, I bought that shampoo you wanted.'

'It was on special. You use it too!'

'There was your birthday—'

'That doesn't count and you know it.' Kate twisted her hands inside each other. 'Birthday gifts aren't something you should be mentioning. Remember? You even let someone else buy my first bed... for my birthday.'

Nora ran her thick fingers through her greying hair. 'That old one. You'll never forget that, will you?'

Kate spoke softly, 'No, I won't. But fortunately for you, it's because it meant so much for me to have *someone* think I was worth spending money on. Not because you wouldn't.'

'So, does that mean you won't even take me to the pub?'

'I wouldn't think you'd want to go. You never stop blaming the pub for your woes.'

'To eat! To eat! Not to bloody drink the place dry.'

Kate raised her hands, palms towards her mother. 'Okay, we'll go for a nice meal when I get my first pay. Then that's it. Nothing else.'

'I think you should pay board. Cover the food you eat. Electricity. You do know I have to pay for all that, don't you? It's not paid for by the fairies.'

Considering this for a moment, Kate realised if she had her own place, she'd have these expenses. 'Righto. But I'm not paying for all the extras you eat.'

'Extras? What extras? You eat what I eat.'

'Come on, Mum. I've seen the things you hide at the back of the fridge. I can't imagine what you hide in your room. Nup, not those things. If you bring home the receipt from the supermarket, we'll split the bill, but we buy our own treats. You can add something for the electricity. But that's bloody all.'

Not wanting to discuss "extras" further, Nora agreed. 'You were going to tell me which job you were going to take. I'll boil the kettle again.' She placed the plate with the smaller piece of cake on Kate's lap as she walked towards the kitchen bench.

Kate sighed. *Mothers!*

Over a fresh pot of tea, Kate explained, with minimal details, what had transpired at the interviews. She added her opinion on the annoying, time-wasting experience of job hunting. Nora wanted to know if the people were nice.

'The receptionist at Phillips seemed lovely. The bit I like, that might sway me on this one, is that the boss said I'd be the one going to the bank. I'd be able to window shop, maybe pop into Culley's, pick up something to take back.'

'I thought you said you wouldn't be seen dead in there once you had another job.'

'Yeah, but as a *customer*. I would like to go in there as a *customer*.'

'Honestly, girl. You'll get your comeuppance one day.'

Kate pouted.

'Stop pouting. Tell me, what was the boss like?'

Kate drummed her fingers against her leg. 'Yeah, Mr Creighton. Dreams could be rather nice with him in them.'

'Don't be stupid, Kate. The age-old boss and secretary... never works, you know.'

'Mum! He might be dreamy, but he was wearing a wedding ring.'

'I don't want you crossing that line, girl. No good will come of it.'

'Would you approve of a young doctor who isn't hitched?'

'Doctor?'

'At the one in Subi.'

'Oh, yeah. That sounds good. Although the distance...'

'It's only a maybe. I think I'll go for the one in Perth. More opportunity for advancement. And the office is modern. Yeah, and I could spend my lunch hour in the shops.'

Nora shook her head. 'I can't believe you'll be gone all day. It won't be the same.'

'Can't wait. I'll be able to buy new clothes. I'll need a coat. It's bloody cold on the bus in winter.'

'You'll have to clean up your language. I can't imagine swearing will be allowed in front of patients.'

Kate chuckled. 'Bloody oath!'

Nora joined in the mirth, then picking up her empty cup, stood. 'We'll be fine. We've done okay so far. We'll get by.'

'That's just it. I don't want to "get by". I want to be rich. Have everything I dreamed about.'

'And what, may I ask, do you expect that to be?'

'A beautiful house, modern stuff. TV, telephone—'

'Yes, I'd love a telephone. I could ring Doris.'

With her mum now leaning over the sink—the podgy bulge of her stomach hard up against the cupboard door, her dress straining over her backside, the varicose veins showing on the back of her knees—Kate couldn't understand why her mother's dream was to ring Doris.

'You ring Doris all the time. Why would that be top of the wish list?'

Nora turned, tugged on her ear. 'I could also ring Janice whenever I wanted. Find out about family. I wouldn't have to walk to the corner to that dirty phone box only to find the thing jammed.'

'Mum! When was the last time you did that? Get real. You ring someone from the laundromat nearly every day. And then you use the phone at Yeo's. I've caught you.'

'Yeah, well, it's not the same, is it? They can't ring me. I'm the one who takes the risk. It'd be lovely to sit in my own home and chat.'

'We'll put it on the list.'

'Cut the sarcasm. It's alright for you. You have no friends. You don't need a phone.'

Rather than try and refute that insult, Kate left the room, consoling herself with a chat to Benji. 'I'd have friends if there was someone worthwhile being a friend with. Maybe I'll find a workplace friend.' Benji thought it might be possible.

KATE'S DIARY

1964

2 September: The long road to success. I have a job. Started last week. Excited. It's a bit of a pain having to catch the bus all the way, or to the station and then into Perth.

16 September: First pay in fourteen days. Had to take Mum to the pub. She reckons I promised. Anyway, it was nice. If I had MONEY, I'd never eat at home.

Now I want to go shopping, put some clothes on lay-by. Maybe some slacks. And that coat I saw in Aherns.

19 September: Ran into Fiona. Away from those bitches she seems okay. Posh. Money. Her bag was real leather.

26 September: On Saturday, I got picked up in a bloody MERC! How's that? Jealousy level sky-high. Shorthand. Fiona knows shorthand. Would like to add shorthand to my abilities. That'd be cool.

3 October: What a fab coat. Store Account. Wish I had one. Still have to pay—that might be an issue!

And everyone is expected to have a phone in their house. Shit, it's so difficult using Mr Yeo's. Mum's a bloody pain.

6 October: Hell of a lunch. Mrs Noble turned out to be a friend of Mrs Fothergill's. Coral and Elspeth—could they talk! I should have gone by myself. Maybe next time will work in my favour. Elspeth! I mean she's a nice old lady, and so posh, Elspeth sort of suits her.

Chapter 10

The following Monday, Kate rang Leighton's as instructed. Apparently, she didn't have a choice of jobs. Only Woods and Baker had offered her a position. Nora wasn't pleased as now Kate wouldn't arrive home early enough to start dinner.

The thrill of employment faded when the spring breeze tossed aside Kate's carefully groomed hair, forcing her to finger-comb it into place as she stood in the foyer. Annoyance bubbled over her nervousness, and if Woods and Baker hadn't been a few blocks from the centre of the city, her need for a wage might have been ignored in favour of the perfumed counters of David Jones.

To top off a mundane day of producing tax returns for people with money, rain soaked her feet as she walked from the bus stop on her way home.

Kate reckoned this simple typing of figures could have been done by a monkey. At morning tea, the silence was anything but golden when Kate told the other six girls this.

'A monkey wouldn't know when something wasn't quite right,' Jane said.

'It's a metaphor.' Kate narrowed her stare as several blank faces looked at her. 'You know, a... never mind. How long have you been in the tax form area, Gail?'

'Six years.'

'How long?' Kate couldn't imagine surviving six months. 'Why?'

It seemed Gail, Jane and the other girls liked the mediocrity, the reliability of having a job they could leave at the door each evening on the dot of five o'clock. They had another life.

'Like what?' Kate asked.

'I can't wait for the weekends,' Jane explained. 'I have my baby for two whole days. His grandmother gets a break. Grant has made him a big boy's bed. He's almost walking now.'

This provided the catalyst for the rest of them to ask for the latest picture of baby Charlie, what he ate, what he said. Kate lost track of the details of how to test if the bathwater was too hot or too cold for a ten-month-old baby and returned to her desk early. If she could get through a couple of extra tax forms, maybe she'd reach her target and not have to suffer another lecture from the supervisor.

When the bell announced the close of the day over the annoying Tannoy, some girls hovered at the staff exit delaying their goodbyes. Kate eased between them. A couple said a polite goodnight. She muttered a reply and walked away. She strode out, hurrying towards Wellington Street, enjoying the activity after sitting for most of the day.

While waiting for the train, she purchased a newspaper determined to find a job that offered something more than mind-destroying repetition. Once seated, she opened the paper to the Situations Vacant page. As the train pulled out, someone called her name.

'Kate! Good to see you.'

Someone sat down, squashing David Jones shopping bags into the small space, bumping Kate's arm, making the newspaper fall apart. Kate grabbed the pages, turned to see Fiona Noble nodding at her.

'Didn't expect you.'

'Sorry about your paper. I'm doing a shorthand course. I did some shopping, so I'm a little later than usual.'

As Kate organised the paper, folding then rolling it, Fiona shifted her shopping onto her lap.

After several moments of awkward silence, Fiona asked, 'And you? Been shopping?'

'Not likely.' She glanced sideways at Fiona. 'I've been working.'

'You have a job?'

'Yeah.'

'How's it going? Where is it? How long have you been there?'

This was three more questions than Kate had heard Fiona ask—ever. 'Um, yeah. It's okay.'

'Sorry. I guess I shouldn't be so nosy.'

Kate shrugged. 'It's okay.' She looked down at the newspaper reading half a headline, wondering what the rest could be.

'I'm sorry.' Fiona said again.

'I said it's okay. No need to go on.'

Fiona gave a jerky nod. 'Look, it's not just about all these questions. I should have been a little nicer. You know, at typing class. I just didn't have the nerve to speak up against Lola.'

'Yeah.' Kate looked closely at Fiona, wondering if she meant what she said. 'Have you seen them since?'

'No way. Lola asked me to go to her party, but there weren't going to be any parents so Dad wouldn't let me go.'

'If you wanted to go, you needn't have told him.'

Fiona's eyes widened. 'Lied? No way. I couldn't. Dad trusts me. Anyway, parents have the unique talent of finding out.' She chuckled. 'I didn't really want to go. Lola's parties are a bit wild. She actually brags about it. Can you believe that?'

'Yeah, Lola does a whole lot of bragging about everything. Cow!'

'So, you forgive me?'

'Course.'

'Good. Tell me about the job.'

'You first. Why are you doing shorthand? Don't you want to get a job straight away?'

Fiona explained her father hoped she'd eventually work in his construction company and as her allowance was already more than a junior clerk earned, it seemed unwise to hasten into a job without a necessary skill.

'I can be a private secretary.'

'Good idea. More money.'

'You should do the shorthand course. It's a sinch.'

'Nup, can't afford to. Got to have a job. Even a boring one.'

'Why is it boring? Haven't you made some friends?'

Turning the paper over, wasting time, wishing she didn't have to answer, Kate shook her head. 'Yeah, lots of friends.' Her eyes glazed over as she thought of all the times she'd enjoyed listening to the tea lady relate stories of her European holiday, instead of standing through another session on babies and car repayments.

'Good for you. I was going to suggest we could get together. But if you've got lots of new friends, you probably don't want to do that.'

A strange sensation flipped Kate's stomach. It filled the empty space in her chest, warmed her cheeks, and made her smile. 'I'd like that. They… anyway, they all seem to live north. Don't reckon I'll bother to see them outside of work.'

'Right, let's see. Would you like to come to our house on a weekend? Nothing special. Dad will probably start the barbie. We can watch the telly. If there's anything decent. Or a movie.'

The overwhelming feeling struck again, but Kate wasn't sure of Fiona's motive. 'Why?'

'Why what?'

Kate rubbed at the grey marks the paper had left on her fingers. 'I'm not exactly your best friend. I mean, this is the longest we've talked. Why would you suddenly ask me to your house?'

Fiona put her hand on Kate's arm. 'You never know, maybe we *could* become best friends. Despite what you may think, I don't make friends easily. Because… well, who knows why, but I think we could be friends. What do you say? Maybe if you give me a ring on Friday, we could arrange something for Saturday.'

'Oh, I don't know.' Nora's apt description of the phone box on the corner sprang to Kate's mind.

'Or Sunday.'

'No, Saturday's fine. It's just… well, I… No, it's okay. I'll ring. Give me your number. I'll ring Friday when I get home from work. That's not too late, is it?'

Fiona wrote her number on the top of a page of the paper, clicked the gold-coloured ballpoint, and tucked it into her leather handbag.

Kate tugged the newspaper over her vinyl version of much the same bag.

They giggled over the stories Kate told of her workmates and the antics of Fiona's cat. Engrossed in the shorthand tutorial, Fiona had to scurry from her seat when the train pulled into her station.

After an automatic wave as the train left Victoria Street station, Kate leaned back and relived the encounter. This could be another step in her reinvention. A ticket into the life of the wealthy. But as she kissed her crossed fingers, she couldn't ignore the floaty new feeling of the possibility of a real friend.

Kate's lack of enthusiasm made another day of mindlessly typing figures onto a tax form seem endless. Ignoring the Friday night chatter of the others, she hurried to the early train. Her purse held several coins and Fiona's phone number.

With the phone box roped off with plastic tape because of three broken windows, and the handpiece dangling forlornly, Kate fingered the tape, imagining her chance of a pleasurable Saturday disappearing as fast as the summer rain racing down the drain beside her. She swiped the water from her face and dawdled back home.

Fortune sometimes smiles. On the kitchen bench, a note from her mother advised that because of the unexpected storm, Mr Yeo had called by and insisted on taking her in for an unscheduled mopping up session, and could Kate start on the veggies. Kate changed her clothes and waited impatiently for the bus to go the few stops to the cluster of shops which included the grocery store.

'Mum! Mum!' Kate thumped the front door of Yeo & Co. The rattling brought Nora scurrying. She thrust the door open, swearing at being disturbed, but anxious—something must be wrong for her daughter to front up at her work.

'What's happened?' Nora's eyes flicked over Kate. 'You okay?'

'Sure. I did get your message but I want to use the phone.' She saw annoyance flash into Nora's eyes. 'If it's okay. Please, Mum.'

Nora locked the door again behind Kate. She held a soggy towel at her side as she toddled to the back room. 'It'd better be urgent. And you'll have to be quick, Mr Yeo is coming back.'

With the scrap of paper with Fiona's number in her fingers, Kate stepped carefully across the damp floor. 'Flood?'

'The window was left open. He wants it cleaned up before stock gets damaged.' She frowned at Kate. 'Who are you ringing that's so bloody urgent?'

'Fiona.'

'Right urgent.' Nora scowled. 'Anyway, Fiona who? Someone from work?'

'No way. All they can talk about is babies and boyfriends.'

'Ah, and Miss High-and-Mighty wants to talk about Paris and London.' Nora held out the handpiece. 'God forbid that teenagers might want to talk about boyfriends.'

Kate dialled slowly, considered hanging up, but a creamy male voice answered before she could. 'Good evening, Noble household. Can I help you?'

'Mr Noble? May I speak with Fiona please?'

'Is that the lovely Kate?'

It took her a moment to answer—the fact that Fiona had talked of her visit surprised Kate. 'Yes.'

'Good, just a moment. I think my daughter is here... somewhere.'

Mr Noble chuckled as Fiona said hello, then spoke away from the mouthpiece. 'Thanks, Dad. You can leave me alone now.'

Kate heard Mr Noble chuckle again.

'Sorry, Kate, my dad is a pain sometimes.'

The chit-chat around Fiona's giggles continued until Nora prodded Kate, scowling and pointing towards the front door. Fortunately, the teenagers' arrangements had been finalised. Kate smiled as she hung up the phone and took the mop from her mother.

'Just finishing up,' Nora said as Mr Yeo entered the back room. 'Kate's helping.'

The rain cleared overnight and Kate cheerfully included Nora in her excitement of Saturday's outing.

'Fiona said her mum would pick me up from the bus stop. Do you think I should have bought something for her?'

'I wouldn't go that far, but I'm sure Bill won't mind you snipping off a couple of his roses. Last time he did the lawn, he said I could have the ones hanging over the fence.'

'Fab. Where are the scissors? How many do you think? I might pick some of your fishbone ferns. What should I wrap them in?'

The flowers lay on the kitchen table while Kate changed her mind about what to wear. Armed with a jumper in her bag, the posy sticking out of a corner, and a book to read on the bus, Kate nodded her goodbye to Nora, told her not to worry if she was late, and she probably wouldn't want dinner, and—

'Just go, Kate. The bloody bus won't wait.'

Throughout the bus trip, the book stayed in her bag as Kate fiddled with the strap of the bag and her fingernails, and worried about the clothes she'd chosen. She alighted, looked around for Fiona. Fiona waved enthusiastically from beyond the rolled-down window of a silver Merc.

'Kate, Kate, we're here.'

Taking a deep breath, Kate stepped towards the car. *Holy shit! A Merc.*

Seated in the back, and an awkward introduction across the top of the front seat of the car completed, Kate lifted the roses. 'Um, these are for you, Mrs Noble. Shall I hang onto them for now?'

'How lovely. Thank you. Yes.' Mrs Noble pointed to the steering wheel. 'Needs my full attention.'

Kate ran her hand over the seat's soft leather. 'Nice car.'

They discussed the weather and the inconvenience of public transport on the short trip to Fiona's home. Kate gave brief answers as she tried not to stare at Mrs Noble's five—*holy smoke, diamond*—rings.

When the garage door slid open with a press of a button, Kate's eyes widened again. As she squeezed between the Merc she'd arrived in and another bigger model, a shiver of delight hit the back of her neck. Manners demanded she didn't comment on the manicured garden, the marble stairs, the glass-fronted door, the chandelier in a substantial entry hall, and the size of the kitchen with two ovens and a double-door fridge. Her eyes couldn't take in everything; her brain fretted over how one family had so much.

Aunt Janice and to a lesser degree, Aunt Jennifer, owned houses Kate envied as a child. Chidley House had been described as "grand" but the Nobles's home oozed all Kate could imagine and more.

Seated on Fiona's bed, bare feet tucked under a luxuriously padded quilt, the girls shared their views on Miss Trantor. Kate waved away Fiona's repeated apology, glad to have someone agree with her opinion on annoying Wanda and the subtle bullying of Lola.

'We all change,' Kate surmised. 'Getting a job is a big change. And I expect a lot of changes, you know, as we get older.'

'And wiser! Can you imagine being thirty?'

'Well, I promise you I'm not going to be working at Woods and Baker when I'm thirty.'

'Why not? It's a reputable firm. Dad uses them sometimes.'

'It's just so damn boring. There's even a bell, for God's sake. For morning and afternoon tea, lunch, and knock-off time. It blasts out, scaring me half to death. You can't stop one second before it rings. And if you want to go to the toilet, you have to ask the supervisor. They don't actually stop anyone, but you still have to ask! Isn't that the pits?'

'I guess. Why did you leave your last job? Wasn't that closer to home?'

'Culley's? Yeah. Dead-end. I didn't want to be still working in a tea shop when I turned thirty.' She shook her head. 'I think Edith's not far off thirty, already.'

'You didn't like it there?'

'Sort of. They were fair. I didn't have to ask to go to the toilet. We got a discount on the food they couldn't keep for the next day. And some of the customers were great.' Kate told of Mrs Fothergill and her typewriter and wasn't surprised when Fiona said the name seemed familiar. *Did all the rich and famous know each other?* 'She even said she'd take me to lunch. I have her phone number somewhere. Probably won't go.' Kate ran her tongue across her teeth. 'Would you come with me if I did go?'

'Sure, it would save you being stuck with her. But depends on when you go.'

'It wouldn't be like that. I get on with old people. I'll tell you about Syd and Stan one day. They were great. Far more interesting than those stupid girls at work. If I do go, I'll ask if you can come too.'

'Why'd you leave then? You could have learned enough to start your own café. Imagine that.'

Kate hadn't imagined that possibility. 'Maybe. Be hard work.'

'Would be. I'd rather not have to work. You know, be like Mum. She can go into the office if she wants. Or just be at home. She does charity work and goes to lots of lunches. Looks good to me. What about you?'

Drifting away to a posh restaurant dressed in glamorous clothes, showing off diamond rings, Kate missed Fiona's question.

'Kate?'

Fiona's insistent voice destroyed the imagery of glamour. Kate answered, 'Your mum is married. Obviously to your dad. He has a lucrative business. So, maybe that's where we should be headed. Finding a rich bloke.'

Considering her family's dynamics, Fiona replied slowly. 'How do you know if someone is rich? If a boy asks you out, you can hardly ask to see his bank balance.'

'No, but you just don't fall in love until you know their potential... or bank balance.'

'Dad wasn't rich when he married Mum. She said it was love at first sight. For her. Dad took some convincing, apparently.' Fiona chuckled. 'Mum said he was determined to have a big house on the beachfront. That's why he went into construction. I reckon he's pretty used to having money.' She pointed out the view from the window. 'Great isn't it. And what about your dad? How did your parents meet?'

'Nah, Dad...' Kate, caught between truth and lie, hesitated. 'Um, not sure. Never asked.' She rolled over and checked out the ceiling. 'I'm not settling. Ever.'

As the two teenagers considered a future where choices were theirs to take, Mrs Noble knocked on the door announcing lunchtime.

After ham and cheese sandwiches, a chocolate slice, and sweet, sugary tea, Fiona brought out her shorthand book. 'Would you help me with this? You just have to read a sentence, and I'll try to write the shorthand.'

Fascinated by the squiggles, dots and dashes, Kate promised to read as many sentences as Fiona wished if she'd let her copy down a few basics. They were still working over the shorthand when Mrs Noble leaned in through the doorway and announced it was time for Kate to go.

'Damn!' Kate winced. 'Sorry.'

Mrs Noble grinned. 'It's okay, Kate. We're in the building industry and on any given day, the lads on site can come up with much worse. But young ladies should watch their language.'

'Can't you stay a little longer?' Fiona pleaded.

Kate hesitated, but Mrs Noble spoke first. 'Kate's mother will be worried if she doesn't arrive home at the right time. She might not let Kate come again.'

It crossed Kate's mind that her mother was probably devouring treats and some soap opera on TV, not even noticing the time. 'Mm, maybe.'

'Does your mum work, Kate?'

'Yes.'

Mrs Noble waited for more information, but Kate gathered her things, tied on her shoes, and ignored the inference.

'What does she do?'

With another expletive hovering, Kate said, 'She works in the office at a grocery store.' Nora did have to clean the office as well as the shop.

'Good. Is that why you're interested in office work?'

'Dad used to work in Singapore, in the embassy. Interesting stuff. Yeah, office work can provide the opportunity I'm looking for.'

Mrs Noble ushered them out of the bedroom and towards the car. 'Good for you. That's where Fiona's heading, but she'll be working for her father. Won't you, Fi?'

Fiona said yes but pulled a face behind her mother's back and shrugged towards Kate.

The girls sat in the back of the car whispering their arrangements to meet in the city next Saturday to go shopping. The nights were still cold and Kate needed a coat.

With a hint of a smile, Mrs Noble let them think they had invented the act of keeping secrets from parents.

Chapter 11

Sunday meant chores for Kate, while her mum pulled a few weeds before demanding refreshments.

Kate's weekday routine of public transport bookending the monotonous completion of tax forms was only slightly better than having to poke at the veins in the liver set before her at dinner time.

Saturday arrived, and with her purse holding a few pounds she'd saved, Kate hurried from the station towards Boans Department Store in Murray Street, not wanting to keep Fiona waiting. She paced several times between the staircase and the front door, impatient to browse through the women's department on the first floor.

Positive it wasn't only two minutes since she'd last checked the time on her watch, Kate walked up the stairs in case Fiona had meant the *top* of the stairs. As she plonked her way down each step, slightly annoyed, Fiona, waving frantically, caught her eye.

'Sorry, I'm late, Kate. I just had to stop for a look at the perfumes.'

'It's okay. I was just worried you'd changed your mind.'

'I wouldn't do that. Come on, let's find you a fabulous coat.'

They hurried up the stairs, Kate checking out Fiona's straight lines of her fine denier stockings, wishing she had made time to wash hers instead of wearing thick, unfashionable ones.

As they pushed the coats along the racks, Fiona asked, 'Are you going to get black?'

'Nup. With my dark hair, Mum reckons I'll look like I'm in mourning.'

'No way. It's the fashion.'

Kate held up a brown version of the one Fiona had indicated. 'What about this?'

'Yuck.'

She'd almost given up the search when she spotted another rack tucked in the corner near the lingerie department. 'This is it!' She held a multi-coloured coat against her chest. 'And it's my size.'

'It's rather daring. Are you sure you won't get sick of yellow?'

Kate put her arm into the sleeve. 'No way. I love the houndstooth pattern. And the yellow is subtle enough between the brown and beige. No, I love it.'

'How much is it?'

'Don't care.'

Her money didn't cover the expensive purchase, so the assistant suggested lay-by.

'I guess.' Kate fingered the lapel. 'I really need it now; it's so cold going home on the train.'

'What if I put it on Mum's account? You can pay her back.'

Kate stared at Fiona, her heart racing. 'You would do that?'

'Course.'

'Shouldn't you ask her first?'

The assistant stopped preparing the required paperwork. 'You can't use another person's account.'

Fiona pulled a card from her wallet and held it out. 'I have her permission. Here's the account number.' She looked at Kate. 'I use it all the time. I'm pretty sure Mum won't mind.'

'Gosh. Are you sure?' Kate removed her arm from the coat. 'I certainly could do with it now.'

Over iced chocolate in the cafeteria, Fiona waved away Kate's numerous versions of appreciation. 'It's payback for all the awful things I did at typing school. Let's call us quits.'

'Okay, that's fair enough. But I'll pay you back as quickly as I can.'

'Stop it. We're quits, remember. Let's talk about something else.'

'Right. By the way, I rang Mrs Fothergill. She said you could come.'

'Come? Where? When?'

'Next Saturday. You know, you said you'd come with me. She wanted me to go to her place, but getting there is too hard. Somewhere in Cottesloe. Knight Street? Nup, can't remember. Anyway, she said we shouldn't go to Culley's. Seems *I* wouldn't relax.' Kate grimaced. 'Too damn right. Imagine me being served by Edith. Em-barr-a-ssing.'

'Right, and so where?'

'Seasons Bistro, on Stirling Highway. I'll have to find out the bus route. It's a proper restaurant. For lunch. Wow!'

They dawdled back to the station. On the train, they sat in comfortable silence until Fiona poked Kate's arm. 'What if you come to my place?'

'I can't. Not today.'

'No, silly. Not now, I meant next Saturday. Then Mum could take us both.'

Kate considered this alternative. 'Um, maybe.'

'It'd be cool.' Fiona clapped her hands.

'Hang on, I didn't say yes.'

'Well, why not?'

'Look, what if I get the bus there. Then, I assume your mum will pick you up afterwards, she could take me back to the bus stop. That'd be cool, and I wouldn't be putting you out.'

Fiona's face drooped; she crossed her arms. 'I just thought... Don't you want to come to my house again?'

'It's not like that.'

'Then how is it?'

Flashes of Nora insisting Kate read her book in the washhouse and not wear out her welcome in Miss Chidley's front room crossed Kate's mind as she stuttered through an explanation. Fiona insisted it would be okay but Kate continued to worry.

In the end, Kate said she'd get her own way to Seasons Bistro but relented and accepted the offer of a lift back to Fiona's after lunch, where she'd stay a few hours.

As arranged, Kate caught the bus, arriving with five minutes to spare. Taking a deep breath, straightening her top, she pushed open the door to a room full of unfamiliar aromas. The white tablecloths and an array of cutlery and sparkling glassware added to the quality of the upmarket bistro. She paused at the front desk hoping she hadn't arrived before Mrs Fothergill.

Mrs Fothergill's queen-like wave caught Kate's eye and with a sigh of relief, she headed towards the table in the corner.

Kate hesitated over the greeting, but the elderly lady pointed to her cheek and said, 'A kiss, I think.'

After Kate obliged, she explained, 'My friend should be here soon. Her mum's bringing her.'

'She's not late yet. However, I always prefer to be early. A good trait to have, I think. Sometimes you can catch people out.' She chuckled. 'Find out things they want hidden.' On seeing Kate frown, she added, 'but not too early. It goes against good taste to be too early.'

Kate mumbled her agreement.

'I'll order juice.' Mrs Fothergill turned a water glass upright. 'Now, before your friend gets here. How's the typing going? Have you found a worthwhile job?'

Kate's answers were interrupted as Fiona and Mrs Noble entered the restaurant. Mrs Fothergill ran her hand over her chin. 'Good heavens. Coral Noble.' She turned to Kate. 'Don't tell me your friend is a Noble!'

'Is that a good thing?'

Mrs Fothergill stood, gave a regal wave in Fiona and Coral's direction. 'Well, I never.'

'El! How nice to see you after all this time.' Coral exchanged a lingering hug with Elspeth Fothergill. They kept their hands entwined as they looked each other over, exclaimed how neither had changed a bit, added some 'remember when...' and 'is it really twenty-six years!'

Insisting Coral stay, Elspeth took charge ordering juice for the girls and white wine for herself and Coral. In between browsing the menu, Elspeth explained to Kate how she had engaged Gene Noble to expand and renovate her Cottesloe property. Elspeth had helped with the interior choices, and the two women had become friends but lost touch when Coral spent more time in the ever-growing building company's office.

While Kate enjoyed every mouthful of the pan-fried snapper and apple crumble, she felt cheated out of the expected tete-a-tete with an elderly friend who might help her find a way out of State Housing and into "society". Fiona and Kate whispered their news, frowning at the older women enjoying themselves a little too noisily for teenager's sensitivity.

Annoyed at the afternoon not turning out as she'd hoped, Kate refused to stay at the Noble's for dinner, making the excuse that Nora would worry. 'Anyway,' Kate said, 'I'm still full from lunch.'

Kate had intended to give Fiona some money to pass on to her mum against the outstanding amount for her coat. But as she opened her purse, a rare moment of silence from the older women meant the exchange didn't take place.

As they left the restaurant, a gust of wind made them grimace.

'Should have brought a cardigan,' Fiona said.

Mrs Noble agreed, then spoke to Kate, 'I believe you bought a coat. Fi said it's rather nice.'

'Yes, it's the one—'

'The one I helped her pick out.' Fiona grabbed Kate's wrist and dug in her fingernails.

'Um, yes.' Kate raised her eyebrows at Fiona in question.

Mrs Noble rubbed her bare arm. 'Let's hope summer kicks in

soon and we won't need our coats at night.'

So, as they sat in the back of the car travelling towards the bus stop, Kate stared at Fiona, waiting for an answer.

'It's okay,' Fiona whispered. 'I paid for it.'

'What?'

'I told you, it's even-stevens now.'

Mrs Noble glanced at Kate in the rear-view mirror. 'Everything okay, back there?'

'Yes, Mum.' Fiona glared at Kate. 'Sush, not now.'

Kate's mind did somersaults as she rehashed the day, considering it an error on her behalf to include Fiona in the lunch, and certainly not at all pleased with how it turned into a reunion between the "old" ladies. However, she repeatedly shook her head when going over the brief exchange concerning her coat. She couldn't believe Fiona had lied. Barefaced lied! It came to her as she struggled towards her home against the strong cold wind that maybe she wasn't the only one who took a rather inventive way through life.

KATE'S DIARY

1965

9 October: This job is soooo booooring. I think I'll die if I have to stay here much longer. And the dribble they talk about at morning tea. Who the hell cares if the baby cried all night or if nappies won't dry? A few single girls, but they want to talk about their boyfriends. Boring, boring, boring. Wish Stan and Syd were still alive. They'd be more interesting than this bunch of twits.

14 October: Sweet Sixteen today, Benji. Thanks for the love. Not a lot from Mother Dear. Although she did bring a cake home. And the blouse fitted. Hilarious card. Getting too old for this diary crap. It can stay in the cupboard.

15 October: Simply had to add something. I can't believe how disappointing the business world is. And what an old bag. No wonder she's a MISS.

17 October: Yep, out the door I went. Didn't plan it, but honestly. Couldn't put up with the crap and the boredom. So glad I did. But now what?

18 October: Mum, of course, went ballistic. Think she saw her desire for a phone fly out the window. Would be cool to have one at home.

19 October: Getting a job should be easy—now I've got experience.

I need a job.

24 November: Exasperating. I didn't expect to start at the top, BUT now it looks like the bloody bottom.

Chapter 12

Life at Woods and Baker continued with repetitive boredom. Kate had previously been called into Miss Atkins's office and reprimanded for her audacity in suggesting improvements to the antiquated filing system and the rearrangement of the school-room array of desks. The latest infringement to attract Miss Atkins's ire was for daring to ask, in writing, for a promotion to the secretarial typing pool.

'Miss Wallace, you've been with us for eight months and your work, if not your attitude, has been satisfactory. But I don't think you're ready for advancement.' Miss Atkins laid her hand over a standard buff-coloured file on her desk. 'We have several memos in this file that show a complete lack of respect to management. I'm sorry, but your request has been denied.'

Kate opened her mouth but held back words that would have made the lads at Noble Construction balk. 'Lack of respect? My... giddy aunt!' Although she wanted to thump the desk and yell, Kate lowered her voice. She knew glass walls had ears. 'I don't see how making suggestions is a lack of respect. Surely any good manager would *want* to improve the workplace situation.' She folded her arms and glared at Miss Atkins, who shifted in her seat and primped the cuffs on her blouse.

'There is always the correct way to do things and, I might say, you have yet to experience tact and thoughtfulness.'

Kate rolled her eyes. 'Tact, eh? You mean... oh, never mind. This place is locked in the dark ages. All I was trying to do was... Like, it wouldn't hurt to stagger the tea breaks. It might even give poor Nancy time to go to the toilet. Oh, no, she'd had to ask for permission first, wouldn't she? And then she mightn't ring the bloody bell on time.'

Miss Atkins's neck turned pink. She flapped the file in front of her face. Several pages fell to the floor.

'I think I should probably go.' Kate stood.

'Miss Wallace, please sit. I haven't finished with you.'

'Oh, but Miss Atkins, I've finished with you.' Kate picked up the pieces of paper from the floor and placed them on the desk. 'Maybe you could add my resignation to this glorious file. Yeah, then you'll be finished with me after all.' Kate tugged open the door, looked over her shoulder and said quietly, 'Is there a form to fill in, or do I just wait for the home-time bell like a good little girl?'

By the time she'd reached her desk, Lillian, her supervisor, was cradling the phone and waiting for her. 'I believe you've resigned.'

'You'd better believe it.'

'Miss Atkins said if you leave tonight, you will forfeit pay. There is a two-week notice which must be observed.'

Kate grabbed her handbag, two pens from the desk, looked around at gaping girls, and replied, 'Two frigging weeks. No way. Two more minutes, and I'll be scarred for life.'

'Please, Kate. I've got to have a Finalisation Form from you. Please.'

'Honestly, Lillian, if that's all it takes to keep you happy, where's the damn form?'

Miss Atkins came through to the section as Kate thrust the completed form at Lillian. Other girls had hovered around her desk, a couple voicing honest regret at her departure while most whispered their opinions about someone they *just knew* would never fit in *here*.

'Your proportionate annual leave entitlements will be available at the end of the week. I suggest you call in and pick up the cheque.' Miss Atkins's bird-like face puckered into a grimace. 'It is most unfortunate for your employment to end this way.'

Kate glanced around the group of girls. 'Yeah, it was never going to end well, was it?'

'Of course, we *all* wish you Godspeed, don't we, girls.' Several murmured their agreement. 'Maybe a more *progressive* company might be for you.'

Kate thanked Miss Atkins for her *kind* words. Not wanting to blow the burnt bridge to smithereens, she shook Lillian's hand and accepted a half-hearted hug from Jane.

As she walked from the circle of workmates, Kate cupped her ear. 'Is that the tolling of the bell I hear loud and clear?'

Some girls sniggered. Miss Atkins clapped twice. 'Back to work. We can't be standing gawking all afternoon; targets must be met.'

Nora couldn't believe her daughter could be so stupid, so childish, so inconsiderate, so damn—

'Shut up, Mum. You wouldn't believe what it was like to work there. I mean, you wouldn't believe the total sum of what I learned while I was there. Syd and Miss Tillman taught me more in one evening than that place.' She pointed to an imaginary document on the table. 'Read an amount, type it in this space. Oh, look a name and address. Isn't it exciting? *This* farmer comes from Kondinin.' She bit into a buttered scone, kept talking around the mouthful. 'Or Kulin, or Geraldton.' She paused in her condescending diatribe.

'Well, there you go. You've probably never heard of Kulin before.'

'It's a small place near Albany.'

'How could you possibly know that?'

'Miss Tillman said one of the teachers she worked with had come from there. We found it on the map.'

'Bloody hell!' Nora added jam to a scone and ran her finger along the side of the blade, relishing the extra. 'I'm not even going to ask about Kondinin.'

'The most exciting thing I learned was that an *undulating* section is preferable to a rocky outcrop on your spare paddock.'

'What?'

'And...' Kate rolled her eyes, 'when I take up farming, I'll look out for one with *undulating* paddocks.' Kate took a scone with homemade strawberry jam from her mother's plate. 'You just never know when *undulating* paddocks will rear their ugly *undulating* heads.'

They giggled their way through another scone each. Kate made comments about the undulating surface of her scone. Nora nibbled on an edge, asking if that was a rocky outcrop or an undulating section.

Over breakfast, their conversation turned to job opportunities, budgets, social service applications, and what Nora wanted for dinner.

Kate explained she'd look for a job but first, she wanted a break. Then she'd ring Leighton's Agency. They would still have her details on file and she now had office experience, making her more employable in any fancy office.

With two lazy days of nothingness, Kate called in at Leighton's without an appointment. She waited impatiently, reading nonsense in out-of-date magazines, watching and judging each young woman who entered.

After twenty minutes of fidgeting and with her pulse building, Kate sat in Miss Fellows' office knowing she'd have to pull out an exceptional performance—feigning calmness and enthusiasm.

Miss Atkins's refusal to give Kate more than a Certificate of Work meant Lucy Fellows frowned when reviewing Kate's possibilities. Potential employers considered a lack of a reference from a previous work situation a warning sign. It could be difficult under that opinion to encourage employers to take a chance.

Four weeks later, Kate still mooched around the house doing minimal housework and avoiding Fiona's invitations issued through an irritated Nora at the laundromat.

A visit to Social Services for Unemployment Benefits meant more frustration. Rules couldn't be broken, and Kate simply had to wait six weeks before receiving payments.

In financial desperation and a need to be free from domesticity, Kate told Lucy Fellows she'd consider "anything".

Benji bore the brunt of her exasperation the night before she started work at a supermarket in Fremantle.

She tossed her diary at the wall and vowed her life was never going to have anything worth writing about ever again.

KATE'S DIARY
1969

6 April: Four years! And nothing to show for it. I hated the early mornings – especially in a hot bakery. And then that freezer aisle in the supermarket. Barely tolerable. Fiona doesn't understand why my moods change hot and cold like those places. She doesn't have to earn a living.

It's hardly been worth writing about my mundane life but this last week takes the prize! Have to record it, just because it's so bad no one would believe it!

7 April: Pissed off at work. They're all such idiots.

20 April: Belinda Appleyard honestly!!!!! No brains that one.

21 April: I can tell them anything. Suckers.

28 April: Need a different job. Mum's giving me shit again.

3 May: Have to up my game. I'm not being a check-out chick for the rest of my life.

8 May: Paris cancelled. Huh! Imagine what old Mrs Vaughan would say if she knew the full story. And that pain-in-the-butt Belinda? Well, it's too bad she won't get her chance to gloat.

Chapter 13

'Doing anything special this weekend?'

Kate was either the speaker or the listener of this sentence… repeatedly. Sometimes, she wished none of the customers would bother to speak—just stand there, unpack the trolley, watch, pay, and leave. Didn't anyone know silence is golden?

But no, even if the customer only grunted as they dropped their items onto the counter, management expected one to say something pleasant. What was it they said in the training she had to sit through a month ago? Engage the customers. Get to know them. Make them happy to come back.

What a load of rubbish!

She arched her back and stretched her neck. *What's that tired platitude about love making the world go around? Bullshit! It was money that turned the globe on its axis. Look how the world gathers fiscal momentum when the stock market flourishes. Try telling all the financial benefactors they should rely on love to keep their world happy. Anyone in love realises they still have to pay the mortgage, and most of them still want to eat. Not to mention the other half of one's love nest always expecting a token of that love. That usually means purchasing something expensive on credit. Yes, it's definitely money that keeps the world spinning.*

Kate's mood darkened while she waited impatiently for a dour young mother with a whimpering child to place her items on the counter. She'd tried love, albeit the brief and teenage type, and the so-called spinning that made the world go round was not conducive to reflective satisfaction. Now, she wanted to actively try "money" but it would take more than working in a supermarket to achieve wealth.

'What exciting adventure are you up to this time, young lady?'

Kate looked up, focused on the regular customer. 'Hi, Mrs Vaughan. Let's see. I'm taking a week off and flying to Paris.'

'First class, I hope!'

'Of course. Mum wouldn't go otherwise.'

As blue vein cheese, pate, and other items from the deli filled the plastic bag, Mrs Vaughan frowned as she asked, 'Kate, isn't it?'

'Yeah, so it says.' Kate pointed to her name badge.

The woman formed a half-smile. 'I seem to remember you were going away last week. Wasn't it to Vienna?'

Kate paused and held the carton of double thick cream for a moment before she placed it into the shopping bag. She laughed and shook her head, making her hair clips shake as if ready to let the long dark curls fall from their grasp. 'Vienna, well, that didn't happen. Mum had an important engagement at the last minute—again! Paris is to make up for it.'

'Vienna, Paris, surely not on the salary you get here.'

Kate squinted at her chipped nail polish before answering, 'No. Mum's paying. Birthday present.' She pressed the final button on the machine and then asked, 'Credit, Mrs Vaughan. Thanks. I'll just get this okayed.' Kate waved towards her supervisor, changing from one foot to the other to ease the building pressure on her tired feet. 'Check, please,' she called.

Mrs Vaughan took the docket, the authorised credit card slip, and slowly organised her handbag. 'Thank you, dear. Enjoy your holiday. I'll expect to hear all about it.'

'Paris. Wish I was going somewhere that exciting,' said the next customer. 'I'm lucky to be taken to the movies.'

'It's not all it's cracked up to be. Mum insists on dragging me to all the poncy art galleries and museums. If I have to go and smile back at the Mona Lisa *one more time*, I'll... well anyway, cash or credit?'

'Poor you! Swap you any time.'

Kate's mood slipped further into misery as her thoughts drifted around a weekend of chores and disagreeable conversation with her mother while she waited impatiently for a spindly young man to place his few items on the counter.

'How's your weekend happening?' he asked.

The performance continued all day. Her forced greetings and automatic responses became shorter until a shrug replaced inane replies. Fed up with over-talkative and under-polite customers, Kate wanted the comfort of a seat and silence when she entered the staff room at the end of her shift.

'Overheard you talking about Paris. Surely you didn't mean *you're* going to Paris.'

One of Kate's workmates, Belinda, her chief antagonist, cornered her in the staff amenities room at closing time. 'Miss Wallace, who has to catch public transport to work, brags about sitting at the front of the plane. Miss La-de-da. How's that possible?'

'None of your business what I can afford,' Kate answered as she changed her regulation shoes for sandals, allowing her red toenails to show.

'It just might be if you can't explain *how* you can afford it.'

Kate swung around, ignored her friend, Rhonda, and glared at Belinda. 'I don't know what you are inferring, but my register always balances.'

'There, there. I think you protest a little too much.'

'Shut up, Belinda.' Rhonda eased herself onto a chair and opened her cola.

'It's okay, Rhonda.' Kate smirked. 'Belinda is just jealous.'

'Jealous! You've got to be joking. Jealous of you! Just for that, I hope it's raining in Paris.' With a sniggering glare at the younger person, Belinda swung her bag over her shoulder and left the room.

'Don't take it too hard, Kate. You know she has to say something to upset someone, otherwise, her day isn't complete.'

'It's okay. I don't like her either.'

'But Paris! Are you really going to Paris?'

'Probably.'

'I didn't know you'd asked for leave.'

'Didn't. Mother will ring in and explain it to Mr Nirav once the tickets are confirmed.'

'Just like that!'

'Yep.'

'And they'll keep the job open for you?' Rhonda asked.

'Yep.'

'Are you sure?'

'Sylvia Bennington can make anything happen.'

'Your mum?'

'She who must be obeyed... by all.'

'Oh.'

Kate nodded, grinned. 'You coming for the train?'

'No, my husband's playing taxi driver today. Pity you're not going our way.'

'Lucky you. See you when I get back.'

Rhonda wasn't surprised when Kate didn't return to work but she spent two days defending her friend from caustic remarks made by Belinda. Unfortunately, several of the other staff seemed to agree with Belinda. Kate's absence made her the chief topic as the cashiers prepared for the first shift.

'She told me her mother was connected to some politician and they lunch at parliament house all the time.'

'That can't be true.'

'Don't know, but she also said her mother's French.'

'Hoots mon!'

'That's Scottish, you idiot.'

'Well, what's French for bullshit?'

'She could be Russian for all I know... or care,' Belinda added.

'No, Kate's definitely Aussie.'

'Mother of said storyteller is, so she says, filthy rich. Lives in Subi and owns some boutique or something.'

'And you believe it?'

'Can't possibly be true. Why does Kate shop at Tar-Shay? No, I don't believe it.'

'She's only been here for a few weeks, and we know nothing about her.'

'She's lived in London.'

'She told me she lived in New York.'

'New York? I thought she said New Zealand.'

'Told you... she makes everything up. You should hear what she tells the customers.'

'Customers like old Mrs Vaughan, who believe anything?'

'Yeah, and the old dear won't have anyone else serve her. Calls Kate her own "type". Maybe she means a snob.'

They all laughed. Mrs Vaughan's reputation for demanding the best products for the lowest price was legendary.

Rhonda jumped in, 'Well, maybe they extended their stay in Paris. Maybe they went to Vienna. She said they were going last month and had to cancel. Anyway, something's happened. Why would Kate make anything up?'

'Because she's a bloody liar.'

Everyone stared at Belinda. Their own thoughts had been voiced. Liar? Kate must be a liar. One just didn't toss in a job and fly to Paris. Did they? They had seen Kate's cheap handbag and shoes. No one had missed the scant lunches and her constant refusal to join any social event. Eighteen-year-olds usually jumped at the chance for a drink after work but just because she always had something better to do, did that make her a liar?

'No, you're wrong,' Rhonda said. 'All of you should just stop talking about her like that. It's impossible to tell why some people act the way they do and anyway, the Paris trip was a birthday gift from her mother.'

'That's another thing,' Belinda lifted her chin, 'who's this Sylvia who can make anything happen? The last day Kate was here, she said Sylvia Bennington was her mother. I thought you said her mum's name was Norma or... yeah, Nora.' Belinda pointed at Rhonda. 'Uh? You did, didn't you? Explain that, then.'

'I can't. Maybe a maiden name? But anyway, she definitely said her mum was buying the trip as a birthday present.' Rhonda crossed the room, trying to emphasise her belief in her friend with a stern look and defiantly crossed arms, when the door opened and Mr Nirav entered.

'Who's birthday? Did we miss someone's celebration?' their boss asked.

'Apparently, it was Miss High-and-Mighty's birthday being celebrated in wonderful Paree.'

'I beg your pardon, Belinda. Who do you speak of?'

Belinda had the decency to look contrite. 'Kate. It's Kate's birthday?'

The manager of the supermarket considered this information for a brief moment before shaking his head. 'I can't remember the date of her birthday, but I'm sure it is as she said. Now, come along. Get ready for opening. And staff, please don't speak ill of Kate. Her mother died, and she won't be coming back.'

KATE'S DIARY
1969

16 May: Have to find work.

17 May: Really have to find work. Wish I didn't have to find work. Wish I had a rich dad. Can't ask Mum for any more money.

18 May: How can I get rich? Must be a way. I'll have to rub shoulders with more than just Fi.

20 May: Looking forward to Fi's birthday party. Yeah. 19th. I bet she gets more than a blouse from Coles.

Chapter 14

Kate wandered through the streets of Fremantle determined to find work. It didn't matter to her if she worked front of house, in the kitchen, in sales, or in an office. Just needed to be free from standing all day, making inane conversation, and having a pasted-on smile.

It had been too easy to give a convincing reason for the quick departure to her gullible coworkers at the supermarket.

Kate chuckled. Nora would be furious with her daughter. 'Tempting fate,' she would have yelled. 'Don't tell people I'm dead, the devil could be listening.'

Kate didn't believe in the devil or God, but if a deity did exist, she reckoned they could do a better job with creating an interesting and financially rewarding employment.

With four knockbacks, Kate returned home, sulked over a slutty novel, the grey of the evening diming the reading light from the window.

When Nora slammed the door, chucked her handbag on the couch and screamed for her daughter, Kate leaped to her feet, the book tumbling to the floor.

'Kate, get here this instance.'

Realising it was way past the time she was supposed to have started peeling spuds and carrots, an apology preceded her entry into the kitchen.

'Sorry, Mum. I was just—'

'If your friends keep…' Nora surveyed the empty bench. 'You haven't even started dinner!'

Ducking behind Nora, opening the fridge and bringing out the dish containing the vegetables supposed to be in the pot, Kate said, 'Doing them now.'

Nora stuck her foot out stopping the door from closing, grabbed a bottle of ginger beer, twisted off the cap, and gulped down the bubbly liquid. 'Ah.' She pushed her hair behind her ears. 'I'm fed up with stopping my hard work to answer the bloody phone. And then, what do I find? *Your* bloody friends wanting to leave a message.' After another quick swig, she pulled the vegetable peeler out of Kate's hand. 'Listen to me. Tonight, it rang when Mr Yeo was there. Try telling him your daughter's friend's call was urgent. Did he believe me? Not on your nelly.'

Kate's eyes flicked from her mother's grim mouth to the peeler being waved around like a murder weapon. 'Was it Fiona?' Kate whispered.

Nora tossed the implement across the bench, just out of Kate's reach. 'You get those veggies done, real quick. I'm going to put my slippers on and you'd better have them done by the time I get back.' Her rotund backside jiggled as she strutted from the kitchen while emptying the bottle of soft drink.

With yesterday's savoury mince re-heating in a pot next to the vegetables, Kate set the table and poured two glasses of water. She wrapped the scraps in newspaper and dropped them in the outside bin. A watched kettle never boiled, nor did watched vegetables cook in a hurry. Kate paced seven steps between the stove and the table, keeping an eye on the passage doorway. Any minute Nora would burst through and start badgering. Kate wanted to cry. The day was bad enough without having to tread warily around an exasperating mother.

'Now see here, young lady.' Nora entered the kitchen, pointing at Kate as if she was three years old. 'How many times must I ask you?'

'Sorry, Mum. I had a rotten day.'

'You! Did you have to scrub the inside of a freezer?' Nora lifted the lid of the mince's pot. 'Eh? No, I'm pretty sure you didn't.'

'I think the mince is ready,' Kate said.

Nora pulled two plates from the cupboard, placed them under the pot's lid to warm. 'Well, it's a pity the veggies aren't.'

'Sorry, Mum.'

Nora sat at the table glancing through yesterday's Daily News she'd acquired from the discard pile at Yeo's. Snorts of derision and spurts of disbelief covered the otherwise silence as Nora disagreed with most of the reports. Kate stood by the stove begging the boiling water to do its thing quicker.

'If you'd cut the pieces smaller, they'd have been cooked by now.'

'I did, Mum.' Kate stuck a fork into a potato, glad it proved to be soft. 'I'll mash.'

Halfway through the meal, Kate ventured, 'Who rang?'

'Bloody hell, Kate. Can't a woman even finish her meal without your going on about a telephone call?'

As she finished her last mouthful and placed her fork down,

Nora pointed towards the sink. 'Get the kettle on, would you?'

Placated by a full stomach and a hot cup of tea, Nora said, 'It was that posh friend of yours. Wants you to ring her. She's having a birthday party. Can't remember when.'

Kate wanted to knock her mother's favourite cup from the saucer, but she smiled and said, 'You mean Fiona?'

'Look,' Nora said. 'we don't have a phone, so I know she can't ring you but... it's annoying.' She rolled her eyes for effect. 'You try getting off the floor in a hurry. My knees aren't what they used to be.'

'No, Mum.'

'Just ring her, then maybe she'll stop ringing *me*.'

'Yes, Mum.'

Fiona and Kate's conversation covered everything from infuriating family members, lack of employment, handsome young men, new dresses, weather that might spoil the poolside event, and anticipated birthday gifts. It ended with an invitation to a sleepover on the day of the party.

'Come early,' Fiona insisted. 'You can get dressed here. Bring your stuff.'

This was a sticking point for Kate. She wasn't sure which particular "stuff" Fiona referred to, but she knew she wouldn't have the same array of beauty products that would be on the vanity in the bathroom attached to Fiona's large bedroom. It wasn't a matter of purchasing more as she already lamented over having to dip into her savings to buy a new dress. The one her friend had described needed to be rivalled in style if not in currency.

Nora's one lipstick and tent-sized clothes limited the option of borrowing. Unlike the actions of Fiona and her sister, Linda, as eloquently explained to Kate many times. Their wardrobes were accessible to either girl, despite Linda having moved to Wembley after her marriage seven months ago.

The Saturday of Fiona's nineteenth birthday shone brightly. Kate finished her chores before lunch without the usual prodding from Nora. With her mother comfortably settled over a two o'clock cuppa and three biscuits, Kate said goodbye.

'Got everything?'

'Yeah, think so.' Kate stood with a small suitcase of "stuff" by her side.

'Clean undies for tomorrow?'

'Yeah, and an extra set. Just like you've been nagging about for the past two hours.'

'Did you do the salad?'

'Yes, Mum. It's all on a plate. All you have to do is eat it.'

'No need for sarcasm, young lady. You're off enjoying yourself. I'm stuck at home.'

Kate grunted. 'Yeah, right. Stuck with some movie and that ice cream.'

Nora wriggled ever so slightly. 'Ice cream?'

'It's okay, Mum. I know there's a tub in the back of the freezer.' Kate chuckled. 'Enjoy it.'

'Well then, off you go. Don't want to miss that bus. And Kate...'

'Yeah?'

'Just be careful.'

'Careful? I'm staying over. I told you. I'll be catching the bus tomorrow at about ten-thirty. No need to worry.'

Nora's eyes widened; she spoke quietly, 'No, I mean, there'll be boys at the party, won't there?'

'Course. Fiona's brother and his friends. Chaps who work with Mr Noble. I already told you that.'

'Yes, you did. And I told you about what can happen with boys.'

'Mum!'

'Don't Mum me. Just you don't—'

Kate kissed her mother's forehead. 'No, Mum. I won't. Enjoy your movie.' Just before she shut the front door, she yelled, 'And the ice cream.'

1969

22 May: What a day! Fiona's party was totally cool. What a blast. But felt totally out of my depth. Have to learn to tread water as the lifeguards are very cute.

Peter!!!!! Nice!!!

No-kids pill. Now that's interesting. The no kids bit, for sure. Sex? Yes. No. Possibly.

There's something about MONEY. Maybe it's just that my life is so... Beaconsfield! It's incredible staying at the Noble's place. I mean—honestly. But having money isn't as easy as it looks. I'll have to learn everything I can if I want to end up wealthy.

I cringe when I think of marriage, but a rich boyfriend might work. Let's see.

Boy, oh boy. Lesson Number 2 or maybe 22 from Fiona—*Daddy!!* Honestly. But it worked. How can I turn that around to work on *men*?

Anyway, these mags have lots of stuff about the rich and famous.

Chapter 15

The backyard of the Noble's home presented a party atmosphere ready to spring to life with only a few final touches required. Streamers and dozens of balloons hung across the pool. Rented chairs filled the space under the patio; blue tablecloths were draped across several small round tables. Containers of serviettes sat next to wooden toothpicks and metal forks. Huge galvanised tubs were ready for ice and drinks. A long table with glasses of all shapes hid under tablecloths. Kate couldn't believe the amount of food in the fridge and the rows of little pies and sausage rolls being thawed.

'How many people have been invited?' Kate asked Fiona. 'There's so much food.'

'Not sure. I think there's about forty.'

'I don't even know that many people, let alone have that many friends.'

Fiona laughed. 'I let you into a secret. Neither do I.'

'How come they're coming to your party? I mean, it's not even your twenty-first.'

Fiona took Kate's hand and pulled her towards her bedroom. 'Dad insists on having a party for all our birthdays. He invites *their* friends, and we get to choose some of ours. All the aunts and uncles, great aunts, grandparents.' Fiona pushed open her door and directed Kate through. 'And if we go a couple of months without someone's birthday, he invents a reason for a party. Even Linda had to come home for a "party" last month.'

Flinging herself on the smaller of the two beds, Fiona scowled at Kate. 'You could have come but you didn't answer my message.'

Kate scowled back. 'Mum doesn't like you ringing, you know, at her work.'

'She didn't say.'

'Oh no, she's much too polite.' Kate smirked. 'To you.'

'Didn't she pass on the message?'

Kate shrugged. 'Think I'll unpack. My dress might crease.'

The confusion of the introductions to so many guests left Kate exhausted. Most of the adults greeted her with, 'Hi, Kate. I've heard Fiona talk of you.'

With the teenagers at one end of the patio and the older people seated around tables, she clutched a glass of lemonade and shrunk back against the wall of the house watching the frivolity, the naturalness of old friends, and the casual interaction. Mr Noble caught her attention as he strolled between the groups, his deep laughter easily audible. He shook hands with men and kissed the women on the cheek. Kate watched as he waylaid one of the hired staff and directed them to guests who didn't have a drink. They responded immediately. When Mrs Noble walked past, he stopped her, whispered something that made her smile. His look lingered as she walked away.

Kate couldn't take her eyes off him. She wondered if money alone gave someone the charismatic charm oozing from this good-looking man.

When someone kissed her neck, she jumped, spilling her drink. 'Don't do that,' she shrieked.

The young man stepped back. 'Sorry, but you look so serious.'

She held out her glass. 'Maybe you could top this up.'

'Certainly. Wine? Beer?'

'No way. Lemonade.'

He took her glass. 'Just lemonade? It's a party, you know.'

'I know that. Just lemonade.'

'Alright, but don't blame me if you don't enjoy yourself.' He strode away. She watched him put her glass down, fill his glass with beer, then turn and talk to Fiona's cousin, leaning closer with each sentence.

Mr Noble stepped in front of Kate. 'You don't have a drink?'

Switching her gaze to Mr Noble from the erstwhile man who hadn't returned her drink, she stammered a reply, 'Um... no, um... not at the moment.'

'Seems he's far from a gentleman.'

'Who?'

'The young man who took your glass and didn't return.'

'It's okay. There's only so much lemonade you can drink.'

'Sure. I agree. Would you like a shandy?'

Her stomach flipped. She glanced around, spotted Mrs Noble handing around a tray of sausage rolls. Fiona was thanking another guest for a gift. 'Um, no.'

'Good girl,' Mr Noble said, his grin adding to his approval. 'Now, come with me. I want to introduce you to one of the more studious young chaps. Peter would never leave a girl without a drink.' He held the back of her upper arm and led her towards the other end of the poolside, dropping her arm after a few steps. 'Fiona's a little busy, but we can't have one of our guests standing alone.'

Peter was in a circle of young people but his uneasy demeanour stood out. He didn't respond to the chatter, only nodding occasionally as he sipped a beer and glanced into the distance.

'How are you all going? Enjoying yourselves? Make sure you eat something, otherwise I'll have it for lunch for the next two weeks.' Mr Noble shook one young man's hand. 'Hi, Brett. Didn't see you come in.'

'Naw, slipped in. Thanks for the invite.'

'Invitation.' Mr Noble corrected the teenager. 'You're welcome. But no hangovers. I need you all to front up on Monday.'

The young men laughed, assured their boss they had Sunday to recover from any hangover. The girls shook their heads in a way that told Kate they knew of hangovers and missed work.

Kate had watched the exchange, amazed at Mr Noble's ease. Uncomfortable at being a stranger, she looked behind her, hoping for a way of escape, but Mr Noble put his palm across the middle of her back.

'This lovely young lady is a friend of Fi's. Kate, this is a bunch of reprobates who work for me.' One girl's eyes widened at hearing the expression. 'Sorry about the language, ladies.' Mr Noble bobbed his head at her.

The "ladies" grinned, seemingly ready to forgive this man almost anything. The reprobates jeered, a couple slapping each other on the back as if they'd been given a compliment.

Kate forced a smile, wanting to shrink behind the hibiscus. 'Hi,' she whispered.

After they offered a brief greeting, Mr Noble said, 'Don't forget, eat all those bloody sausage rolls.' He nodded at Peter. 'Peter, can I see you a moment? I have a question.'

While she answered the usual question about her friendship with Fiona, Mr Noble and Peter spoke quietly, Peter nodding a great deal at his boss's words.

As the group's focus shifted from Kate and returned to their previous chatter, Peter re-joined the circle. 'Can I get you a drink?' he asked Kate.

'I guess.'

'Want to come with me?'

Kate couldn't move quickly enough. At least she wouldn't have to contend with the stares of the others, who seemed astounded at many of Kate's serious answers to their flippant conversation.

'Whew!' Kate let out a long breath.

'You too?'

'What?'

Peter glanced at the group. 'They're hard work. I mean, nice chaps, but not a serious thought among the lot.'

'I noticed that. Although one of the girls said her brother had just left for Vietnam. That shut them up for a bit. I mean, how awful.'

'Yeah, shocking really. I wonder whose idea it was to have a lottery for conscription. I mean... a bloke from our office left to do his training at Pukapunyal. Scary to think of what is happening.'

Peter glanced up and down, left and right, then back to her face. 'Sorry, not exactly a pleasant topic of conversation.'

Pouring herself some orange juice, Kate agreed, 'You're right, and it *is* a party.'

'True. Do you go to many? Parties, I mean.'

They moved to seats at the other side of a table and introduced themselves to Auntie Flo and Uncle Joe. Kate found the rhyming names amusing but thought she'd hidden her giggles until Peter wanted to know what she found funny. He leaned over so her whispered explanation wasn't drowned out by the explosion of Neil Diamond's *Cracklin' Rosie*.

He laughed and added that he had an Auntie Ollie from Collie.

In the course of their conversation, she learned he was studying accountancy at night school and worked full-time in Noble Constructions' office. She was explaining her disastrous experience at Woods and Baker when Mr Noble clapped his hands and asked for attention.

The speeches were short, and after a toast to the birthday girl, Linda's husband announced it was time to dance. With the music echoing off the walls, the older guests disappeared into the house.

'Come and dance.' Fiona pulled Kate to her feet. 'You too, Peter. Come on, everyone's up.'

With light-hearted banter between the dancers, everyone joined in swapping partners or dancing singularly in a circle. They collapsed onto a chair one by one, begging to be allowed to sit out at least one song.

Towards midnight, Mr Noble turned the music down. Amid boos and jeers, he said, 'Time for the quieter ones. Unlike you noisy lot, the neighbours may want to sleep.'

Some guests announced they were heading off, organising who would drive and who would squeeze into the other seats. Fiona begged everyone to stay but reluctantly waved from the front porch as a Holden FJ squealed its tyres as it raced away.

Kate was stacking the dirty glasses onto trays when a hand caressed her waistline. 'Leave those. How about one more dance.' She turned around, grinned as Peter held out his hand. 'No music,' she said softly.

'I'll fix that.'

Once Elvis Presley started crooning *Love Me Tender*, Peter took Kate's hand, pulled her into an embrace, and kissed her lightly on the mouth.

As they swayed in time to the music, Fiona, now back from her goodbyes, grabbed Andrew and, along with two other couples, joined them.

'Can I ring you?' Peter asked. 'Would you go to the movies with me?'

Kate stopped dancing but didn't move from his arms. 'No.'

'I thought you'd enjoyed tonight. I did.'

'It's not that. I haven't got a phone.'

Peter laughed gently. 'Well, thank goodness for that. I thought you were turning me down completely.' He eased her back into the rhythm of the music. 'You could ring me.'

'I don't know much about you.'

'That's what dates are for.'

'Date?'

'Yeah, you know, boy, girl, going out.' He chuckled. 'A date.'

The song ended and no one put on another record. Fiona and

Andrew smooched behind an abundant palm; one of the other girls sat on her boyfriend's knee feeding him peanuts; the other couple had left without farewells.

Peter pulled Kate closer; she cuddled into his chest as his hands ran across her back and over her backside. His kiss, gentle at first but with her response, became eager and demanding. After a while, she pulled away.

'Um, I should finish these glasses.'

'Please, Kate.' He retook her hand. 'Another... dance?'

She shook her head and pointed to the large window, which revealed adults enjoying coffee.

'I suppose it's time to go. Do you need a lift home?'

'No, I'm staying the night.'

He smirked at her. 'Lucky, Fi.'

Tugging her hand free, she emptied dregs from a glass into the garden and stood it in a tray. 'What sort of car do you have?'

'Just a Viva. But it's new.'

'Lucky you.'

'Dad bought it for my twenty-first. Said I'll need wheels when I open my own accountancy business.'

'Gosh, you're ambitious.'

'Aren't you?'

'Between jobs at the moment. I told you about Baker and Woods. Been looking. Might go live in Melbourne. I believe opportunities are great there.'

'Melbourne? I have a cousin in Melbourne. When are you going?'

Kate's face went blank as she searched for a feasible answer. 'Well, depends on Mum and Dad. I can't just up and leave, can I?'

'Guess not. Is there a problem at home?'

'No way.' She turned her back on him, shifting the already packed glasses. 'Mum's always in demand. Works in an office. Dad travels a lot. Just have to fit in with their plans, don't I.'

Peter put his hand on her shoulder, easing her around. 'Come on, Kate. Kiss me again before I go.'

Fiona interrupted their kiss with unsubtle coughing. 'Kate, Dad said I have to get rid of the stragglers.' She glared at Peter. 'Well, he didn't say exactly *that*, of course. But the party is over. I've managed to lever Jill and Robbie apart, and my cousin's inside trying to convince her parents she can go home with... whoever he is.'

'I'm going,' Peter said. He turned to Kate. 'Ring me at work. Fi will have the number.'

Kate asked, 'Is it okay for you to have calls?'

Peter glanced at Fiona. 'Yeah, as long as it's important, as your calls will be.'

Fiona laughed. 'Dad won't mind, but you'll have to make up a story if the switchboard demon catches you ringing too often.'

Once the young guests had left, Mrs Noble shooed the girls to bed.

They removed the gifts from the beds, grimacing over some choices, being delighted by most. It seemed the aunts had intentionally added to Fiona's glory box with expensive crockery items and wonderfully soft towel sets.

'Do you have a glory box?' Fiona asked.

'I'm never getting married. So, no, I don't intend to have a bunch of stuff sitting in a box or shelf, waiting for the big day.'

'What? Of course you are. You have to.'

'No, I don't. Why would you even say that?'

'You can't have children unless you're married.'

Kate sniggered. 'What if I don't want snivelly brats?'

'Kate!'

'What?'

'I don't know anyone who doesn't want children. I mean, it's part of being married. You know, sex, then children.'

Kate tossed her clothes onto a chair and hurried into her pyjamas. 'Sex. Children. That becomes a problem.'

'Only if you're *not married*.' Fiona hung up her dress, let her underclothes fall to the ground, and stepped into her pyjamas, carefully buttoning the jacket.

As they cleaned their teeth, Fiona asked, 'Have you done it?'

Kate's toothbrush almost jammed through her cheek. 'It? Sex? You mean with a boy?'

'Yeah! Who else?'

'Well, no, I haven't. Not sure I want to if it means children.' She spat toothpaste into the bowl and rinsed her mouth.

'You can, you know.'

'What?'

Fiona finished rinsing her teeth. 'Linda said.'

'Linda said what exactly?'

'Get into bed, and I'll tell you.'

'Tell me what?'

'How to have sex without getting pregnant. Without a condom, even.'

Kate scrambled into bed, pulling the sheet over her chest. 'Go on.'

Fiona ambled from the bathroom, slowly arranged the pillow and sheet, wriggled down, realigned the sheet, switched off the bed lamp, and sighed.

'And?' Kate demanded.

'It's easy, apparently. You take a little pill every night for three weeks, then you have your period, then you start taking the pill again.'

'That's all? What sort of pill? Does it work?'

'It does. So Linda said.'

'And you can have sex whenever you like?'

The conversation lingered around sex, boys, and the lack of children before the gaps in their questions and answers became longer, and ultimately, they fell asleep.

Kate's lingering thoughts were of how she could find a rich husband who only wanted sex and not children.

'Fi? Are you awake?'

'Mm. Sort of.'

'Where do you get that pill?'

'What pill?'

'The no-kids pill?'

Fiona sighed. 'I'm sorry I told you. Are you planning on having sex with Peter?'

'Not necessarily. But I would like to know, personally, what all the fuss is about. Wouldn't you?'

'Don't know. I mean, I've read books, and you know, I've had…'

'Yeah, well, so have I, but not the whole way. Like they do in movies.'

Fiona sat up quickly. 'What sort of movies have you watched? They all just disappear into the bedroom in the ones I've seen.'

Kate stepped across the small space between beds and wriggled in next to Fiona. 'Mum has this movie… It was in the back of the cabinet.' Kate smirked. 'She works nights sometimes, so I watched it.'

'You mean a sex movie?' Fiona's face contorted as her thoughts jumped to conclusions. 'Wow! Did she find out?'

'Of course not. I put it back.' Kate poked Fiona in the ribs. 'Want to see it?'

'No!' She moved away from Kate.

'Want'a see a dirty movie?' Kate's American gangster accent wasn't very accurate.

'No.' Fiona sucked on her lip. 'I might.' Her eyebrows shot up. 'No, I shouldn't.'

'Treat it as education, Miss Noble. Didn't some teacher ever say to you that education is power? Case in point.' She put on the accent again. 'Want'a see a dirty movie, young lady?'

Mrs Noble entered a room full of giggles that stopped abruptly. 'Glad you're enjoying yourselves, but it's time for a shower. Breakfast in fifteen minutes, girls. And, Fi, you know your father will expect you to be immaculate.' She picked up the clothes from the floor and dropped them on the foot of Fiona's bed. 'So nice that you stayed, Kate.'

Mrs Noble disappeared as quietly as she'd entered.

'Holy shit!' Kate exclaimed. 'Immaculate? It'll take a while.'

Fiona climbed over Kate and headed for the bathroom. 'Dad's standards never slip. He's an ogre on *standards* and finance. But a girl can always get around a man, and he's no exception. Well... maybe the standards bit is difficult, but the getting of money, Miss Wallace,' she bowed, 'be prepared to be *ed-u-cated*.'

'There you are, girls.' Mrs Noble held out some cutlery. 'Pop these on the table, please.'

Fiona took the spoons from her mother. Kate took half from Fiona.

'And Kate,' Mrs Noble smiled, 'you look nice this morning.'

Kate sucked in a breath. 'Um, thanks.' She stood motionless, glanced at the small round table by the patio doors, then back to Mrs Noble. Fiona had disappeared through an open doorway beyond the kitchen. Confused, she followed Fiona.

'Fi?' Fiona was setting down the spoons in a formal dining room. 'Are we having breakfast in here?' Kate whispered.

'Sure, we always do when we have visitors. And you're the visitor. Well, you and Gran.'

During breakfast, Mr Noble sat like a king at the top of the table making amicable conversations with "his" girls, quizzing Kate on her family, making light of her evasive answers.

Kate watched in awe at this casual breakfast: in the formal dining room, with linen serviettes, toast in silver racks, teapots, marmalade, vegemite, strawberry jam, and manners she'd seen in 1920 movies.

She answered when spoken to, tucked her elbows in, and declined the third piece of toast.

'Well, young ladies, what are you up to this afternoon?' Mr Noble asked.

Kate's eyes flicked nervously to Fiona, hoping to be saved from inventing something more exciting than going home and washing her undies. 'Going to Paris' wouldn't work with this upper-class family—they'd probably been there more times than she'd invented.

'Oh, Daddy, we were so hoping to go to the movies, but I've spent my allowance.' Fiona forced a broad smile, placed her hand on the table near her father's. 'Do you think...'

Mrs Noble tutted. 'Now, Fi, you know you're not supposed to ask for more.'

Fiona crossed her arms across her chest and pouted. 'But, Mum, those shoes were just adorable.'

'Let's see.' Mr Noble pulled out his wallet. 'But Fi, you'll have to earn it.'

'But, Daddy,' Fiona smiled from lowered eyelids, 'Not today. Not when I have a *guest*.'

Kate wriggled in her seat. She hadn't heard Fiona call her father *Daddy* before. It seemed so... babyish... undignified, and Kate knew she was being used. She raised her hand but Fiona glared across the table at her, so she wimped out.

Mr Noble laughed as he took out a note. 'You girls! Wrapped around my little finger. I'll go broke if I'm not careful.'

Taking the money, Fiona stood and kissed her father on the top of his head. 'Thanks, Daddy. I love you.'

'You never learn, do you, Gene Noble.' Mrs Noble stood, gathered some plates, and headed for the kitchen.

'Perhaps not. When it runs out, I'll send *her* out to work.' He turned to his daughter. 'Now off you go, help your mother first, or I'll charge you interest.'

Back in Fiona's room, Kate cross-examined her friend.

'Why were you calling him "Daddy"? It sounded awful. And I didn't say I'd go to the movies. I have to go home. You shouldn't have used me as an excuse.'

'Oh, come on, Kate, my father won't even ask what picture we saw. He won't even miss the money.'

'But "Daddy"?'

'Look, he's always talking about his "little" girl. Even in the office when I'm typing letters with other women around. Get *my little girl* to type this one, he'll say to his secretary. I mean, I'm nineteen! So, if he thinks that, I'm going to use it. When I call him "Daddy", it appeals to his fathering instincts.'

Kate nodded slowly, understanding the wiles, saving the knowledge. 'I see.' She walked to the window, stared past the marble stairs into the manicured garden. 'I see.' She turned around. 'But I do have to go home.'

Fiona flapped the crisp note in front of Kate's face. 'Want to help spend it.'

'Sure. When?'

'Now. We'll get Mum to drive you to the train station. There's the newsagency there. Let's get some magazines.'

'Help me pack.'

Kate arrived home with two magazines, promising to swap them with Fiona's choices when they met next.

Even more determined to find a well-paying job so she could start on her way to wealth, Kate scoured the Saturday's paper Nora had left on the kitchen bench. All the prestigious positions required experience.

She tossed the paper into the air—job searching was so frustrating.

KATE'S DIARY
1969

2 June: Have to get a job. It's a little awkward going to Fiona's and not having ANY money.

3 June: I'll try Fremantle again. I like Fremantle. Reminds me of Syd and his Guinness. Stan and his make-believe. And Miss Chidley. I wonder if she still has that terrible orange hair. I wonder if she's still alive and kicking. And Miss Tillman. I wonder if she is settled in England. She was such a sweetie. Calling me Katherine. If only I could be Katherine. So much posher than Just Kate.

But first. A job. Yeah, perhaps tomorrow. Yeah, I can feel it.

4 June: Happy days. Yep, I LOVE Fremantle. I might try a Guinness. Think I pass for twenty-one. I'll celebrate. When I get a job. Nup. Champagne. I think I'll be Katherine and celebrate with bubbles. Might change my luck.

15 June: It's exhausting. Peter wants to bring me home. Pick me up—in his brand-new Viva. Can't have that. Mum would act like a dating Nazi. And it's all, *so not Cottesloe*.

22 June: The thought of knobbly toes and smelly feet—nup. Anyway, I certainly wouldn't pass for sixteen. Then, almost got a job I would hate in two minutes. Can't do that again.

Huh! She believed me. Good old Cousin Veronica. If only!

Chapter 16

Kate passed several shops with scribbled signs announcing the availability of casual or part-time jobs. Buddy's Burger Bar wanted someone capable of working the night shift.

Kate refused to work nights.

Drunks in alleyways. Sailors wandering in two and threes as they looked for their last beer before returning to their ship in Gauge Roads. Women with long glamorous dresses tucked into the leg of a G-string and others with their six-inch-heeled shoes dangling from their painted fingertips. These people who had misused their evening always seemed to think it necessary to have Kate join in their attempts for a final bout of joviality. Kate never did.

These people were bad enough, but the misshapen mass of clothing crumpled in a doorway or a bus stop shelter frightened Kate. *Why did they always wear so many clothes?* she asked the hot night air waiting in vain for the Fremantle Doctor. *Maybe it's easier than carrying them, or perhaps it ensures they aren't stolen when they're asleep*, she considered. She was petrified one of these unfortunate persons would beg her for money, not take no for an answer. Worse still, they might insist they were her father.

The shoe shop looked promising. *Everyone needs shoes,* Kate thought and looked at her feet, which stepped proudly in new ballerina flats bought yesterday, emptying her purse. They were cheap and made in China but they made Kate feel… bouncy. Her feet were pleased they didn't have to endure the rubbing of the safety pin holding together the strap on the pair which now lay in a rubbish bin outside the minuscule cubicle at the Fremantle Markets.

The spidery script in the shoe shop window stated they were after a sixteen-year-old. 'Few years too late,' Kate announced to a passer-by who moved on quickly.

Entering the cool of a long arcade, Kate sat down at the table outside a café that declared: "new owners, new menu". She browsed the menu noticing the expensive nature of each item.

'One dollar!' Kate exclaimed loudly as her finger ran along the line of the hot drink items.

'Can I take your order?'

Kate looked up, a little embarrassed, not for the declaration of the expense of a coffee but to be caught talking to oneself.

'Surely you can't justify charging that much.'

'Yes, our tea is the very best. It's served in a pot and usually serves two. And it comes with a Custard Cream each. See here on the menu.'

The waiter pointed to the menu with many items under the heading: "Things to Share".

'Well, I'm by myself.'

'That's fine. Would you like tea, or do you prefer coffee? A single cup without the biscuit is thirty cents and we still use the best ingredients.'

Kate wriggled in her seat. She didn't want anything to eat or drink, just a rest from walking in new footwear. She had been unable to resist this spot where the breeze reached down past all the colourful shops in the arcade.

'I'm sorry, I wasn't going to order. My feet are sore. New shoes.'

The female waiter gave an understanding chuckle and said, 'It's okay, stay for a minute. I could do with joining you. We've been so busy, my feet hurt even in these old things.'

Kate assessed the sensible footwear before asking, 'Are you allowed to sit?'

'Good heavens, no.' She turned to go but looked back at Kate. 'Sorry, I didn't mean to sound rude, but there is so much to do even when we don't have customers. We're rather short-staffed.'

'Mm. I'm between jobs at the moment.'

'Experienced?' asked the waiter, who ignored whatever it was demanding her attention a few minutes ago and sat opposite Kate.

'Mm, yes. Worked tables in a few places. Here and overseas. London last year, Brazil the year before.'

'You wouldn't have your CV on you by any chance.'

'But the sign says sixteen.'

'Yes, but at the moment I'll take anyone. Do you have your CV?'

'I don't really have one. My things were burned a few months ago.'

'Oh, I'm sorry about that. Did anyone get hurt?'

'It's okay. No. No one hurt, just lumps of my life disappeared.'

'So, no copies.'

'You don't ever think it'll be necessary.'

'Too true,' the waiter said as she stood and wiped at imaginary spots on the table. 'By the way, I'm Carmel, Carmel Greenaway. One of the new owners. Are you interested in the job or not? If not, I must keep going. Dom will be wondering what's taking me so long.'

'Yes, I'm a bit low on funds. Would be good.'

'When can you start?'

'Tomorrow? Even now, if you wish.'

'Really?'

'Yep, can do.'

'I think today's a bit sudden.' Carmel nodded towards Kate's feet. 'You would need comfy shoes.' She chuckled. 'However, if you pop back at six when we're shut, we can sort things out.'

Kate stood and glanced down the arcade, reconsidering her spontaneity. 'Six o'clock. Okay, see you then.'

With three hours to fill, Kate spent most of them sitting outside the town hall under the dappled light of the Plane trees, almost wishing for a habit of smoking to give her hands something to do. Avoiding the obligatory acknowledgment that goes with catching people's eyes, she watched feet go by, fascinated by what shoes could tell of the wearer.

Shabby shoes often stuck out from expensive trousers. *Not one for attention to detail*, Kate thought. High heels without the tip—a bad sign. Kate supposed the wearer might have lost it on that particular outing but refused to give the wearer the benefit of the doubt. Sensible shoes, invariably on ladies with grey hair. Brightly coloured footwear often revealed a young owner. Many rubber thongs seemed to be chosen by default rather than with forethought. A group of shoes challenged the observer. Fashion next to the aforementioned thongs, work boots next to flimsy sandals and the flip-flopping of too large ballet pumps next to ubiquitous sneakers, all walked to their destination. Kate decided the unmatched pairs were the epitome of opposites attracting.

When she became tired of contemplating footwear, Kate hovered outside Culley's but didn't enter, and instead, bought a sandwich from a small lunch bar near the Post Office. Returning to the bench in the mall, she had to squeeze on the end of the seat next to three uniformed teenagers.

Ah, school. I wonder if they still have sport on Friday afternoons.

School, supposed to be the best years of one's life, although you never believe it at the time. Perhaps it is because you make so few real decisions and school springs relatively few surprises.

Nora didn't like surprises. She said it was enough to bring bad luck to the one being surprised.

'What if the reaction is not what is expected. I mean, it would be bloody awful if it was supposed to be a pleasant surprise but turned out to be an unexpected disappointment,' she told her sister Jennifer one year when she'd tried to convince Nora to help arrange a surprise party for their younger sister, Janice.

Kate understood about unpleasant surprises. She'd found a huge surprise when reading her mother's diary. The elaborate cover seemed hardly touched, but the inside pages were crinkled, unmistakably turned repeatedly. Kate's throat gagged and her pulsed increased as she read the entries. She had hastily shoved the diary back into the drawer, hoping she'd remembered how the folded underwear had been arranged.

Tired of looking at a watch that ticked so slowly, Kate rang Noble Constructions from a public telephone.

'May I speak with Peter Ackroyd please.' She held her breath.

'Who may I say is calling?'

'Miss Wallace.'

'Is he expecting your call, Miss Wallace?'

Kate inwardly sighed. 'Yes.'

'One moment, please.'

While she waited to be transferred, Kate stepped from one foot to the other and rubbed an elbow across the fogged-up glass.

'Hello, Miss Wallace.' Peter laughed, then dropped his voice to a whisper. 'I hoped you'd ring.'

'Hi, Peter. I didn't know if you just said… or that you really wanted me to ring.'

'Of course, I did, but I can't chat too long. Can we go somewhere, say Saturday?'

'Huh? You're assuming I'm free.' Kate held her breath again.

'Well, sure. You rang, didn't you?'

'Mm, but I still mightn't be free.'

'Sunday?'

'Maybe.'

'Look, Kate. Did you ring just to annoy me, or can we go somewhere on the weekend?'

Kate had given much thought to a date with Peter. He seemed nice, had a new car, was ambitious… but…

'Kate. You still there? I have to go. Saturday?'

'Sure. Movies?'

'I'll pick you up at five. We can go for a drive, say, to the beach, we can have fish and chips. If you want, we can find a late movie after that.'

'What if I met you in Fremantle?'

'That's stupid, Kate. I can pick you up.'

Her brain jolted. He wanted to pick her up. From her house! *Oh, no.* 'So, you think I'm stupid. I'm not sure I want to go out with someone who thinks I'm stupid.'

'I didn't mean that. It'd just be easier if I picked you up.'

'No, it wouldn't. Forget I rang.'

'Kate, don't be stu— Don't...'

She hung up before Peter could work out what he should say.

Kate folded her arms and leaned back against the wall, swearing. She should've anticipated Peter would want to pick her up. Although their front garden was neat and the house exterior tidy, it didn't rate next to the likes of Mr Noble's house. A small tidy home in a row of State Housing homes wasn't going to impress someone as ambitious as Peter. She'd have to find another way. She'd have to have a place of her own and that meant she'd have to find a job—a well-paid job.

She dialled the Noble's number, spoke politely to Mrs Noble and greeted Fiona tentatively before saying, 'Fi, want to help me go shopping?'

'Who better?' Fiona replied. 'I'm always up for a new dress. When?'

'What about tomorrow?'

Fiona paused. 'Yes, I think so. I've got to work on Thursday and Friday. Someone's sick. Yeah, Wednesday will be okay. Will you want to come here first?'

'No. Let's meet in Freo.'

'But, Kate, there are so few shops there. We'll go to Perth. I'll show you all the best places. Try and get the train that goes past my stop at about ten. Mum goes to tennis and will drop me off.'

Kate returned to the mall and watched the passing parade of people moving between shops. She shook her head at the way some girls were dressed. *Doesn't she check a mirror?* Her eyes followed two thirty-something females as they came out of one boutique, arms full of bags.

'Must have shoes I can dance in,' the bottle-blonde said.

They tittered as they passed Kate and walked into a shoe shop.

The building blister from her new cheap shoes throbbed. No way could Kate just stroll into Betts & Betts and try on every second pair of displayed shoes. Firstly, she couldn't afford *another* pair of shoes and her pink nail polish needed attention, not to mention she should have shaved her legs.

'Money,' she whispered. *It's all about having money.*

At six o'clock, she tapped on the door of Carmel's Café. Dom adjusted the CLOSED sign and opened the door to Kate.

'You're Kate, I assume,' Dom said.

Kate nodded.

'Have a seat. I'll get Carmel.'

All but one table had upended chairs covering them, so Kate hovered over the clear table, gripping the back of a chair.

After the initial greeting, Carmel motioned for Kate to sit.

'I... I can't take the job,' Kate blurted out. 'It's not...'

Carmel's eyes flicked over Kate. Her brow wrinkled. 'You gave me the impression you were desperate.'

'I'm sorry. It's just that... I forgot about... Sorry.'

'Look, if you want to just say no, that's fine, but I do have things—'

'My cousin is coming. From New Zealand. I forgot about it when I was here earlier. She'll expect me to drive her around.' Kate stood taller, tipped her chin up. 'It's her first visit. She wants to go to all the... museums, art galleries.' She nodded, as if trying to convince herself. 'She is a bit older than me.' Throwing sad puppy eyes, she spoke softly, 'I'm so sorry. Your café is lovely. Maybe I'll bring... um, Veronica, next week.'

Carmel shook her head as she closed the door behind Kate.

10 July: I feel awful about Carmel but I have to do better than a cafe. I bet those two bitches from typing don't work in a shop of any type. They only *shop* in a shop! I've got to find a way.

16 July: How can I get a rich, rich, RICH chap? Peter? Good option. But I need money now!!! I wonder how rich Fiona's boyfriend is. Mind you, her father has pots, so maybe she doesn't even need to marry Andrew.

20 July: Holy crap! They landed on the moon. Neil Armstrong! Although there's some talk of it all being a ruse just so they seem more advanced than the Ruskies. Talk about a big lie. How could they pull that off? It looked real enough for me. But who can tell? Won't affect me. I'm still trying to live better on *Earth*.

23 July: Remember, quiche not sandwiches—Lesson 56. Can you believe that Benji? Ordering lunch is a minefield.

3 August: Ha! Fi hadn't been to Grande café. I'd only had coffee last time as I couldn't afford to eat there, but no need to tell anyone that.

6 August: Double dating last night. That worked. Solves the pick-up problem. Peter, yum. Peter!!! Lessons 625-635 all in one night.

Chapter 17

On Wednesday, Kate peered out the train's window, spotting Fiona on the platform. Following an affectionate hug, they caught up on recent happenings and whispered about the couple snuggling in the corner at the other end of the carriage.

After arriving in Perth, they wandered through Forrest Place into Murray Street, deciding which shops to go to first. Kate wanted to try the department stores but Fiona insisted she knew several boutiques which had clothes "to die for".

The first boutique catered mainly for older women and although Kate picked a crazy-patterned dress from the rack to try on with no intention other than amusement, Fiona insisted they move on.

'You can't pretend you would buy something. The shop assistants can tell. And you were so flippant.'

'Now I'm offended.' Kate pouted. 'Can't we have some fun too?'

'Yeah, but...'

'I'll just have to get better at pretending.'

'No, you shouldn't—'

'You're a snob, Fi.'

'Huh! And you're not!' Fiona slapped at Kate's arm. 'Good heavens, Kate. You look down your nose at anyone without money.'

'*I* don't have money. How the hell am *I* a snob about someone without money.'

'Maybe you aren't rich but, you know, you're as bad as anyone when it comes to wanting money. I've seen you checking out what people wear, especially shoes and rings. I remember you saying you'd only fall in love with someone with money.'

'Is that so bad? To want to have enough. Not to have to worry about where it comes from.'

As they walked along Hay Street, Fiona took Kate's arm. 'Let's not argue.' She bumped her shoulder against Kate's. 'It's true. Money is lovely. I'm glad my family isn't, you know, poor. And you're lucky your Mum works, and what is it your father does? The embassy? That must pay well enough.'

They entered another boutique and Kate avoided answering those difficult questions by picking up a tiny, bejewelled clutch purse.

Fiona held out a silky top. 'Try this, Kate. You would look fab in this.'

'It's too bright.'

'What about that pale blue one?'

Kate and Fiona enjoyed trying on several dresses, parading in front of the mirror and exclaiming how beautiful they looked.

'You've got to get that one,' Fiona said as Kate stepped out of a long black evening dress. 'It'd be perfect.'

Kate caressed the skirt as it lay over her arm. 'It is beautiful.'

'Get it. I'm taking this floral one. It's a good price.'

The ticket on the black dress showed an amount that made Kate stifle a gasp. *That's more than I can earn in a whole week.* She swallowed hard, stumbled over making an acceptable comment. 'Oh, I don't know. I don't go anywhere to wear it.' She placed it on the chair, glancing at the adored article as she replaced her slacks and top.

'Everyone has to have a little black dress.'

'I'll think about it,' knowing damn well she wouldn't—couldn't—afford it. 'It's the first place we've tried.'

Fiona purchased the floral dress, saying, 'I love this one. But, if I find something else as well, I can always use Mum's card.'

After three more boutiques, Fiona purchasing a red skirt and demurring over a light-weight cardigan, Kate dragged her disgruntled friend into Bairds. 'I need some work clothes and I'm not going to get them in those posh places.'

'You didn't even buy that scarf. It was a bargain,' Fiona complained.

'Nothing seemed quite right. I'll probably go back and get that black dress. They might even have something knee-length. Might be more useful.'

Purchasing a floral blouse and a light blue pullover costing a total of six dollars, Kate breathed a sigh of relief when Fiona offered to buy lunch.

'Let's go to David Jones. They have a café. I've been with Mum. She never goes to Coles Cafeteria!' Fiona tugged on Kate's arm. 'Come on, DJ's is lovely, and we can check out their cosmetic counters on the way.'

It wasn't the black dress Kate continued to dream about but the aura of each boutique they'd entered. The selection of clothes might be minimal but the obvious class of each garment was indeed "to die for".

'Kate, you didn't answer me.'

'Sorry, what did you say?'

'Should I get this perfume?'

Kate had drifted away to extended shopping trips where limits didn't matter. She nodded absentmindedly as Fiona deliberated over the perfume in the pink package, or the one she'd read Marilyn Monroe had worn.

'Which one, Kate?'

Catching the last question in time, Kate said, 'Both. Why don't you get both?'

Arm in arm, they sauntered into David Jones' café. Kate suggested chicken and salad sandwiches. 'No, Kate, we're having the quiche. Sandwiches? No way.'

Kate cringed. Even in a department store, style obviously mattered. She had a lot to learn if she wanted to be accepted into a class above state housing level.

'Sure, I was going to say that, but...'

'And coffee. We must have coffee.'

Kate tipped one shoulder forward, hoping it showed nonchalance. 'Sure. Not tea.'

With the last mouthful of quiche on her fork, Kate said, 'Fi, I have a question.'

'Shoot.'

'You know you said about that pill. To stop pregnancy. Do you just get it from the chemist?'

Fiona carefully placed her knife down, wiped her mouth with the serviette and asked, 'Are you seriously going to have sex with Peter?'

Kate answered quickly, 'Not necessarily. I probably won't be seeing him again.'

The pros and cons of Peter exhausted, Fiona asked, 'So, sex with anyone?'

'No, but at some point, I guess, with someone and then, I certainly don't want to have a baby.'

'I'd love to have a baby. They're so cute. I'm sure Andrew wants kids.'

'Holy hell, Fi, are you going to marry him?'

'He hasn't asked, but, yeah, I've dropped lots of hints. I just have to work out how to get him to think it's his idea.'

After several silly suggestions, Kate circled back, determined to get an answer. 'So do you have to get a prescription, you know, from a doctor?'

Fiona sighed, 'How the hell should I know? I guess. But I'll ask Linda if it's that important.' She placed the cutlery neatly across the plate. 'Come on, let's go through the lingerie department on the way out.'

Over the next two weeks, Kate applied for six more office jobs. Leighton Agency suggested a warehouse position, which Kate turned down without asking for the details.

She caught the train to Perth each Wednesday for window shopping and for dreaming of the day she could afford to live, work and more importantly, play in the trendy part of town.

On the third Wednesday, she arranged to meet Fiona outside a café in Kings Street she'd passed by when wandering near His Majesty's Theatre.

'It's nice here,' she said to Fiona as they entered. 'I've been several times. Imported coffee.'

'It's new to me.' Fiona spotted a table. 'There, that one. That'll do.'

With their coffee ordered, Fiona asked, 'Anything special going on with you? Found a job?'

'Still looking. It's bloody hopeless. All office jobs want experience, and the few months I spent in prison at Woods and Baker doesn't seem to count. Who would've thought?'

'I could ask Dad. Maybe there's something at his company.'

'You'd do that?'

'That's what friends are for, isn't it?'

'Yeah, but... I don't know, it's dicey. What if it doesn't work out? That would be embarrassing.'

Fiona pouted. 'Well then, I won't ask.'

The coffee arrived during the awkward silence.

'Sorry,' Kate said. 'I'm just so sick of being without a job. I mean, I'd love to get my own place. Give Mum some privacy.' She swallowed hard. 'With Dad.' She licked her top lip. 'You know, when he's back from Singapore.'

Touching Kate on the arm, Fiona said, 'I understand.' She paused, then with no preamble, asked, 'Would you double date with me and Andrew?'

'What? Where'd that come from?'

'It's just that Peter keeps asking why you won't go out with him. Every time I go into the office, he's talking about you. Kate this, Kate that. I think he's more than a bit keen. He said you rang but hung up in a huff.'

'I wasn't in a huff.'

'Well, can I tell him you would?'

'Would what?'

'At least come with Andrew and me to the pictures.'

'Maybe.'

'Only maybe.'

Kate was frantically trying to solve the problem of being picked up. 'What if I come to your place and they pick us up. If I stay over, we can be out a bit later. That'd be nice.'

'That'd be great. When? This Saturday?'

'Sure. I'll ring you Friday night.'

'Kate, you really should get a telephone. It'd be so much easier.'

'Yeah, yeah. Just pluck one from the telephone tree that grows next to the money tree, shall I?'

After a second coffee, this time with a torte, Kate eagerly showed Fiona the boutiques she'd discovered along King Street. They lingered outside *La Joie*, deciding which delicious creation they'd buy for their date on Saturday as if they were dining at the Ritz in London and not going to the pictures in Subiaco.

However, Kate refused to go into *La Joie* or any other boutique, stating they were surely too expensive, even for Fiona.

'No way,' Fiona said. But she did understand Kate's excuse, so relented. They returned to David Jones, browsed for over an hour; neither buying anything.

The Saturday matinée movie proved a little scary but ideal for clutching a young man's hand. Kate wriggled into Peter's shoulder and accepted several kisses as the screen hero battled the enemy. With Andrew's hands wandering under Fiona's cardigan and their faces locked in long passionate kisses, Kate thought they probably wouldn't know the murderer suffocated under an unrestrained mudslide.

As they came out of the theatre, Fiona said she needed to powder her nose. Andrew and Peter nodded wisely and headed for the toilet as well.

'Rather keen, isn't he?' Kate said to Fiona.

'You should talk.'

'Tuck your t-shirt in and comb your hair.' Kate smiled, as she peered into the mirror. 'Did you bring any lipstick?'

Fiona chuckled, neatened her clothes and pushed her bag along the vanity to Kate. 'In there. I really do have to go to the loo.'

Searching through Fiona's bag, Kate noticed a lavish compact, two lipsticks, mascara and eyeliner. She fondled the compact before placing it back, then pulled out the two lipsticks. Choosing the orange, rather than the bright pink, she puckered up to the mirror and replaced the lipstick that had disappeared with Peter's kisses. She reckoned this was better than being at home with a mother who only wanted to watch romance on the TV, not participate in it. *Well,* she thought, *surely the much-talked-about garlic prawns at The Witches Cauldron will be better than fish and chips from any local shop.*

Kate soaked up the atmosphere in the dimly-lit restaurant. She observed the relaxed but stylish way other diners enjoyed themselves. The quiet frivolity, the expectation of immediate attention, and bottles of wines constantly replaced—seemingly without a thought to the expense. She sighed, looked at her companions, seeing young people who knew of this luxury while she was an outsider. *One day*, she thought. *One day, I'll be the one getting out my purse.*

By the time they'd finished three courses, Andrew had drunk too much and disagreed with Peter over who should pay the bill. After negotiating with Peter, Fiona pulled Andrew outside telling Kate they'd wait in the fresh air. 'Might do him some good.' Kate grimaced as they left but stood quietly while Peter handed over the money.

With Andrew losing his inhibitions and wanting to talk about anything and everything that came to mind, and Fiona trying her best to quieten him, the train ride back to Victoria Station was strained. Peter caressed Kate's hand with his thumb, glancing at her with a cheeky smile. When the train pulled into the station, she pulled her hand free, kissed his cheek, and walked to the doorway. She skipped a few steps down the platform, laughing at Peter's frown. Fiona and Andrew walked steadily from the train and, without waiting for the others, straight to Andrew's car in the car park.

Kate poked Peter in the ribs, jumped out of his reach as he playfully tried to grab her hand. By the time they reached Andrew's car, they had their arms around each other, snatching kisses as they walked.

'Peter, you'll have to drive. I'm not letting Andrew.' Fiona held out the keys.

'I'm not drunk,' Andrew insisted.

'You might not be drunk, but your sense of anything has disappeared. I don't want to have an accident.' She pushed him away from the driver's door. 'Just get in the back.'

They arrived safely back at the Noble's home. Fiona snapped at Andrew as she woke him. 'For God's sake, Andrew. You're ruining the date. Peter and Kate won't do this again. Just get out, you can sleep in the spare room.'

Kate opened the door, ready to get out but Peter grabbed her other arm. 'Wait,' he said. 'Let them go first.'

Fiona linked her arm through Andrew's, called back over her shoulder as they headed to the house. 'Kate, come in when you want. I'll leave the door unlocked. Mum and Dad will be in bed. Or Mum will be. Dad might still be in his study. Anyway,' she looked past Kate to Peter, 'don't do anything I wouldn't.'

They watched silently until Andrew and Fiona closed the front door. Two seconds later, Fiona reappeared, waved, then disappeared again.

'They've gone,' Peter said, raising his eyebrows at Kate.

'Yep. They have.'

Fifteen minutes later, Kate snuck in through the front door and up the stairs to Fiona's bedroom. She eased open the door, hoping Fiona was asleep.

'You didn't take long.'

Kate's breath caught. 'Sorry, did I wake you?'

'Not likely. I want to hear all about it.' Fiona sat up in bed, the bedclothes up to her chin. 'Might make up for my night. Did you hear Andrew snoring away?'

'Nup. I heard nothing.'

'Do you like him a lot?'

'Who? Andrew?'

'Don't avoid the question. Peter, of course.'

'He's okay.'

'What! Okay? I think you lie, Miss Wallace. Methinks you think he's a little more than okay. Otherwise, why all the kissing and who-knows-what in the car.'

'Don't want to talk about it.'

'Does that mean it was that bad... or that good?'

'Let it go, Fi. Surely you shouldn't talk about such personal stuff like it's... a new handbag... or something.'

Kate undressed, put on her pyjamas and went into the bathroom, ignoring Fiona's gaping mouth.

'Must have been good, then,' Fiona shouted.

Kate finished in the bathroom, slipped into bed, turned off the light, and snuggled down.

'Goodnight, Fi. I do appreciate you letting me stay.'

Fiona sat with the bedclothes scrunched under her chin for several minutes, unable to understand why Kate wouldn't want to spend at least a half-hour discussing the evening, the *whole* evening, with her. Linda always had.

Nora had repeatedly warned Kate not to share family matters. When nine-year-old Kate replied to Doris Baird's inquiry of her father with "we don't want him to come home. He's a no-good drunk", Nora tugged her daughter out of the kitchen and made her stand to attention against the back wall.

'Never, and I mean never, talk of your family to strangers.' Her strained, high-pitched voice was just above a whisper but Kate's ears tingled with the intensity.

'But, Mum,' Kate looked down at her shoes, 'Mrs Baird's not a stranger, and... you said it, too.'

Nora slapped Kate's arm. 'I don't care what I said. You are not to repeat it. Got it?'

It was a lesson hard to learn. The difference between "family matters" and stories about where they went on Nora's day off confused her. She'd been allowed to tell Miss Chidley about going to a concert in the town hall but not, according to the lowered eyebrows scowl of her mother, to tell they'd bought a pretty dress from the Salvation Army Op Shop.

As Kate pushed her feet towards the end of the bed, she enjoyed the memory of Peter's soft touch on her breasts and the fervent kisses that stirred passions she wanted but didn't dare take further. She'd pulled away when Peter placed her hand on the hardness inside his trousers.

Kate and Fiona slept late and because Kate wouldn't give in to Fiona's begging questions, their mid-morning brunch chatter cooled quickly, and Kate announced it was time for her to go.

KATE'S DIARY

1969

9 August: God, I must hide you. Think Mum read the last entries. Thank goodness I didn't expand on Lesson 628 with Peter.

Fi reckons there isn't that many lessons on sex. It's just a made-up number. Choose any number! But I must find out about those no-kid pills. Then, off we go to Lesson 629.

Chapter 18

Kate called out as she pushed the key in the lock, 'Mum, Mum, you home?'

She stood in the narrow hallway for a moment, then pulled wrapped chips from her bag. 'Good. All mine.'

After tossing her handbag on her bed, she hugged the warm packet and went to the living room, slumped onto the lounge, and created a hole through the end of the paper. Steam burst out and Kate enjoyed several chips before she spotted her diary on the sideboard.

Forgetting the chips, she wiped her hands on the seat of her trousers and grabbed the diary. Fire shot up her neck and her pulse rose.

'Shit!'

She flicked through to her last entry—a cryptic reminder of Peter's hands on her eager body. 'Bloody hell.'

The chips lost their appeal as Kate continued to worry about having left her diary in the lounge. Despite arguments over privacy having been resolved when Kate was fourteen: 'I won't touch a thing in your room, and same goes for mine,' Nora wouldn't have been able to resist the opportunity to browse through her daughter's life when carelessly left for easing viewing.

Still in a mood dangling between fury and resentment, Kate pounced the moment Nora entered the house.

'You read my diary, didn't you?'

'For God's sake, let a person get in the door.'

'You did, didn't you?'

Nora eased past Kate and walked through to the kitchen.

'You promised you wouldn't.'

'Promised what?' Nora took a bag of sweets from her handbag. 'Want one?'

'Mum!'

Nora took a Liquorice Allsort from the bag, pulled off one sheet of liquorice, and studied it. 'Worried I might have, eh? Done something you shouldn't have, eh?'

Kate grabbed the packet of chips, holding them under Nora's nose for a few seconds before storming to her room. The door shuddered on its hinges as she flung it shut. She flopped onto the bed, her mood creating tears as she opened the diary. *Peter, yum. Peter!!! Lesson 625-635 all in one night*, she read.

She stood, strode across the room, hit the door with her open hand, and yelled, 'You shouldn't have. It's *my* life.'

Shaking her hand to relieve the sudden pain, she opened her wardrobe and pulled out her keepsake box. 'Nup, not writing any more. Ever.' She turned towards the door. 'Ever,' she yelled. 'You won't mess with my life. Ever! Ever!'

KATE'S DIARY

1969

12 October: It was all too much. Mum reading my old diary.
Have to be careful what I write.

13 October: See Mum, nothing to get your knickers in a knot
about!!!

14 October: Another birthday. Jolly nice diamond bracelet from
him. Things looking up!

23 October: Tears, sad, sad tears. Thank goodness for Benji.

28 October: Have to... do what? Not sure I can write about this lot.

29 October: Ha! Must say between Benji's listening skills and the
cathartic benefit of diary writing, I got over that experience. Good
idea to put it in a separate notebook. Thanks, Benji!!!

Chapter 19

The coldness between mother and daughter gradually dissipated. They were used to their battles, so life chugged along through hours of ignoring each other, days of being polite and without any apology from either woman, finally settling back into a comfortable routine of sharing spaces and daily happenings.

Friday evening, Kate entered Yeo & Co Grocery intending to make a quick apology to Fiona, hang up, and leave Nora to her tasks. But with Fiona begging Kate to stay over and have a weekend of nonsense, the intended short telephone call turned into a long conversation that tested her mother's patience.

Nora stood with one hand on the broom and the other on her hip. She scowled at Kate in a way that could have curdled custard. 'Hurry up,' she mouthed.

When Kate shrugged, Nora added aloud, 'Mr Yeo might be in soon.'

Kate turned her back and continued talking into the phone. 'I just can't.'

The person on the other end had a lot to say because Kate nodded, sighed repeatedly before interjecting. 'But, no, look...'

More frowning before she said, 'Fi, listen. Listen to me. I know I said I'd come this weekend, but I can't keep taking advantage of you and your family.'

Nora tapped her daughter on the shoulder. 'Get off the phone.'

Ignoring the hurry-up, Kate said, 'No. Not to your place. We can meet in town.'

A brief silence followed as Kate listened to more pleading.

'Not even for a party. No Fiona, and I have to go,' she turned and pulled a face at her mother, 'Mum's giving me that look. I have to go.'

She hesitated, listened to Fiona, interrupting with broken sentences.

'Peter? No, we've broken up.' 'Yeah, he is nice.' 'You marry him then.' 'Course I don't mean it.' 'No, I won't come.' 'You've got to be kidding?' 'I'm sure your father didn't say that.' 'Okay, okay, but say hi to your mum.' 'Fi, I got to go. I'll ring sometime.' 'Bye.' And she plonked the phone down and sat on the nearest chair, slumping forward, shaking her head.

'What's that all about?' Nora asked. 'Not even for a party—since when?'

Kate lifted her head. 'Not now, Mum.'

'Yeah, bloody now, if Miss High-and-Mighty doesn't mind.' She leaned the broom against the wall and faced Kate. 'You've been all uppity for weeks now. And I don't reckon it's because we argued.' Nora folded her arms. 'If you want to know what I think, you're thinking you're too good for ordinary folk. Messing about in Cottesloe as if you're one of them upper-class sort. All those late nights.' She sniffed her annoyance.

'Messing about! What's that mean?' Kate stood. 'Think I'll just go home. It's a right old mess when your mother thinks you shouldn't better yourself.'

'It's not that. You haven't been yourself lately. Have you two had a fight?'

'Yeah...' Kate tap-danced her thoughts. 'That's it. She... well, you wouldn't understand.' Kate foraged her creative mind for something feasible. 'She... wants to... I feel like a poor cousin. I want a break from making excuses about my clothes, about why I can't saunter into a boutique and buy two outfits, why I don't have an account at every department store, from explaining why... why we don't have a phone.'

'If she's a true friend, she'd understand.'

'Come on! Do you think someone with loads of money can understand when you say you can't afford it? She... well, I'm just sick of it.'

'Knew it would come to that. So much time spent with the Nobles. I know their sort. I've always said you should stick to our type. What about that nice Shirley Bennet? Why couldn't you be friends with her? You went to the same school. You should look her up.'

Kate turned the lock and opened the back door of the shop. 'You don't get it, do you? I don't want to be friends with the likes of Shirley bloody Bennet. She's probably engaged to some mechanic, putting doilies in her glory box, dreaming of kids.' Kate shivered at the thought of nappies and pureed carrot. 'Forget it, Mum.'

'Then why did you fight with the wonderful Fiona. I would've thought you had the nous to wheedle your way through a girly spat.'

The back-handed compliment triggered a moment of remorse. Fiona *was* a good friend, and Kate valued the time at the Noble's house. After all, hadn't her education into society been ramped up!

'You've always said not to take advantage, so I'm just following your advice. Mrs Noble's lovely. Gene... Mr Noble is generous, but...'

'Ha! Gene, is it? My God, Kate, don't go down that line.'

'Sorry, Mum.' Kate glanced over her shoulder at the dark alley, turned back to her mother. 'It's just he gets everyone to call him that. I was surprised, you know, at the parties, all the blokes from his work... the ones my age.'

'Well, you just watch yourself. I bet *he's* a charmer. *She* sounds like a bloody superwoman, and I reckon sugar won't melt in their mouths.'

'You're hopeless. You don't even know them.'

'I know the sort. Super smooth, glib, showy with money. Yeah, it might surprise you to know, I *know* the type.'

Kate avoided her mother's eye as she thought how true the description of Fiona's father was. She didn't like the inference Nora had placed on "know" and chased away the image of her mother succumbing to the wiles of any man.

'I'm getting out of here,' Kate said. 'And by that, I mean out of Beaconsfield. Why shouldn't I have nice things? Rich, rich I say. I could get used to being rich.'

'And how do you think you're going to do that.'

'I'll think of something.'

Nora humphed. 'Stuck up, that's what you are! I never raised you to be stuck up, missy. You bloody get on home and start the dinner.

I'll be there within the hour. You'd better have the veggies done. Peeling potatoes, that'll bring you down to earth.'

Kate closed her eyes, begging the tears to stop building.

Tears didn't fall often in the Wallace household. If emotions were high, they usually showed themselves as anger. Nora, shocked at the liquid emotion, stood stock still for a moment before placing a hand on her daughter's shoulder.

'What's up? You're not pregnant, are you?'

Kate turned so quickly Nora lost her balance and had to grab Kate's arm.

Flapping away the closeness, Kate said, 'Been reading between the lines of my diary again, have you?' When Nora shook her head, Kate yelled, 'What if I were? What if I get married and never come back?'

Steadying her balance and her racing heart, Nora checked the time. 'Mr Yeo is due soon. You'd better go. We'll talk when I get home.'

Kate laughed. 'Honestly, Mum, it's a bit late for a mother-daughter sex talk. But, no, I'm not pregnant. And I'm never getting married, so you can stop thinking about grandchildren and all that. I just think I spend too much time at the Noble's place.' She tipped her head, looked down her nose. '*You* said one shouldn't overstay one's welcome. I'm just obeying orders.'

'That'd be the day.'

'Yeah. But not anymore. In future, I'm the one who's going to be in charge.'

Nora spent the rest of the cleaning time figuring out what may have caused an argument between good friends. She was sure Kate wasn't telling the truth.

Raconteur

Years of teenage angst and the establishment of her twenties introduced Kate to mind-numbing work just to earn some money.

Adulthood also came with a repetitive life of arguments with Nora, occasional shopping trips with Fiona, dates with young men with names like Ramon, Tony, Clinton, Juan. She might have even let some of them pick her up from home.

Above all else, Kate was determined to shape her own life, trying her luck at being a receptionist, a PA, and a debt collector—failing pretty much at them all. She found it hard to follow rules, and even harder to smile at demanding and sexist bosses. She needed an escape plan: from Beaconsfield and the lower step of life (as she called it).

Kate's diary enabled her to reminisce over past jottings. She laughed at some and grimaced at others, noting the one constant theme was money—the lack of it and the desire for more.

With spasmodic contact with Fiona, mostly in Perth city, the years ticked by. She tucked some incidents away into forgetfulness by choice, took all she'd been through and decided it was time to move forward to better things.

KATE'S DIARY

1977

6 February: Hey! I might start writing again. It's time to alter my life. I'm sick of being thought of as everyone's POOR friend. And why not record it. Yeah, why not indeed!

7 February: I need a new exciting plan. No way I'm ending up like Nora. Surely there's a way out of this situation.

8 February: Off with the old. You won't see me for *gold* dust!

9 February: Time to work on Plan B. Or should that be Plan F, after all, most of my plans have failed—so far. Maybe Plan S—S for success. Yep, it's time to step things up. Time to be part of the wealthy society.

10 February: I've had the training for it. All that stuff must have rubbed off from the Nobles. Let's put that to good use. If I can't be rich AND famous, let's try the RICH bit. Okay, Plan M for money is about to start.

1 March: Know what I want. Seen where to start. Let's go... Goodbye Kate.

I'm now Katisse. Much classier. Yeah, that should do it.

Chapter 20

Katisse caressed the soft folds of a grey silk cocktail dress, and the end of her self-manicured nails bumped over the beading clinging to the neckline. She hummed to the mellow music, which added to the calm ambience of the boutique, pushed a few hangers along the shiny rod and assessed each creation, nodding as she recognised the individually designed items from the brochure she'd picked up from the French polished table near the front door. Pictures showed originals by Yves Saint Laurent, along with other famous labels and some newer designers Katisse didn't recognise.

She chose a bright top with as much material hanging from the bodice as in the bodice itself. Draping a second and third article over her arm, she made her way to the generously proportioned change room.

'Does madam require assistance?' The velvety voice of a tall, angular woman who appeared by Katisse's side asked.

'*Merci*, I am just fine,' Katisse answered.

'If mademoiselle would like to try something else, please feel free to call me.'

'No, these will do, *merci*.'

Katisse faced the mirror. Her plan hadn't included purchasing this indulgence but she liked what she saw. Her tanned legs protruded from a swinging red skirt and once she removed the plain black tee shirt, the firm abdomen and toned arms made her grin with approval. She held the Dior top against her chest before poking her arms into the sleeves. 'No, no—it isn't me,' she announced to her reflection. She removed it quickly and draped it over a cushioned chair. Next, she chose the top, which resembled a brightly coloured gift wrapped by a child let loose with ribbons. After wriggling into the garment, Katisse swayed back and forth, making the strips dance around her torso. 'Totally unsuitable,' she said but continued to view the piece from all angles. 'Mm, I like it.'

'Need any help? Are the sizes right?' The sugary voice announced the assistant, who tapped on the side of the booth.

'No. *Oui, Oui.*'

Being interrupted during her delight in the garment annoyed Katisse. She tugged at the edges of the caramel-coloured curtain, eliminating the small gap. Her mirrored form now looked cheap and dishevelled. *No. I can't.* She didn't bother to try on the remaining article and flounced from the cubicle and held the three items towards the assistant. 'I will not take any, I think.'

The young assistant took the garments, offering apologies. She didn't know how she had displeased this French-accented woman and hoped the boutique owner hadn't overheard.

'I'm sorry you didn't like any of them. Have you seen our shoes at the rear of the store?'

Katisse softened. It wasn't this young person's fault her mood had darkened so quickly. She'd entered the boutique with one quest; now, she was being taunted by luxury.

'Ashleigh,' Katisse said as she peered at the elaborate name tag, 'It is I who should be sorry. So many lovely things, but... it is difficult.'

'Would you like to start again? I can help you choose. Is it for something special? Perhaps *someone* special?'

Katisse realised, despite her reticence to elaborate, Ashleigh would be hoping for a sale. 'Mm. Maybe. It is tempting to try on that grey dress with the beads.'

'It's one of our very newest. It would suit you. Your dark hair.'

'*Oui*. Maybe—maybe not.'

'Are you French?' The question slipped out before Ashleigh could stop it. One was supposed to engage the "client" but becoming too familiar wasn't encouraged.

'*Oui*. Yes, but no as well. My father... we lived in France for many years. I was very young.'

'How lovely. Now, are you going to try on that dress? I'm sure you could carry it off.'

By this time, the young assistant had removed the dress from its hanger and offered it to Katisse.

'It's lovely, but I came not to buy anything.'

'Well, there is no cost to try it on.'

Katisse hesitated, touched the grey dress with one finger. 'No, thank you. It is not for me.'

She walked the few steps towards the door, then paused at the counter, aware that Ashleigh watched her closely. After placing the hanger now holding the silk creation onto the display stand, Ashleigh moved towards Katisse.

Two laughing customers entered and scanned the shop before they continued towards the racks.

Katisse rubbed her fingers across the counter and looked up at Ashleigh with half-closed eyes.

She paused with a flash of recollection.

After a disappointing morning trailing aimlessly through the city, she'd sat in a café opposite *La Joie* pondering her options.

This end of town attracted many of Perth's wealthy. The socialites, needing their weekly fix of retail therapy, were regular clients of *La Joie*. The French-sounding name of the boutique added to the aura of international glamour when displayed on a receipt.

Two middle-aged women tittered as they showed off their purchases to each other. The waitress placed expensive salads on the women's table. After polite acknowledgement, they seemed oblivious to the cost of their simple lunch.

Her envy had prickled. 'I need to get a foot in the door to this life.'

She stared through the window watching another woman enter *La Joie*. Her outfit reeked of money.

'*La Joie*,' she whispered. 'I can be French. *Bonjour, mademoiselle*.' She recalled the hated language lessons of her youth. 'Maybe not wasted after all.'

As she assessed Ashleigh's watchfulness, Katisse's voice crept out in a whisper, 'Is it at all possible... would there be a position vacant?'

The intensity of the question shocked Ashleigh. She'd become perceptive to ladies who came into this upmarket boutique. Some wanted quality and exclusiveness, the price tag meaning little.

Others came in pairs, out for some fun trying something they'd never be able to afford. Many customers came somewhere in between. Ashleigh hadn't quite been able to make out the woman with the haunted eyes. There had been something that set her apart, something that didn't sit quite right. She had kept an eye on the neatly dressed but nervous customer. The client's darting glances around the shop, the reading of the brochure in apparent detail, and the quick appraisal of seemingly unsuitable items made Ashleigh doubtful at the beginning. Now she had an explanation and could relax.

'Well, as a matter of fact, there is. Part-time, but could become permanent if trends continue.'

Katisse sat on one of the glamorous Parisian-styled chairs near the counter and flapped the brochure in front of her overheated face. 'I'd like to apply, please.'

Katisse's Diary
1977

5 March: Barely surviving. Plan M or *More Money* is a must. Fingers crossed.

9 March: Katisse—Ha! People are so gullible. My French is nearly as good as my shorthand. *non*.

Yes!!! I mean *oui!* The money that looks like it comes—and goes— in this place. I have to find a way for it to land in my purse. LEATHER purse.

Chapter 21

Katisse sat opposite Rachel Bentleigh-Rowe, the owner of the King Street boutique *La Joie*.

'May I ask how you would like your name pronounced?'

'Car teesh. My mother's choice.'

'Katisse... okay. Was your mother French? Ashleigh said you speak some French.'

'Only a little. Father was a diplomat. We moved many times. Paris was one of the cities we lived in for a while.'

'He was Australian, then?'

'He used to say he was a world citizen.' Katisse repeated her father's apparent explanation, '"From nowhere and everywhere".'

'Interesting.' Rachel twiddled the pen in her hand. 'And your mother?'

'My mother?' Katisse paused. Explanations of her parents were always difficult. 'She was born in Australia, but my mother also wanted to be a citizen of the world. She loved France. Always dreamed of staying longer.'

'Well, Katisse, let's get down to the necessary. Tell me about your experience. May I see your resume—references.'

Katisse swallowed. 'I must explain.' She licked her bottom lip, then worried about smudging her lipstick, continued speaking. 'I'm sorry, but I don't have documents to offer. You see, I've travelled so much, so many places; firstly, as a child, then I couldn't get the travel bug out of my system. So many places, so many jobs. There are no references, I'm afraid.'

'I don't know how I can employ you without something to go on. This is a highly reputable boutique. We have many high-powered clientele. Our stock is very valuable. You must have something. A police clearance, perhaps.'

Katisse looked down at her knees, which were poking out from the same skirt she'd worn the first day she stepped into *La Joie*. She turned her hands around each other and looked at her freshly painted nails. The silence had gone on long enough. She would have to say something or lose the opportunity.

'I've worked in Prague, Seattle, LA.' Katisse nodded with confidence. 'I *know* fashion.'

'That as may be. But I need a little more. Why haven't you any references? It certainly isn't smart to leave an establishment without a reference.' Rachel raised her eyebrows. 'Doesn't give the right impression.'

Lifting her chin, Katisse spoke clearly, 'I agree, but there was a fire. Paper burns easily. People move on. Memories are short.' She sniffed as if to hold back tears. 'I'm willing to be put on probation, even work for a week without pay. I really would like to work here. I have a good knowledge of fashion, am excellent at looking after any clientele—even the fussiest—and certainly know how to treat the wealthy. I just need a chance to prove it.'

'Enthusiasm is one thing but experience doesn't count for

anything if I don't feel I can trust my staff.' Rachel tried to see beyond the eyes of the young woman who seemed to be begging for this job. 'Why *La Joie*? Why not apply to the agencies? Tell me, why here?'

Katisse fingered her long earring. 'It's all about the clothes, Mrs Bentleigh-Rowe. Can you imagine working at a supermarket? I couldn't do it. I'm twenty-nine and have seen enough of the world to know what I want. Luxury villas, beautiful clothes, opera, food to die for—I've seen it all. I just want a chance to build a better life.' She sighed. 'It would be ungracious of me to ask of your background, but you know the thrill; *La Joie* has the best of the best. Could you serve in Big W?'

Rachel didn't answer, internally shuddering at the thought of being stranded behind a check-out counter. She opened an empty file with the title "Katisse Blanchard" typed neatly on the white label. 'I'm a businesswoman. I'm supposed to have many pieces of paper in this file—your file—but I have nothing. What can we do about that, Katisse Blanchard?'

An awkward silence hovered. Katisse spoke first. 'Do you have a staff form? I can give you some information.'

A relieved sigh escaped from Rachel. She shut the empty file, retrieved two papers from the tray on her desk, and passed them across the table.

'I suppose one has to take some risks.' Rachel remembered her interview four years ago with a surly bank manager who wanted assurances from her. "I certainly didn't get where I am today without taking risks.'

As Katisse pulled a notebook from her handbag, Rachel said firmly, 'You'd better not let me down.'

Pausing over entering her details, Katisse looked up. 'I—'

Rachel interrupted, 'It won't be plain sailing. I'm going to put you on a bond, then three months' probation.'

'A bond?' Katisse's hand hovered over the space for her signature. 'I have no money for a bond.'

'One week without remuneration will cover the bond.' Rachel shifted in her seat, already doubting her decision. 'If you... if we survive three months' probation, at base rate, you'll get paid for the first week as a bonus.' Rachel gathered the forms. 'It's up to you. I have to have some guarantee against this... the risks.'

'*Oui*, I understand.'

With the rest of the interview proceeding in a convivial manner, Katisse relaxed as Rachel outlined the boutique's methods, the stock, and her expectations.

Minutes later, Ashleigh watched Katisse nod to a mannequin, skip down the steps and disappear up the street.

On the way to the train station, Katisse repeated *La Joie* in her best French impression.

Katisse's Diary

1977

16 June: Been busy. Sorry, Dear Diary.

20 June: Yes, *Oui*. Done it. Got through those three months in a breeze. Knew Katisse could do it.

29 June: Some real snobs come in. The worst is the old dears. They think money makes them more important. The sorry thing is it does. Plan M will prove that. I'll prove that. I've met some lovely people as well. Not all the rich and famous people are horrid.

4 July: Mum's having a fit. Surely she didn't think I'd stay at home forever. I'm thirty-frigging-eight.

6 July: One rather generous bonus coming up. My own flat. Phone? Oh yeah.

Chapter 22

'So,' Rachel said as she motioned for Katisse to sit. 'Three months is up. I've been impressed.'

'Thank you. I've enjoyed it.'

'Our regular clients tell me when they're not happy. Not often when they are.' Rachel tipped her head, indicating the vagaries of customers. 'But just yesterday, Lynne Williams gave me a glowing account of your worth.' Rachel chuckled. 'Mr Williams must faint when he gets our account each month.' Her quick smile disappeared as she added, 'That's no casual recommendation.'

'I put myself in their shoes,' Katisse said. *Platforms and all.* 'They're happy to spend money; I want to make it as pleasant as possible.'

'Good. Just make sure it continues.'

Katisse asked, 'Will I get the back pay this week?'

'I want to discuss that,' Rachel said.

'It's due.' A prickle of annoyance built. 'I've earned it.'

'Yes, yes. You'll be paid. I wanted to discuss your hours and rate.'

Katisse relaxed. 'More of both, I hope.'

'Mm, yes. I'll put you on full-time from next week. Ashleigh's going on holiday, you'll fill in for her, and the agency will send a part-time temp.'

'Oh, I thought you meant full-time permanently.'

Rachel stood, took a file from the draw behind her. 'I did. Now let's see about the rate, then I have a question for you.'

Katisse didn't like questions. Her life consisted of either questions *she* had that people wouldn't answer or questions *they* had that she didn't want to answer. She certainly didn't want her boss probing into her past and making life difficult.

With the discussion on pay rate settled, Katisse waited anxiously, hoping the generous salary increase meant the question wasn't negative.

'That's done. We'll review again in six months,' Rachel said as she committed the details of the pay increase to file. 'Now, my question.'

Katisse's stomach churned. She uncrossed her feet, scratched an imaginary itch on her neck.

'Would you be available to help at a fundraising event next month? Saturday the tenth.' Rachel placed a leaflet on the desk in front of Katisse.

Picking up the leaflet, Katisse could feel the relief race up her throat.

'Yes? No?' Rachel asked.

'Of course. Yes. Happy too.' Katisse scanned the leaflet again. 'Sure. What would I have to do?'

Rachel nodded slowly, considering if it was the perfect time to ask a personal question of this enigma. During the last three months, Rachel had watched Katisse closely. Her rapport with *La Joie's* clients made one think Katisse came from the same mould. However, Katisse spent little, ate even less, and never spoke of her leisure time. Ashleigh had mentioned Katisse's rejection of after-work coffee or shopping trips to more affordable boutiques.

Although she had no complaints about her work, Rachel knew something kept Katisse from revealing her true self.

Rachel scanned the document on the table, decided against raising her doubts. 'You'd have to look after those spending their money. Much like here.'

'It says here that it's an auction.' Katisse turned the leaflet over. 'That's a little different.'

'Yes, but before the auction starts, they have time to browse. We've donated seven dresses. We'll have three sizes of each for the ladies to try on... if they wish. That's where you'll come in.'

'Won't Ashleigh be back by then?'

'I need both of you to be there. We need to schmooze as much money out of their pockets as we can. For the charity.' Rachel, not known to smirk often, smirked. 'Then it's up to you and Ashleigh to convince those who miss out to be on our doorstep the following Monday.'

Katisse stopped the building cheer. 'I'm sure I can help you out. Saturday the tenth. *Oui*, I am free.'

She left work that day with an extra bounce.

Schmooze... I'm an expert, she thought. *Just let me at them. I'll show you schmooze. I might even schmooze me a personal millionaire!*

With a substantial pay increase, regular employment, overtime at the fundraisers, and the possibility of more tips, Katisse searched for a place of her own.

Nora disapproved vehemently. 'How the hell will I manage?' she yelled at her daughter.

'Just as well as you always do. You won't have to feed me. Think of all the space you'll have.' She pointed in the direction of the bedroom she planned to vacate. 'Take in a border. Maybe one of those sexy foreigners who come into your laundromat.'

'All well and good to joke about it, but have you thought they might take the house from me.'

Katisse certainly hadn't thought of that. She folded her arms, pursed her lips in concentration. 'Would they give you a smaller place?'

'Holy hell, don't even suggest that.' Nora's mind whizzed over options. It might be advantageous to get a new place, something smaller, but she complained anyway. 'I'd be stuck in four walls without company.'

'Mum! We don't do *anything* together. You're working. I'm working. We hardly see each other.'

'Will you get somewhere close? So you can call in every day?'

Katisse shoved her chair back, went to her room, and came back with a page of a newspaper showing real estate advertisements. 'Victoria Park. There's one here I like. Near to the bus that goes straight across the Causeway.'

Nora yanked the paper from beneath Katisse's hand. 'Vic Park! That's not even close. I'll *never* see you.'

Biting back the words *that's the plan*, Katisse said, 'It'll save money on my fares. Anyway, I just can't go on living here. It's the back of beyond, and I intend to get off the bottom rung of the bloody ladder once and for all.'

Shoving the paper away, Nora slumped back in her chair, twisting her hands as she said, 'It's that stuck-up job you've got. *La Joie*! What sort of name is that? *Oui* this, *Oui* that. Holy crap, and you changing your name. Deed bloody poll and all. Why wasn't Kate Wallace good enough?' She banged her palm on the table. 'I blame Miss Tillman. Katherine indeed. That's when it started, she—'

'Mum, please. I have plans. I just don't want to end up like you.' She waved her hand around the room. 'Stuck in an awful bloody place with no chance of ever getting out.'

'Now see here, whatever you want to be called, I can't stop you, but I won't have you criticising my home. There is nothing wrong with it. It's clean, tidy, and you've never gone hungry.'

'I know, and I'm grateful, but I want more than that. Don't you see, I want bloody more than neat and tidy.' She stood grabbed the newspaper and stalked to her room.

'Pride cometh before a fall,' Nora yelled at her daughter's back.

As a token of understanding of Nora's situation, Katisse spoke with the State Housing Authority, who promised to look into moving Nora into a flat. Authorities were keen to have the Beaconsfield house available for migrant families.

Six weeks later, as a farewell gift, Katisse offered to pay for installation and the rent on a telephone. After all, it would save her visiting as often—no matter where her mother ended up.

10 July: It's pretty late. Need to slow down after all that hype. Let's see. It wasn't too bad, this gig, this auction. The food was fabulous. Didn't need to cook anything for dinner. Boy, those women can shop. All that money on a couple of dresses. And they pretend they're spending just for the donation to Red Cross. I ask you!

James Waterman? Reminds me of Gene. But now I can handle that sort. Pity about James's ring. But the man—and the money!!

Get to do another auction next month. For some local church. Missionaries need money, apparently. Well, so do I. Although, my savings are doing okay. The tips help. Socialite Josephine Della thinks I'm wonderful. Half into the bank. Half on a new dress. Have to look the part.

15 July: This unit is better than a Beaconsfield state house. Quite nice. I'll get somewhere better to live as Plan M advances. Subi, or Leederville? Maybe somewhere on the river.

27 July: Spent a boring time at an art gallery. *Monied folk* go to art galleries. Tried to chat up some old bloke, Ronald something or other. Unfortunately, his wife grabbed him, wanting him to buy some God-awful splash of colour. Shame—his Rolex matched his suit.

12 August: Old Ronald recognised me at the next auction. The grabbing woman wasn't his wife. Sister. So, here we go. I'm going to schmooze me a millionaire. He's taking me to dinner!

15 August: Ronald was boring. Old and boring. But still. Top restaurant.

19 August: Ronald wanted me to attend some football gala event. I went. Boring again.

He talked to his OLD buddies, me on his arm. Several raised eyebrows and sideward glances, but I'm probably just the *current* one, not the *only* one. At least it's another night out. Free food.

26 August: Work is okay. Great tips this month. And with staff discount can afford something from *La Joie* stock.

27 August: Said no to Ronald. Told him I didn't have anything new to wear. Worked! New dress from *La Joie* and stupendous shoes. Killer heels. Fortunately, it's dinner, not dancing.

28 August: And you wouldn't believe who was at the next table. James Waterman. I tell you.

1 September: Dinner with James. Boy, oh, boy.

Chapter 23

The auction preparation filled the quiet times at the boutique but on Saturday 10th, time was of the essence.

Katisse and Ashleigh straightened the expensive outfits hanging on the racks. Their slim-fitting black dresses were unadorned except for enamel name tags pretending to be gold lettering on black onyx.

'This is hard work,' Ashleigh said.

'*Oui,* but it's worth it. I mean, Rachel pays us well, and the tips are good.'

'Certainly. It makes it worthwhile.'

'*Oui.*'

Ashleigh frowned. 'Are you actually French?' She glanced away as she added, 'Sorry, didn't mean to pry, but your accent comes and goes. I mean... sorry.'

'It's okay.' Katisse chuckled. 'Sometimes I feel very French.' Her accent became stronger as she added, 'Surrounded by the glamour, the high-end clothes. I'm reminded of the European boutiques, then the French influence takes over and I am, as you can say, indeed very French.' She touched Ashleigh's arm, her French accent disappeared. 'Then, I see the streets of Perth, the casualness of the

216

people, and, *POOF*, suddenly, the French is no longer there.'

'Oh! And... how long did you spend in Paris. It must have been exciting.'

Katisse showed her indifference by tipping her head sideways. 'You know. It is like anywhere. Once it becomes the familiar, it is the same as, you know,' she pointed towards the doorway, 'anywhere.'

'Surely not Paris,' Ashleigh whispered.

'Let's get these racks through. Rachel will be yelling for them soon.'

The guest numbers expanded quickly. Many only dropped a donation in the strategically placed boxes, tried on clothes they couldn't afford and, after consuming titbits of food, ogled the persons who could afford to bid ridiculous amounts for over-priced garments.

Katisse and Ashleigh smiled through the nightmare of women intent on trying on the smallest possible size, attempting to find compliments that didn't sound false or condescending. They handed out flyers advertising the open hours of *La Joie*, taking names and addresses of potential customers.

Once the auction was over, the models and staff mingled with the guests who had been successful with their bids and were now paying their account. Lesser mortals had been gently ushered out, receiving a decorated flacon of perfume as a departing gift. Although the champagne flowed freely, Katisse topped up her flute with water.

'Gorgeous, simply gorgeous.' A man, impeccably dressed, held out his hand towards Katisse. 'James. James Waterman.' His cheeky grin disarmed her.

'I bet you introduce yourself to all the girls the same way.'

He sighed. 'Just the rather ravishing ones.'

Katisse rolled her eyes. 'Well, all of that won't work on me.'

'Sorry,' he said. 'Trying to make up for all this standing around. Waiting. I hate waiting. Such a waste of time.'

Looking around for the person making him wait, she said, 'And who is keeping you here?'

He stepped closer, touched her arm lightly. 'It could be you.'

'Sleaze,' she whispered.

'Sorry. Again.' He sipped his wine. 'I'm a bit of a bastard, even a "sleaze", as you so correctly noticed, when I'm tired, hungry, and... waiting. All because my wife wants to spend more than all the other women who want to spend more than the next one.' He tugged his ear. 'Do you want some more wine? I could be at least useful to someone.'

'No, I'll finish this one, but thanks anyway. Do you need a refill?'

'I can see my wife heading this way. Hopefully, she's ready to go. It's been nice meeting you.'

With a chuckle, Katisse rolled her eyes again. 'Even though I called you names.'

'I think I'll live. Next time, I'll be on my best behaviour.'

'Next time?' Katisse's stomach did an unexpected tango.

His eyes lost their impudence. 'I'd like that.'

'And Mrs Waterman?'

'No, she wouldn't like that. But...' He touched her arm. 'Anyway, I know where to find you.'

'And Mrs Waterman?' Katisse said again.

'Don't worry about Brooke. She wouldn't be seen dead talking to someone who works for a wage.'

With her mouth open, Katisse watched James walk away.

Taking an armful of bags from his wife, he nodded at something she said, then turned and raised smiling eyes at Katisse.

'You okay?' Ashleigh asked, following Katisse's eyeline.

'Um, yes, I guess.'

'That's Brooke Waterman. Husband James.'

'James. James Waterman.' She laughed at her imitation of the well-known James Bond line. 'I just met him. Quite something.'

'If you like that sort,' Ashleigh said with a laugh.

'That sort? Explain.'

'Rich. Very Rich. Wife. Awful wife.'

'Wife. Yes, he said. And a wife of any sort is not good.'

Taking Katisse's glass and smelling it, Ashleigh grinned. 'You need wine. Real wine. James Waterman would be the catch of the season, bucket loads of his own money but, and it's a huge but—he's married.'

'But,' Katisse emphasised, 'to an *awful* wife.'

'Don't get involved.'

'Money. Lovely stuff. Might be worth the risk.'

Ashleigh stopped, turned to her friend. 'Money? Don't you want more than money? Love? Marriage?'

'I've yet to try marriage. I'd like to try money first. Anyway, it takes two to tango, and I own dancing shoes.' As she turned away, she whispered, 'Pretty ones.'

KATISSE'S DIARY
1977

3 September: Oh yes, dear diary. Money is one thing. A man like James Waterman is another. Fortunately, it seems like they are a well-matched pair. James/money, I mean. Pity about the wife.

15 September: Have said no often enough. Time to say yes.

18 September: If only one didn't have to send him home to her.

28 September: Seems he flirts a lot, doesn't often get taken up on it. But he hasn't met me before! The trouble is, how is a poor working girl going to keep a wealthy lover. You know what is said: necessity is the mother of inventions. Invention is another word for avoiding the truth. And I'm good at that. Yes, you better believe it.

10 October: Weeks of bliss and now, just when it's settling nicely into a glow of... who knows what... cold tippy-toes come to the fore.

Chapter 24

'James.' Katisse whispered into the phone, her French accent noticeable. 'What took you so long.'

'Honey, I've been away. I've missed you.'

Katisse purred her acknowledgment. 'When will I see you?'

'It's difficult. One dinner out with a gorgeous woman who isn't my wife can be explained, but...'

'Then, it's over?'

'It can't be. I'll... Can I come to your place?'

Last week after a long dinner, James had expected to be asked in for coffee when he pulled up outside an impressive condominium in Victoria Park.

'Look, don't come up. I'm having the place re-carpeted and it's a mess.' She'd walked into the lobby, turned, peeked out the door, and waved. After he'd driven away, she exited the glamorous building and walked around the corner to her compact, sparsely furnished flat on the first floor of a renovated but low-budget building.

Now, with James on the phone, her eyes darted around her

bedroom as she scrambled for a reply, 'Um, carpet delayed. Sorry.'

'Okay, let's see. I'll get back to you. But what about lunch?'

'Today? I can't get away for more than half an hour.'

'If we skip the food...' He chuckled. 'Not entirely joking, but hey, I'll ring you back.'

'James, I can't keep taking calls at work. I'm not supposed to. Rachel has already glared at me. Luckily, it's my tea break. Now, I've got to go. Ring me.'

'Sure, honey. But make yourself available for dinner. We'll go somewhere nice.'

Katisse knew it was time to come clean. She sashayed into the restaurant, thanked the hovering waiter for having pulled out the chair, and plopped down opposite James.

'Hi, honey. You look fabulous.'

'Mm. Ta.' She focused on sitting straighter. 'I think.'

James leaned forward. 'What's up?'

The waiter saved her from replying. 'Wine, sir?'

After they agreed on a bottle of red wine, they perused the menu in silence. Nearby patrons talked loudly about the vagaries of the stock market. James glanced several times at Katisse while deciding between lamb or trout.

With their meals ordered and the waiter satisfied he'd delivered excellent service by fussing over serviettes and correct cutlery, James asked again, 'What's up? Not happy with that stunning dress? I can tell you it could only look better on a hanger by your bed.' He chuckled at his attempt at the beginning of seduction.

'Actually, I'm in a bit of a spot.'

'Spot? What sort of spot? Tell me. Maybe I can help.'

'You know I work at *La Joie*.' She paused. He nodded. 'I thought my wage would cover the cost of the condominium. It does when I get generous tips, but they've dried up. I've not got any furniture except one chair and a bed.'

She re-arranged the cutlery, fiddled with her serviette. 'That's why I couldn't ask you up.'

'Honey, why didn't you say? I wouldn't've minded. You and a bed.' He tipped one shoulder forward. 'That'd be okay.'

Katisse counted to ten with her eyes on his. Then, her eyes moistened. 'Oh, James, I wanted it to be more than just me and the bed. Is that all I am?'

The two plates of trout arrived, along with more fussing from the over-attentive waiter. He filled their glasses. 'Anything else?' he asked.

In between eating slowly, frowning into the distance, and patting her lips with the white serviette, Katisse glanced at James with pussy-cat eyes.

'Honey, is the trout okay?' he asked. 'You don't seem to be enjoying it.'

'It's delicious. It's just... No, it's not your problem. I should be able to sort it out. It's just... oh, never mind.'

He placed his cutlery down, leaned forward and spoke softly, 'Of course I mind. Tell me. I'm pretty good at solving other people's problems.'

Kate explained how she'd been evicted from her "fabulous" home because of non-payment of the lease and moved into a tiny flat with the chair and bed.

'I thought I could manage,' she whispered.

After he'd convinced her to have another glass of wine because the problem was a little one, she wiped the corner of her eye, smiled at him.

'You're too good to me,' she said.

KATISSE'S DIARY

1977/1978

4 November: Fiona! I knew it had to happen. Thank God I was able to fob her off.

15 November: Love my condominium. He didn't realise about the boring flat. He paid twelve months in advance. Furniture is way better than I could afford. Payback = Bed now well used.

20 November: Awful wife is getting suspicious. Keeping tabs. Maybe time to let him go.

24 November: Ronald phoned, came into work. No go, Ronnie old boy.

29 November: Awful wife came into *La Joie*. Dropped hints. Hell, fortunately doesn't suspect me. Not when she's so pally and talking about all the 'sluts and whores' in her husband's office.

24 December: Bye, Mum. I will miss you. I wonder what her dreams were when she was my age. I did care about her—in my own way, but we were... yeah, so different.

8 January: I'm sad. Miss my lovely man.

Chapter 25

Controlling her sudden audible intake of breath, Katisse stepped quickly behind the rack of dresses. She shouldn't have been surprised; Fiona was bound to enter *La Joie* one day. Struggling to find an escape route, Katisse turned her back and unclipped her badge, then spoke with false enthusiasm.

'Fiona! How lovely. Fancy... we meet here.'

Fiona's eyes widened. 'Kate! Since when do you shop at *La Joie*?'

Katisse furtively glanced around the boutique taking in Ashleigh at the front counter and Rachel tucked away behind the office desk. She placed her hand on Fiona's arm and moved them toward the side wall.

'Have you seen this one?' Katisse asked. 'I bought one like it last time.'

Fiona moved her arm away and looked Katisse over. 'Things must have changed if you're shopping here.'

'Well, yes, just a bit. But to be honest, I'm meeting a friend in...' she looked at her watch, 'a few minutes, so I was just filling in time. I've got to go.'

As Ashleigh ushered a customer towards the change rooms, she smiled at Katisse, spoke softly, 'Just check the new stock when you get a moment.'

Fiona shot both women a confused glance. Katisse giggled deceptively, shrugged for Fiona's benefit, waited until Ashleigh was out of ear-shot, and said, 'Apparently, new stock has an item I've been asking for.' She stepped towards the front door. 'I'll come back when she's unpacked it. But I do have to go. Perhaps we could have a quick coffee? But I do have... yes, Lily... um,' she checked her watch again. 'Yes, I could grab a coffee with you.'

'I suppose,' Fiona said, not sounding at all convinced of the need to rush. 'Couldn't we browse instead? I mean, we can talk *and* shop.' She forced a smile. 'We used to.'

Katisse knew Ashleigh would expose her if she didn't act immediately. 'Sure. Usually I'd agree but... Lily... and... well... just a sec. I'll... let her... the assistant... hang on, Fiona.'

She spotted Rachel closing her laptop preparing to leave the office. Katisse paced towards the change rooms, whispered to Ashleigh, 'I'm taking my break now. This customer is a friend of mine. Would like to catch up. Can you cover for me. I'll make it up to you. I'll work late. Do the stock. Just need to get out of here. Right now. Please, Asheigh. I'll explain later...'

She left Ashleigh staring as she grabbed her handbag from the staff room and hurried back to Fiona.

Fiona had a floral blouse draped over one arm and considering another one still on a hanger. 'This is nice.'

'Yes, but, come on, let's go. It'll be great to catch up...'

'Honestly, Kate, what's wrong. Surely, we can spend...'

Katisse held open the door. 'Coffee, I need coffee.' She slung her handbag strap over her shoulder, grinned inanely and waited while Fiona replaced the blouse on the rack, shrugged and accepted defeat.

Awkward silence hovered while they walked to the nearby café and ordered their hot drinks. Fiona dithered over tea or coffee and queried how the café attendant seemed to know Katisse's "regular".

'What's going on?' Fiona asked as they settled at a table.

'Not a lot. What about you?'

'Kate! I'm not entirely stupid, you know.'

'Never thought you were.' She fiddled with her name badge sitting in the pocket of her top. Several scenarios bounced around her mind. She didn't want Fiona to know she was working at *La Joie*. If her portrayal of success was to continue, she had to pull this one off.

'Well, you should explain.' Fiona picked up her cup.

'Explain what? Shopping?' Katisse smirked half-heartedly. 'It's the art of purchasing items you may or may not need.'

'For God's sake, Kate. That's not what I meant.'

Katisse sighed, her shoulders dropped. Not only would she have to explain she was working at *La Joie*, but she'd have to explain why she lied about it. Fiona had always denied any form of snobbery, but Katisse knew the subtle ways of the rich were just well-hidden elitism. Playing for time, she welcomed the interruption of the assistant placing the coffee on the table.

'Your usual,' the assistant said to Katisse. 'Enjoy,' she added to Fiona.

'That!' Fiona said, when the girl had moved away. 'Your usual? I'm surprised you have a "usual" here! Explain that.'

'Why not here? Nice as anywhere.'

'Sure. But that woman in *La Joie*. She knew you too. Check the stock, she said. That isn't "usual". My mum is a regular at a lot of places, she never gets to "check the stock". Explain that!'

Katisse searched for make-believe, even considered the truth. 'I returned a dress last week—'

Fiona interrupted, 'If you've come into some money, it's okay, Kate. You're entitled to shop wherever you like. But we were friends, I thought we were besties, but things change, that's okay, but you don't have to pretend about shopping at boutiques instead of Target... or wherever.'

'Oh, yes, well...'

'It's really great to think your dad's come good. I know it's a little difficult sometimes having to accept money, but men love to be in charge. Go with the flow, I reckon.'

Fiona's "Daddy" came to Katisse's mind, and the power money initiated. She shook her head, thinking of her father's drunken state, thinking of her bonus's sitting in her bank account. She let Fiona continue.

'I often wondered how you survived. I always admired your persistence. I thought you'd find a high-powered career. Did you? Or have you found a rich guy? Whichever! I'm just really glad you've found your feet. We should go shopping after this coffee. It *is* really nice coffee. No wonder you come here. Perhaps we can go back to *La Joie*. That blue blouse was really pretty. You could see if the new stock has the piece you're waiting for. Surely, that assistant would—'

'Take a breath, Fi.'

'Sorry. Just got excited. You know. We were great mates. Shop 'til we drop. Didn't we?'

'*You* did,' Katisse said softly.

'Yes. But can we now go—'

'I have to go. Lily will be waiting.'

'Oh, I forgot. Who's Lily? New friend obviously.'

Fiona's instant jealousy reached across the table.

'No… she's… well, Dad wanted me to meet her. Someone from the embassy—'

'That's okay. Off you go. Don't worry about me.' Fiona then dropped the sarcasm. 'But can we meet next week? Maybe here.'

'I'll ring.'

'That's a fob off, Kate. Not even a clever one.' Fiona stood. 'I thought maybe this was a happy accident. Running into you. But, leave it, Kate. I understand. Might run into you again. Or not! Thanks for the coffee.'

Fiona stalked out.

A chuckled threatened, and Katisse grinned. *Perfect,* she thought. *Not only have I avoided the "working at La Joie" exposure but Fiona is annoyed enough not to expect a phone call. Couldn't have worked out better if I'd planned it.*

As she returned to *La Joie,* Katisse worried about the required discussion with Ashleigh. Their friendship constantly teetered between difficult and grim. Now she would have to construct another pathway to conciliation. Maybe Ashleigh would understand the vagaries of social standings.

Fortunately, Rachel had left *La Joie* a couple of minutes after Katisse, happy to leave Ashleigh in charge while assuming Katisse was in the stock room. Katisse now only had to deal with Ashleigh's exasperation.

'About time!' Ashleigh exclaimed.

'I'm sorry. Old friend. Doesn't understand the need for us to have to work.'

Ashleigh closed her eyes for a second. 'Then she's not worth the friendship.'

'It's more than that. She—'

'I don't really care what you tell *her*. Tell her you own this place! Tell her you're the queen of England!' Ashleigh grabbed Katisse's arm. 'You tell enough stories that you may well be the Queen of Sheba for all I know, but just... just don't involve *me*. You rush in, you rush out. Men! Women! Who are all these people? Who are you? Really? Truly? *Who are you?*'

It took a great deal of fortitude for Katisse not to collapse, sob until every last drop of emotion lay on the floor, and to tell Ashleigh the myriad of hidden lies, but the knot in her chest bubbled until a fresh breath broke free.

'I'm me,' Katisse whispered. 'Not the queen of anywhere. Just me.' She retrieved her name badge from her pocket, held it towards Ashliegh. 'Katisse.'

'Well then, Katisse. You owe me.'

Katisse headed for the stock room. 'Yeah. The queen of the bloody stock room!'

Chapter 26

'Katisse, you want to attend to Brooke Waterman?'

'She's back in again! Wow. Every week. *Oui?*'

'Yes or no?' Ashleigh asked again.

'Not really. You go.'

'You had a thing for her husband James, didn't you?'

'A thing? What are you? A teenager? But no, I don't particularly want to serve her.'

'Go on. You might find out if they're still married. Let me know if he's not? Although, I reckon you'd get the first option. I've seen the way he looks at you.'

'Ashleigh!' Katisse peeked out from the staff room again. 'You go.'

'Nup. I need to replace my lipstick. And toilet first.'

Rachel opened the door. 'One of you, *please*. There are clients waiting.'

Ashleigh pointed to the restroom, which gave Katisse no option but to leave the staff room and offer assistance to someone she'd been avoiding for over four months.

'That one would suit you,' Katisse said to Mrs Waterman.

'Not sure about that.' Brooke turned. 'I like the blue better.'

Katisse draped the yellow shirt dress over her arm and offered the blue version.

'I wondered if you still worked here. You haven't been here when I was in last. So, when was it? Probably that last auction night. Wasn't my husband chatting you up?' She snorted a laugh. 'Mind you, I think he's got more than you on his plate at the moment.' She held the blue shift against her frame. 'Mm, might try it on.'

Katisse chose a patterned navy-blue dress, held it at arm's length, showing off the generous skirt. 'What about this one? More alluring.'

'Bring that one, and the yellow one. If you think it suits me, I might as well try it.'

When they reached the changeroom, Katisse asked, 'Is it for something special? Dinner perhaps?'

'Huh, something special. I wish. But maybe that's what I need to organise.' She frowned as she asked, 'Are you married? No, I guess not.' She lifted her left hand and flashed over-generous rings.

Katisse shook her head.

'And on the subject of special treats, my lovely husband is always too busy with business dinners to take his wife out. I'm a little suspicious. Not sure they're all *business* dinners. His secretary is a bitch. Covers for him. Lies, all lies. I reckon he can't have *that* many interstate and overseas clients. Even in the finance industry. No. He comes home too late. Too worn out even for sex. That's a bit suss.' She took the navy-blue dress from Katisse. 'Don't get married, my dear. Love them and leave them. Best advice I can give. Now, leave me to spend his money. I might even take all three.'

It didn't take Brooke's comments to convince Katisse of the lack of marriage benefits. She knew all too well how badly it had turned out for her parents.

Derek Wallace had drifted off any radar. No one had advised Nora of his death. Katisse thought he could well be one of the invisible, unnoticed people who fade away from reality into the oblivion of alcohol and homelessness. She would shudder with the memory of the encounter with a bundle of rags who said he was her father any time a late-night event meant she had to scurry to her car in the dark.

Nora had been transferred to a third floor one-bedroom apartment in South Fremantle. The lift was a huge bonus—except when it broke down.

Her bulky frame was kept primed with the discovery of Joe's Spaghetti Café two doors from the bus stop that delivered Nora to and from the laundromat on Wednesday afternoons and Saturday mornings. Under-the-counter ironing had stopped the moment she became eligible for a pension.

Nora was often in tears when Katisse rang on Sundays. Katisse bribed away the tears with promises of treats—always delivered by someone else. The few times they'd shared a movie or a lunch in Fremantle, both were on edge knowing Katisse's obligation had fuelled the outing, while Nora did her best to live up to her fashionable daughter. To avoid the strain of being over polite and side-stepping conflict, Nora often included Doris, her friend from Chidley House, in these infrequent outings.

Doris, now a widow, lived a few streets away from Nora and had let slip to Katisse that they spent many hours at bingo, usually spending any winnings at the pub. Sometimes a beer, but when one of them had a big payout, a steak and chips lunch. Once or twice a month, they'd catch the train to Perth intending to see a movie, visit the museum or the art gallery. Nora invariably complained of sore knees, swollen ankles, and would convince Doris she preferred to sit—usually over shepherd's pie or Devonshire tea.

Just before Christmas of 1972, Doris rang Katisse speaking in gasps, saying Nora had slipped down the stairs, injured her leg and, at this very moment, the ambulance was taking a screaming Nora to hospital.

'The blasted lift wasn't working. I almost fell on top of her. She couldn't stand,' Doris said. 'I didn't know what to do. I think she's broken her ankle.'

'Which hospital?'

'I didn't know what to do?'

Katisse reached for the glass of water she'd been halfway through when the phone rang. 'It's okay, Doris. Stay calm. Now, which hospital?' Katisse sipped the water as an image of her obese mother—Kmart dress above her waist—screaming obscenities until help came. She shook the image away, took another sip of water. 'Which one, Doris?'

Nora hadn't broken her ankle but pulled many tendons, which meant an automatic stay in Fremantle Hospital.

Katisse almost gave in to the request to have Nora stay with her. But when the details of the assistance Nora would require were made clear, Katisse shivered with distaste and said it wasn't possible. It was one thing to sit through lunch but to have to shower and dress her mother didn't bear consideration.

Nora refused all attempts to get her active again. She huffed and puffed, refusing to walk further than the toilet. The huffing and puffing were real. Her lungs shuddered as the staff encouraged her past the door of her room. After three days, infection grabbed the battling lungs. Another three days and Katisse had a funeral to organise.

Her own level of emotion during the service had come as a shock to Katisse. Memories snuck back. She'd smiled as she remembered her days in Chidley House and the moments they'd battled to make the garden presentable in the Beaconsfield home. She also remembered Nora always taking the last piece of any cake she'd baked. Katisse's brief smile ceased. Now, it didn't matter. Her mum wouldn't hide chocolate in the back of the fridge ever again.

Katisse realised she'd never told her mother how proud she'd been of the way Nora had worked hard all those years. A flick of annoyance killed the remorse. Her mother had never said she was proud of her daughter, either.

It took little effort for Katisse to talk to a funeral director, insisting they follow her directions to the letter: smoked salmon and roast beef on delicate crackers, tiny *petit forts*, ridiculous amounts of white roses and imported daffodils for the coffin, appropriate classical music and soulful poetry. Doris had burst into tears, sobbed about what Nora would have wanted. Katisse had relented, allowing Doris to accompany her to the funeral director's office but without physically removing Doris from the establishment, she could only sit quietly waiting for the explosion of emotion to evaporate. Doris's tears diminished as each item on the funeral director's pad was altered, except for the excess amounts of flowers.

As the final piece of country music faded and the small gathering stood around a table with sausage rolls and cream cakes, Katisse hugged Doris fondly.

'There, there,' Doris said as she patted Katisse's back. They released each other and Doris wiped away the dribble of a tear from Katisse's cheek. 'She loved you, you know. Despite everything.'

'You really expect... um, yeah, one's parents to live forever. Well, sort of.'

A tiny chuckle slipped out. 'I don't know about that,' Doris said. 'Our ample-bodied Nora wasn't going to live until one hundred.'

Katisse nodded. 'Thanks, Doris. For everything.'

'Have a sausage roll. They're good.'

'No, I'll just have coffee.'

Katisse returned to *La Joie* from the day off without explanation. Ashleigh presumed Katisse had spent the day in bed with James again. Rachel recorded the day off and didn't think anything more about it. Several staff pushed their allowances of days off to the limit.

James didn't know Katisse wasn't at work but rang the following evening to cancel their dinner date.

Then, in the following weeks, with another two dinner cancellations and a cryptic phone call from a formal-speaking secretary, Katisse knew her affair with James was doomed.

After a melancholic Sunday breakfast—an apology coming from James for having to return home for a promised family barbecue lunch with his wife's parents—James and Katisse hugged out their unspoken goodbye.

When she arrived home on Monday, the doorman greeted her

with a smile almost as wide as the bunch of red roses he held.

'Someone's a lucky girl,' the elderly doorman said.

'Very lucky,' Katisse replied.

Her luck held out when she opened the attached card. James's guilt had paid for another twelve months lease and offered an amount substantial enough for a Paris flight and accommodation for at least five days.

'Yes!' She waved the card above her head. 'At last! I will now get to walk under the Eifel tower.'

Over the next few months, James and Brooke Waterman glowed from the society pages. His tight smile aged him, and an overly decorated beige dress made Mrs Waterman's complexion look sallow and washed out.

Raconteur

Kate became reconciled to a life of mundane repetitiveness and recorded nothing in her diary.

Her life at La Joie ticked over one week, one month, one year after the other.

She spent time wishing for her life to be different but not quite knowing how to change more than her selection of high-end clothes and choice of coffee. An unwritten bucket list still held Paris but a wish for a chance at never-ending love didn't include a gold band on the left hand.

Evenings, and a few weekends, were spent with well-dressed, intellectual, monied men, including a geologist, an IT specialist, and a Volvo dealer. Several other men, who she saw as nothing but a distraction to an evening alone in front of the TV, came and went.

Kevin lasted three months, Geoff three days, and Robert three minutes after he asked her to go 'Dutch' for dinner. She tried living with Louie, but his mother had spoilt him, and Katisse refused to play housemaid. Over-attentive Jack couldn't accept she needed time for hair appointments and facials without him patiently waiting in reception, while Abercrombie Arkwright wanted to share her... too much!

Her friendship with Ashleigh never extended past an occasional coffee after work or an extra glass of wine at the end of a La Joie auction. Rachel respected but never really accepted Katisse's aloofness and continually doubted any connection to France. Doris sent birthday and Christmas cards, suggested they catch up for old time's sake. Katisse sent a basket of fruit in return.

As Katisse celebrated her forty-third birthday, alone, she dug out her diaries.

Pushing the memory of Fiona and the Noble family into a corner of reminiscence, she sighed with the memory of Stan, Syd, and Miss Tillman. She returned the box of diaries to the top shelf of her walk-in wardrobe and vowed to forget about the past.

KATISSE'S DIARY

1992

24 May: Huh! Who would have thought I would have fallen for a damn Scot! All that rubbish about sporrans and stuff.

27 May: Is this the ONE?

11 August: Mm, not sure I should have done that. Cutting off the nose... you know. Will miss the place. Ashleigh, even Rachel. It was a good job. And it worked its magic.

15 August: Yeah, sure Mrs Waterman doesn't match me up with James. If for no other reason than snobbery. Up yours. I'm as good as anyone, and I'll prove it.

Chapter 27

Determined to walk the boulevards, sit in sidewalk cafes and buy a painting from a Montmartre artist, Katisse bored her workmates with the countless details of her planned trip to *revisit* her favourite spots in Paris.

A few weeks later, while browsing the window advertisements of Flight Centre, Katisse caught the attention of a fellow browser.

'Going somewhere exotic?' he asked.

Katisse turned, flicked her eye over the tall, bearded man. 'Definitely somewhere more exotic than Scotland.'

'Aye, well lassie, you're missing something fabulous.' The Scot laughed and dropped the exaggerated accent. 'Got me in one. And, if not to Bonnie Scotland, where then are you going?'

'Paris.'

'Oh, the city of romance. A fella going with you?'

'None of your business.'

The Scot laughed again. 'Want a coffee? I'll even burst open my sporran and shout you one.'

Kate shook her head. 'And why would I do that?'

'Mm, let's see. You need coffee. I need coffee. We might as well get one together.' His eyebrows lifted. 'Yes?'

It was Kate's turn to laugh. 'Okay, but on one condition.'

'And what's that?'

'That you stop with the Scottish crap. I mean, sporran... honestly.'

'You don't like my sporran? You *have* to wear a sporran with a kilt. Don't you know anything?'

'Look, Mr Scotland, I never want to see you in a kilt, so the sporran... Oh God, how ridiculous. Let's forget the coffee.'

He tapped her arm. 'Sorry. It's a deal. No more promoting the Scottish... um... crap, as you so eloquently put it. I'll even try to sound ocker!'

'Do that, and I'll leave immediately.'

'Right. Café. Over there. Coffee. Nothing Scottish. Not even shortbread with your coffee, eh?'

Kate rolled her eyes, walked with him to the nearby coffee shop, where they continued chatting long after the waiter had removed their empty cups.

The next day, Arthur Macintyre rang Kate several times nonsense chatting but also begging for breakfast, lunch, or dinner. In her replies, she constantly teased him about his Scottishness, his beard, and the amount of time he spent on the phone. In the end, she agreed to Sunday brunch.

When she suggested the Indiana Tea House, he chuckled and replied, 'The beach? Want to go swimming?'

'No, but a walk on the beach would be nice.'

'Haven't eaten there, but worth a try. At least we'll get great views. I'll ring them.'

She had used her *La Joie* training, that of spotting a wealthy client and, on their first meeting, calculated Artie could afford to pay. Then he backed her assumption by admitting to frequenting trendy restaurants and enjoying the so-called in-people of Perth. This was the other side to this laughing Scot she could get used to.

She remembered telling Fiona it was as easy to fall in love with a wealthy man as a poor one. Now to prove it.

Within a week, Paris faded into the background as Kate couldn't get enough of Artie. She soaked up his generosity, taking time from work to enjoy long lazy lunches and sneaking snuggly coffee breaks in the nearby café. He talked of his house renovation business in detail but Kate let financial numbers drift away as she checked out his expensive briefcase and Italian shoes.

On weekends, they visited Swan Valley wineries for lunch, the casino at night, usually ending up at her place, not surfacing until mid-afternoon for food and more wine.

After three months, Ashleigh complained about having to repeatedly cover for Kate. Rachel issued a final warning after Kate returned at three o'clock, on a frantic day before another charity auction evening.

'I can't have you flouncing in as if you own the place,' Rachel said. 'In case you've forgotten, *I'm* the owner, and *you*, at least you're supposed to, work here.' She lifted Kate's employment file, held it for a moment before placing it down again. 'Remember, I took a risk taking you on. Don't let me down, Katisse. I won't have you jeopardising my business just so you can have long lunches. It mustn't happen again.' She paused, waiting for a reaction. When none came, she added, 'Final warning, I'm afraid.'

Katisse stood, controlled her temper, and spoke evenly, 'I've worked hard for you. I've more than paid back that risk.' She picked up the file from the desk. 'I'm happy to go. Just pay me what I'm due and I'll leave you to find someone else.' The file spewed the interior papers as Kate placed it down. 'I'll go now, shall I?'

'Katisse. Please. We have the show tonight. If you're not concerned about me, think of Ashleigh.'

Katisse sat, sighed. 'Okay. *Oui*. I'll do tonight.' She paused, watched Rachel's panic lessen. 'You did give me a chance when I needed it. So sure, tonight, then will you accept my notice without a working period?'

'I'd prefer you give me some notice.'

'No, I think we both know it will be awkward. Surely one of the casuals will want full-time. Sophie? *Oui*? Or Loren?'

Rachel shook her head. 'If you leave after tonight, you'll be forgoing a week's pay in lieu of notice.

'*Comme il sera*. So be it.' Katisse stood, held out her hand. 'Agreed. *Oui*.'

'Thank you.' Rachel said. 'Oh, and Katisse, one question?'

Katisse held the doorknob, turned back to Rachel. 'Yes?'

'Did you ever live in France? Is *any* of your history true?'

'That's two questions but, *oui, madam*. Much of it is true to me.' Katisse closed the door quietly and went out into the salon where Brooke Waterman held out two dresses and asked Katisse for assistance. 'You shouldn't keep me waiting, Katisse. I mightn't tip as well.'

Tempted to walk straight past the demands of the last customer she wanted to assist, Katisse fake-smiled and replied, 'So sorry, Mrs Waterman. Let's make you look fabulous for that husband of yours.' Katisse's grip on the delicate lace dress tightened. Fortunately, Brooke's attention had already turned to a Cardin jacket, which would match perfectly with the grey skirt draped over her arm.

Katisse's Diary

1992

20 August: Interesting turn of events with Artie.

29 August: He might even be mine forever. He makes me laugh. His accent comes and goes. Yeah, maybe this time I got it right.

30 August: Certainly wasn't my plan to get a proposal. But hey, I can work with that. Moving fast. Didn't think a Scot would be so generous. Oops, I shouldn't take notice of that old myth. He certainly opens his sporran often.

8 September: Bloody hell, bagpipes and all. What a wedding!

21 September: I suck at being married.

9 October: Refuse to go. An island. God help me. In that sort of weather. No way.

Chapter 28

Throughout preparations and the crowded, busy auction, Ashleigh replied to Katisse in monosyllables. Katisse took another tray of miniature quiches from the makeshift kitchen and glared pointedly at Ashleigh. 'Why the silent treatment?'

'Huh, I'll probably never speak to you again,' Ashleigh whispered.

'Never? Never is a long time. Please. Don't do this.'

Ashleigh walked away.

With the auction raising an exorbitant amount of money for Doctors Without Borders, Rachel poured champagne and praised her staff. 'Congratulations. You will all get a bonus after tonight. Well done, everyone. Now, Katisse, can I see you for a moment.'

With her third glass of champagne almost finished, Katisse sighed as she sidled up to Rachel. '*Oui, madam. Ce fut le plus de success ce soir.*'

'Don't waste your French on me.'

'I was paying you a compliment. I said it was a most successful night.'

'Do you still intend to go?'

'*Oui, madam.*' Katisse raised her glass towards Rachel. 'Here's to the future.'

'Well then, good luck.'

With her bridges in flames, Katisse spent the next day making plans. Although she'd lit the match herself, she knew there would be a way to cross to the other side. She'd been out of work before, and resilience was her middle name. Then, while other options faded, she thought of lazy days in bed with Artie.

It took several attempts to contact Artie, but he rang back several hours later.

'Yes, babe, what's so important? I'm between meetings. Can you be quick?'

She giggled. 'A quickie. Yep.'

'Not now, babe. What's up?'

'Are we doing dinner tonight?'

'We can. Eight? I'll pick you up. Book somewhere nice.'

They were sharing a cheese platter after the meal when Katisse told Artie she'd lost her job. She explained that times in the high-end retail market had taken a hit and Rachel had to reduce staff numbers. He sympathised with her, said he hoped the downturn wouldn't affect his business, ordered a whisky, and fiddled with the glass during an uncomfortable silence.

'Babe...' he started, then closely considered the amber liquid.

Katisse watched Artie lick his lips, tip his glass but not sip the Glenlivet.

'Are you okay?' She chuckled. 'Scotch whisky not up to standard tonight?'

He put down the glass and smiled at her. 'Not up to the standard of the company I have.'

'Ha! Now I know you're up to something. Spit it out.'

'Will you marry me?'

Her eyes widened as she processed his words. 'What? Are you serious, Artie?'

'You want me to get down on my knee?'

'Don't you dare.'

'Well? We make a great couple. The sex is good.' He smirked as he reached for her hand. 'I reckon we should do this. And now that you're unemployed, I'd look after you. You'd never have to work again.'

She gripped her bottom lip with her teeth, frowned in concentration.

'Oh, you could,' he added quickly. 'If you wanted. But you *needn't* work. You could... I'd find something in my company. If you wanted.'

Katisse wanted to dance through dandelions, wanted to shout to the stars, but leaned across the table and said, 'How can I refuse such an offer?'

Putting all previous doubts of matrimony aside, Katisse arranged a wedding that ended up being featured in every major paper in the state. Trying to balance out Artie's guest list, most of whom she'd never met, including two second cousins who happened to be travelling through Perth, Katisse invited Rachel and Ashleigh, knowing full well contact on the day would be minimal. She was sure curiosity would have their acceptance in the mail in days.

While compiling the guest list, Katisse thought of Fiona. She remembered the times they'd joked about boys and sex and being married. After arguments, and following stilted and partial make-ups, they gradually lost touch. Fiona fulfilled her dreams of being a wife and mother, and Katisse fulfilled her ambition of self-sufficiency.

On one of their infrequent get togethers, Katisse had just slipped into a chair opposite Fiona, when she, as excited as a puppy with a new toy, gushed out the details of a proposal by her boyfriend. While Mrs Noble and a distracted Fiona did the dishes after Sunday lunch, a nervous Andrew Juntavich had asked Mr Noble for his daughter's hand.

The besotted bride walked down the aisle ten months later, producing two children in four years. Katisse remembered the crushing hurt when she saw a picture of the happy couple in the paper.

Realising their friendship could never be restored after their fateful last encounter at *La Joie*, she scrubbed out Fiona's name from the invitation list. 'Past is past,' she said.

Despite Katisse's protestations, Artie insisted his kilt was perfect wedding attire. When bagpipers drowned out the well-wishes of the guests as the newly married couple exited the church, she threatened to boycott the reception if any more Scottish nonsense interrupted her bliss. However, once in the limousine, she ran her hand up his leg, admitting the wearing of a kilt could work in her favour—if only they were alone.

Within days of returning from four days in Margaret River, Katisse and Artie argued relentlessly. She had so much time to fill. He had no time to be interested in how his wife filled her days.

She still wanted to go to Paris. He couldn't—wouldn't—take time off.

He wanted her to sell her apartment when the lease ran out. She didn't want to tell him she owned it courtesy of James's final generosity. She insisted it could be a future asset, and any rent could be "pocket money" for her. He relented.

He showed her the house he'd been renovating on the river in Applecross, explaining they could now call it home. She didn't like the marble floors or the hideous water feature in the courtyard.

He said she didn't like anything he liked—such as kilts and bagpipes.

She ignored his humour; said she liked classy things.

'Expensive things you mean,' he said.

She was pleased when he went to work. He went to work with relief.

Then, after several months, including an enjoyable Christmas but an alcohol-filled New Year of angst, their lives settled down to an agreeable pattern.

In early March, a buff-coloured envelope teased Katisse as she waited for her husband to come home from a late meeting. She was on her second glass of wine when he arrived. Without greeting, she gave him the envelope. 'From Scotland.'

Artie sighed. 'Probably some family issue. It can wait.'

'No way. It's from a solicitor. Open it.'

Katisse waited as he repeatedly shook his head, glanced at her several times as he read the document.

'Legal stuff. Fairly serious,' he said. 'Here, read it.'

She scanned it, then handed it back. 'For real?'

'I had no idea. Fraser dying wasn't expected. He's quite young. And I didn't know about the island?'

'You've got to be joking. You must have had some knowledge of a family island.'

He sank to the sofa, tossed the document to the floor. 'Bloody hell. That's all I need right now. Looks like I'll have to go.'

'To Scotland? How can you afford the time to go to bloody Scotland when you won't take me to France?' She topped up her glass of wine, took a swig, and glared at her husband.

'It's not a friggin' holiday. My second cousin died.'

'So? Haven't you got seven cousins? Are you going to traipse off when each one of them departs to the great haggis-eating dinner in the sky?'

He stalked off to his study. She finished the wine and topped the glass up again, listening to him clack away on the computer and tug a piece of paper from the printer. He stomped back and stood in front of her.

'Here, read this.' He dropped the page on her lap.

Hands on hips, scowling through the silence, he waited.

'What's it all mean?' she asked. '*You* own the island?'

'Yep.' He sat down next to her. 'Apparently, I inherit a portion of this speck in the North Sea.'

'How lovely,' she said sarcastically. 'I suppose you'll holiday there *every* year. Maybe *that's* when I can go to Paris.'

'No, babe. I have to live there.'

'What? *Live* there. Forever?'

'If I don't live there for at least nine months of every year, then it goes into government hands.'

'Okay.' Her imagination travelled from a stormy Scottish island to sunshine in Hawaii. 'Then you can use the money on somewhere more creative.'

He sighed. 'No, that's not how it works. It's some ancient creed. The line of inheritance must be maintained, or it reverts to the government. No entitlement of reimbursement.'

She shook her head, the dream of exotic island life juddering away with each movement. 'Well, you're on your own then. I'm not going to some remote island. It's bad enough here. Being tied to marriage.'

'Tied? Bloody hell, Katisse, is that what it is to you.'

While he flew off to Scotland, she continually cursed as she flung cushions across the room and slammed doors. With unrelenting anger over losing control of her foreseeable future, she removed her wedding ring and turned bridal photos face down on cabinets.

Artie promoted his manager to partner, acknowledging he could remain in touch via the internet—despite the unreliability of its infancy.

During the second week of his absence, she packed his kilt and sporran, filled the second bedroom with all things male, and rang the estate agent managing her condominium demanding notice be given to the lessee—forthwith.

When Artie returned to finalise arrangements in Perth, Katisse teased him about his broader accent. They called a truce on their disagreements and spent the last few days as if they were characters in an R-rated novel.

She accepted his assurances of continuing support, simpering as he offered a generous allowance and coyly asking if he could replace her two-year-old Audi with something which would show the world he had kept his promise to look after her. He told her to select something and have the account sent to him.

Memories of Mrs Noble picking her up from the train station returned as Kate put the key in the lock of her light blue Merc.

KATISSE'S DIARY

1993

6 March: Bloody Aggie! Gets me going every time. Can do without deep and meaningfuls. I don't lie—I just embellish. Where's the harm in that? And what's more, Aggie, I do have friends. Just don't see much of them.

9 March: What is it with old ladies? They seem to disregard niceties. As if they don't care. Well, maybe that's what age does. Hope I never act that old! Champagne is not nearly as nice on one's own. You can pretend all you want, but it just isn't.

15 March: Bloody, bloody hell. Life is awful.

16 March: I should throw this damn diary away. What is there but horrid, horrid stuff in the world. Even Mother Nature can't leave us alone. 200,000!

17 March: Easter eggs, yum! Ice cream! Thank God for small mercies.

3 April: Maybe I've wallowed a bit too much. That child. Those eyes.

14 April: Let's go, girl. Time to do something. Even if it's just dishes.

Chapter 29

Artie visited just before Christmas of 1992. He showered Katisse with duty-free gifts: perfume, handbag, scarf, and a diamond-encrusted watch. She thanked him by going to dinner but refused to share her bed. Then when Artie left she'd vowed never to be under a man's spell again. His short visit only made her more determined to be self-sufficient. Independence was the name of her game.

Lawyers were handling the divorce application, with Katisse rarely reading the fine print, blindly taking their advice, confident Artie was a man of his word.

Now living back in her apartment in Victoria Park, Katisse still knew no one in the building by name, was only a nodding acquaintance with the owner of the corner deli, but occasionally spoke with her cleaner who came once a week.

'How's it going this week? Been somewhere nice?' Aggie asked.

Katisse ushered the middle-aged woman through to the bathroom. 'Many, and I'm especially looking forward to the concert tonight.'

'Now, which concert would that be?'

'Ah, at the Concert Hall.'

'Is that so? Orchestra of some sort, is it?'

'My friend booked it. Not sure. Just going to please her.'

'Right... If you say so. But you should check with your *friend*. Otherwise, I can tell you, you're in for a bit of a surprise. Can't imagine you'll like what I saw on the program when Tom and I went last week.' She rolled her eyes. 'You'll have to tell me all about this mystery *concert*. Oh, and how you and your friend enjoyed it.' When Katisse failed to react to her sarcasm, the cleaner nodded towards the cluttered vanity. 'Should I shift that lot?'

There seemed no end to Aggie's perception. She'd caught Katisse out frequently. Several times, Katisse had to tap-dance her way out of explanations while suffering her cleaner's smirk. So, casting aside this inference, Katisse answered the easy question.

'Yes, please. Under the sink. I should have done it.' Katisse pulled at a scarf draped over the other items, knocking the hairdryer off the counter. 'I'd better leave you to it.'

'Sure, but you really don't need to... you know. It really doesn't matter to me if you're going to a concert or watching TV on your own, eating a hamburger and chips.'

'Ah, well, that's the thing...'

'No. Listen. People should like you for *you*, not some goddamn fancy-nancy outfit or your ability to pay for a highfalutin meal.'

'It's alright for you—'

'Now look here, just because I'm your cleaner, you think I'm inferior. I can jolly well tell you I am certainly not. Now, no more of your bullshit. Just let me get on. Whatever you're up to, I have *actual* friends, and I will *actually* be having lunch with them.' Aggie tipped her chin up. 'So let me get on.'

Katisse lowered her head as Aggie spoke. She waited milliseconds that seemed like hours before she looked the other women in the eye. 'See, that's the thing, Aggie. I *don't* think you're inferior.' Katisse bit her bottom lip and shook her head, then whispered, 'It's me. I have always felt inferior. I don't want to be that stupid girl from state housing who shops at the local op shop, can't afford nice clothes, eats takeaways, puts on weight, *has* to watch TV because hot-shot events are out of reach.' She lifted her head, stood straighter, spoke clearly, 'See, it's not about *you* being inferior. It's not about other people. *Me.* That's what it's about. Being... I suppose... better than all that.'

Aggie shook her head. 'You are good enough. You're a lovely young woman. There's no need to make things up. Let people see you as you are.'

'Huh, and that would work? How exactly?'

Pulling a pair of rubber gloves from her apron pocket, Aggie sighed. 'Everyone doesn't have to like you. I'm bloody sure everyone doesn't like me. Do I care? No way. But there are enough people to go around. You know, a group for everyone. If group A doesn't like you, move on to group B. You just have to show your true self.'

'I don't think group A or B would like me if they knew my bare bones.'

'Rubbish. You should try it. Might be a welcome change to all the nonsense you give out.'

Katisse's neck prickled; she finger-combed her fringe. 'I do have friends. Maybe I will ring Fiona later. We could eat lunch together.' She knew full well she wouldn't be ringing Fiona or any other so-called friend.

She watched Aggie slip her hands into the gloves, wondering how many friends an older person might have. 'Where are you going for lunch today? Hate to run into you. That could be awkward.'

Aggie rolled her eyes again, handed a bottle of perfume and its lid to Katisse. 'No chance of that.'

After this uncomfortable encounter, Katisse's self-confidence needed a boost. She gathered her handbag and headed for a place where she would lose this lack of certainty; be in her craved environment. Her place in the world wasn't chatting with a cleaner; it was around champagne, caviar and credit cards.

Thirty minutes later, Katisse ran her hand across the leather steering wheel, nodding slowly, grinning surreptitiously while watching the glances of three women as they walked past. It wasn't the first time Katisse had observed the interpreted envy of others. Her attention-grabbing car couldn't be ignored.

While her outward demeanour sparkled: chic attire, salon-perfected hairstyle, immaculate makeup and a Gucci handbag to die for, she battled for contentment.

Last night, with relocating finances finalised, she had made a list, intending to work her way through reducing the number of her shoes, donating useless cooking utensils and binning the dozens of Arti's books she had no intention of reading after all. However, after finishing two bottles of wine while defacing their wedding photos with a black marker, tearing the "happy couple" apart and crying over the loss of a certain respectability marriage had given her, sleep didn't come easily, and she woke with a hangover.

Attempting to be cheerful, she had rung for reservations at a riverside restaurant and, with a couple of paracetamols in her system, dressed intentionally, ready to impress the lunching crowd.

Now, cheered by the attention in the carpark, all went well until ten minutes after being at a corner table, pretending she didn't care about sitting on her own at a table for four.

'No, my friends couldn't make it,' she told the waiter. 'You know, the last moment obligations. Thought I wouldn't waste the booking. You know, celebrate anyway.'

'Okay. That's fine. I'm Vicki.' She held out the menu. 'I'll be your waiter today. I'll be back in a few minutes to take your order.'

The obvious pleasure of companionship emanating from the three women now seated in the centre of the room, irritated Katisse. Couldn't they enjoy themselves a little quieter. She noticed their inexpensive handbags, cheap flowery dresses—although one woman wore crocodile leather shoes.

A lack of close friends had never overly bothered Katisse—she was her own woman, able to create an ideal life without clingy friends, those desperate for attention, or those using up valuable time over trivial outings.

But as crocodile-leather-shoe-woman caressed her friend's arm, frowning with concern and offering a tissue, a jolt of longing hit Katisse. She remembered Fiona, the times they'd spent giggling, teasing... just being friends. She remembered Ashleigh and Rachel, from *La Joie*—not true friends but people who shared her life. Now, without a husband, even a lover, she really had no one.

'Excuse me.' Katisse beckoned the waiter who, with a ready smile, came immediately. 'Can I have another, please.'

'Sure, champagne again. Are you celebrating?'

'Big time. But, as I said, my friends couldn't make it. They would have. Knew I'd be paying.' She nodded towards the three women. 'Friends. Great, aren't they?'

Vicki nodded. 'Those ladies come every week. Apparently been friends since school.' She lowered her voice. 'I hope I still have some decent friends when I'm that old. Now, have you decided. I can always come back.'

After the waiter had written down Katisse's order, she moved away. Katisse then re-examined the older women, who now were giggling, wiping away a different sort of tear. Two had podgy stomachs; one stick thin. Their lipstick had vanished, mostly onto the water glasses. Elbows leaned on the table as they whispered, then heads were flung back in laughter. Katisse wriggled, tried for a more positive position to prove her elegance. She licked her bottom lip, straightened her back even further and smiled as the waiter placed a Caesar Salad and another glass of Bolliger champagne down.

'Here's to whatever,' the waiter said.

'Thanks. New contract. Big one.' Katisse shrugged. 'Knew I'd get it. It's a bit of "who you know". Still a lot of hard work.'

'That's great. I'm afraid I'm stuck here. Need the money.'

'Well, keep at it. Rub shoulders, you know, with the big wigs. Don't be afraid to ask for a step up the proverbial ladder.'

'Gee, guess I could… well, I'd better get on, but thanks for the tip. Congrats again. Enjoy your champagne.'

Katisse couldn't stomach any more of the salad, wishing she could spend the rest of the day drinking but the Merc sat in the carpark, and the last thing she wanted was a dented panel.

The frivolity of the three friends with water, not wine, surprised Katisse. In all her adult years, liquor inebriation enabled casual conversation to flow uninhibited, and this type of relaxed attitude usually came from even more liquor.

She stared at her sparkling wine, downed it in two swallows and indicated for the waiter again.

'I'm going. Where do I pay?' Katisse asked. 'It's not much fun celebrating on your own after all. And I have an important meeting later. Too much champagne and someone might take advantage of me.' She forced a chuckle. 'As if!'

Vicki pointed to the counter by the door. 'And we have card facilities.' As Katisse stood, the waiter added, 'Shame your friends couldn't make it.'

'I'll catch up with them on the weekend.'

'Great. Have a good time. I'm sure you will.'

Accidentally bumping the chair of one of the three friends, Katisse apologised quickly.

'That's okay,' said the woman.

Katisse surprised herself by saying, 'You look like you're having a good time.'

'Oh, darling, we always do,' said woman number two.

'We're celebrating,' said woman number three. 'Want to join us?'

Katisse's breath caught. 'No, thanks. Couldn't interrupt your party.'

'Sure you could. There's a fourth chair.'

'What are you celebrating?' Katisse asked.

'It's Thursday! That's the day we celebrate getting through another week.'

Katisse's frown initiated woman number three's quick response. 'It's okay, pet, we'd be happy to share our Thursday with someone new. We've told all our stories six times over.' She poked her friend's shoulder. 'We've known each other since we wore baggy bloomers under our sport skirts.'

They all laughed. Woman number one added, 'And that's more than your lifetime ago, young lady.'

Feeling conspicuous as their laughter grew louder, Katisse stepped away. 'I'll leave you to it. I've got to go.' She looked at her watch. 'Gosh, is that the time? Sister's off to Barcelona. Have to see her off.'

Katisse left a generous tip for Vicki and hoped the young waiter would find some way to climb the ladder of life.

She drove for two hours, speeding along highways and meandering through side streets, ending up in Beaconsfield, parking outside the shops where Nora had worked. School children hurried from the bus stop chatting as they headed home. One long and lanky kid strolled past her car, stared at her for a moment, then moved on. He kicked an empty drink can into a wall, heaved his backpack into a more comfortable position and ambled around the corner.

Katisse wondered if this loner would go on to great things. Not needing anyone but his own ambition and a drive for wealth.

Her tears came without warning. She leaned back against the leather headrest, eyes closed, and let the tears drip. With a turn of a button, the radio blared, hid her sobs and her gasps for control.

When the emotion levelled, she turned the radio off, wiped away the tears, checked for smudged makeup, and remained motionless for several minutes.

Memories rushed across her mind: her mother, Mr Yeo's phone, Fiona, Doris, Miss Tillman, Syd, Stan, Miss Chidley, Mrs Fothergill and her typewriter, those bitches from typing school, *La Joie*, James, Artie—*it's like I'm dying and having a flashback of my life*—back to her mum, and her mum's funeral.

Who will come to my funeral? Katisse's black mood deepened.

Bloody no one. She flung the car door open, stepped out, and slammed it shut; didn't bother to lock it.

She stood outside Yeo & Co store, side-stepping out of the way as a customer hurried out. The store hadn't changed much but fresh posters across the window spruiked the weekly specials. The laundromat where Nora read old magazines, gained under-the-counter money for ironing, and ate cake her regular customers brought in, was now boarded up and covered with graffiti.

Katisse sagged. Her chin touched her chest, her arms hung loosely, and her fingers tingled. She wanted to curl up on the footpath and let the world trample over her.

Making her way back to the car, she glanced through the doorway of Yeo & Co, sighting a teenager sweeping the floor—a teenager who turned into Nora for one flash of a memory.

She drove without thinking and arrived at the state house, which had been her home. She parked across the road but left the motor running. The asbestos house now had a new front fence and a small frangipani opposite Bill's roses. After five minutes, with the only movement being a tabby cat stalking across the lawn, Katisse u-turned the Merc and headed slowly out of the suburb she'd been feverishly determined to leave so many years ago.

The next few weeks became a ritual of misery.

The morning usually started about 10am, with a breakfast of cold coffee left over from the previous late night. She didn't even bother adding milk; not sure it would be fresh.

Scattered over the coffee table and the couch, several novels had turned down corners before chapter five. Only one made it to chapter ten. Many more remained unread in the bookcase. Spasmodic bursts of housework meant the dishes were unwashed for days and the bed linen unchanged for three weeks.

Occasionally, she'd walk down to the local supermarket for chocolate and ice cream, sometimes stocking up on bread, cheese, frozen meals—basic essentials for someone who didn't care what went into their system.

She scribbled in her diary, declaring the world a lost cause. Not knowing her place, unsure of her way forward in this crumbling society where the Yugoslav War killed innocent people, and 200,000 lost their lives as a cyclone tore through Bangladesh.

The Simpsons, a new TV show, unconsciously captivated her despite not being able to fathom its reputation as the height of hilarity. Because of the need to avoid total silence, which drew impossible gloom, she became addicted to hating what the show threw up.

Then, with an updated computer, she spent hours scanning the unreliable internet and wasting time hooked on solitaire. Katisse yelled at the screen and slammed down the mouse when the new-fangled technology failed to respond.

Lunch consisted of cheese—or not; a tomato—or not; a bread roll—or not! Unless she ventured down to the supermarket again, she relied on baked beans or overripe fruit.

The afternoon copied the morning, except for a nap on the couch in front of the TV. She steadfastly refused to open the wine until two o'clock, declaring she was not an alcoholic, just a full-bodied supporter of the wine industry.

Frozen meals were half eaten after dark. Then more wine and coffee, which kept her awake until three-thirty.

One evening, fuelled by wine, she scanned the telephone directory searching for Fiona—now Fiona Juntavich.

The Nobles were listed at the Cottesloe address she'd visited many times, but there was only one Juntavich listed. Douglas Avenue, Como. She dialled, hung up before completion. Sitting there with the phone in her hand, she shook her head until she became dizzy. The tears came, and she swore them away thrusting the phone into its cradle, then stalked across the room. Back and forth. Back and forth.

Sinking into the couch mindlessly watching TV, she wondered how life dared to treat her so badly. After a run of advertisements on Easter eggs, cereal to make you stronger, special prices for cheese and a dopey-looking bloke spouting where to buy the best hamburgers, a promotion for Red Cross spruiked its message. As the screen flicked back to mundane news, Katisse rolled her eyes and thought about having cereal for dinner.

Because she had three cups of coffee after the cereal, she tossed and turned even longer than usual. In her caffeine-drowned mind, she recalled the hungry children of some poor country looking into the camera, begging for assistance from the rich and famous, or even the not-so-rich and the down-right ordinary person.

Despite promising to donate in the morning, she couldn't settle. With the big brown eyes of the children burning a hole in her conscience, she paddled out to her little-used desk and wrote a cheque.

The next morning, with bleary eyes and skin tingling with sleep deprivation, Katisse dry retched as she examined the dirty dishes half buried in the scummy water in the sink. Then, as if a switch turned, she tackled the dishes, did a load of washing, ignored the TV and made headway of the accounts waiting to be paid.

After a shower, a glass of mineral water and two grapes, she headed to the Post Office with her donation. As she walked, she kept touching her bag—her expensive Gucci bag—knowing she had everything when so many had nothing. It wasn't an epiphany, and she chuckled at the thought of her becoming a Mother Teresa type, but there was something poking her, telling her she was wasting her life.

With the deed done, Katisse wandered through a pocket-sized park, pirouetting occasionally. Wanting to continue enjoying the soft heat of autumn, she sat on a bench poking her feet forward, swinging them in time with the nonsensical music in her head. She considered her generous donation, smiling at the satisfaction of contributing to a worthwhile fund. But just as a cloud covered the sunlight, she wondered if the joy of making a one-off contribution reeked of being a goody-two-shoes. Was her donation made with the right intention? Was it really about the children? Or...

No! it isn't anything else. It is about helping.

Nora had often berated the do-gooders of the world. 'They aren't generous, not without wanting something, those high-and-mighty rich sorts,' she'd said when some property mogul lauded his donation to a charity. 'They're out for the exposure. Bloody goody two-shoes. All "look at how wonderful I am" and then ripping off some struggling couple with top-end prices for a back-of-beyond block of land. Nah, if you're going to do good, you shouldn't be crowing about it.'

'It's alright, Mum.' Katisse stood and signalled towards the heavenly sky. 'I won't tell anyone. That okay with you?'

She nodded as she walked, explaining to herself how she was going to turn over a new leaf. 'Bugger them,' she whispered. *I am good enough.*

She spent the late afternoon cleaning: daydreaming as she leaned on a broom, considering options as she dusted, and making mental lists as she stacked clean dishes away.

17 April: I have to get a job. Not for the money. With Artie's generosity, I've managed. Yeah, really well. Glad I took his advice on getting a financial adviser. But I need to stop wasting my time shopping and this God-awful stuff. I need something worthwhile to keep me occupied.

29 April: Eiffel Tower—yeah, it's okay. Couldn't get in the mood. Disastrous. Waste of money. Should have stayed home. Now home. Back to my senses. Now what?

4 May: Apparently, Brooke Waterman heads a fundraising committee. Now, wouldn't that be interesting? Wining and dining for charity. Yeah, might look into that Telethon luncheon.

18 May: Charity. A wonderful excuse for a new outfit. I like this caper. Suits me just fine.

19 May: Good feed at the book launch. And the author, can you believe, he claimed, he was "rolling in it". Maybe I should become a writer. No, my storytelling talents are elsewhere. Fingers crossed I can pull it off.

16 June: Finally! That's what Lewis said. I felt like that. Immediately. Another chapter coming, I reckon. And this one might be a great one.

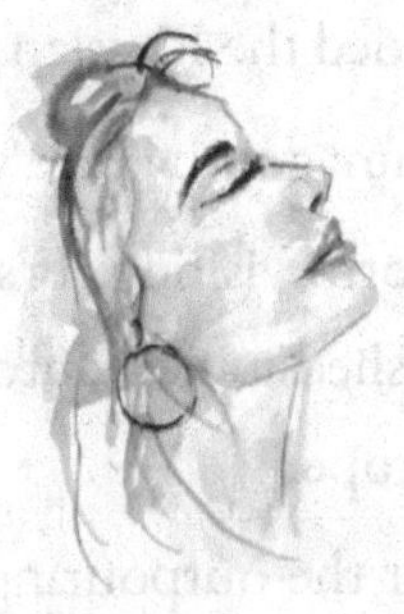

Chapter 30

After paying $250 for a seat at a Telethon luncheon, Katisse anticipated sharing time with the upper echelon of Perth society. Many of the guests in the room were probably hoping for the same thing. She was the only "single" at her allocated table; others had come with female friends. She tried to be interested in their conversations, some politely directed her way. She noticed they only made low bids in the auctions and didn't respond to any luxury items. It was a struggle to look interested in their technology tips and get through to the dessert course where the chocolate mousse, crème fresh and masticated strawberries were briefly tasted and left for the volunteers to take back to the kitchen.

Once the auction had dispensed of all the items, guests were encouraged to leave the table and mingle over coffee. The women invited Katisse to join them at a bar-height table where seating wasn't included. Most opted for coffee. When one angular woman loudly voiced her desire for more champagne "of the true French variety", the conversation turned to travel. Katisse surprised them with her knowledge of the countries they had visited or were planning to fly off to 'when I find time, darling'. A petite red-head had Czechoslovakia on the top of her wish list.

With a silent acknowledgment to Syd, Katisse said, 'The Velvet

Revolution peacefully ended the Russian rule in 1989.'

'Okay... that sounds, um, good. Have you been there?'

'Great Old Town. Worth visiting. It's really authentic.' Katisse finished her coffee and fished in her clutch purse for a tissue. 'One of the better places in Europe.'

It proved a catalyst for the outpouring of each young woman's favourite European city. Katisse nodded sagely, said her goodbyes, thanking them for their company. No one asked to swap phone numbers.

Perhaps it was the simple act of filling in her details on a raffle ticket stub, or maybe the noisy chatter of so many enjoying themselves that left an empty pit in her unsatisfied stomach. She'd be going back to a lovely home—alone. She gave the pen back to the teenager behind the table and sighed.

'Good luck,' the teenager said. 'Rather nice to win a trip to France.'

Katisse looked at the ticket in her hand. 'Is that what I'm going to win? How nice. Haven't been there since...' She looked at the innocence of youth in front of her. 'Well, not since, *ever*.' The teenager giggled. Katisse smiled, took another look at the jovial gathering, and left. She was calming her emotions as she waited for the lift, taking in the view from the third floor, when someone called her name. She turned and inwardly cringed.

'Mrs Waterman. How nice.'

Brooke Waterman came towards Katisse, extending her hand. 'It's been quite a while. And it's Brooke, please. Fancy seeing you here. Coming or going?'

'Going, I'm afraid. Other commitments.'

With a glance back to the room Katisse had just left, Brooke asked, 'Were you in there? I didn't see you.'

'Yep. I was. Hiding in the stalls, I'm afraid. Rather daunting on one's own.'

'Don't tell me you chanced it without company? Gosh, poor you. You should have rung me.' Brooke patted Katisse's arm. 'These outings are the pits if you don't know the right people.' Her pencil-thin eyebrows rose a few millimetres. 'Why don't you come back in? I'll introduce you.'

'Thanks, but I think I've had enough obligatory smiling for the day.'

'It does get a bit like a bride at her wedding.' Brooke lowered her voice. 'I heard things didn't work out for you and the hairy Scot. Are you okay?'

'Couldn't be better. It's great to be able to please oneself again. You know, things being where you left them. No one else's mess to clean up. Yeah.'

'Talking of messes; divorce done?' Brooke asked.

Three women interrupted as they passed on their way to replace their lipstick or just to gossip privately without a cast of dozens. Brooke returned their greeting.

'Look, are you sure you won't come back in. I might be able to change your mind about these sorts of functions. If you're interested, I could show you how to get involved in running something. I'm sure you've got talents we could abuse.' She chuckled. 'And I'm only half teasing.'

Through the doorway, Katisse watched the teenager cajole cash from other guests preparing to leave.

'Maybe another time.'

'Sure. I have to get back. Ring me.' She handed over a business card. 'We can get together. See what you fancy being involved with.'

'Next week, perhaps.'

'Make it after the tenth. James and I are off to Hayman Island. Downtime. We need it.'

Avoiding direct eye contact, Katisse asked, 'How is James?'

'Just between you and me, I think he's only playing at home now. For a couple of years, actually.' Brooke smirked. 'Seems he's finally given up the away games.' She rolled her eyes. 'Thank the Lord. I'd have killed the captain of the other team if I knew her name.'

Completely stuck for a retort, Katisse was relieved when a bustling woman in a grey pantsuit demanded Brooke's attention inside "immediately".

The unsuccessful nature of her tentative trial into attending the fundraising circuit continued to play havoc with Katisse's restlessness. She knew her life had been self-indulgent. The irony of it being James's wife who was giving her the chance to change made her yell at her reflection as she cleaned her teeth.

'Bitch.' Toothpaste dribbled from her mouth. She spat the foaming paste into the basin. 'You're a bitch, Kate Wallace.'

Later, while she rehashed the charity lunch in her mind, she pushed on her pillow and promised that now was her chance to go to Paris—for real.

The luxury of being waited on in first class made for a comfortable flight and a charming chauffeur completed the picture.

With her cases unpacked, Katisse showered, carefully chose an outfit, and prepared for an evening of a slow meal in the hotel's restaurant. The food was superb, the service outstanding, and the bill, added to her account, was momentarily ignored. She lingered in the lounge area, cognac in hand, watching couples, groups, enjoying themselves but, unable to bear the comparison any further, retired to her room so that she wasn't seen to be a lonely person waiting for hours to tick by before bedtime.

After breakfast, she strolled through delightful avenues, tempted by much, succumbing to little. Purchasing a hideously expensive silk scarf didn't ease the longing to share the romance of Paris with someone—anyone. She thought of Artie stuck somewhere in an office, on a God-forsaken island, locked away even from salt spray and roaming wildlife. While sitting in a street café with caramel sauce-covered crepes in front of her, she tapped in his mobile number; three times, she pressed delete. Even delicious crepes can taste disappointing when eaten solo.

Back in her room, she threw herself across the bed. Her handbag tumbled to the floor, spilling the contents. When she returned the coins, Brooke's business card stood out from the French banknotes. Thoughts of Brooke and James cavorting on sunny shores and sharing a glass of red wine as they snuggled in a hot tub, did nothing to cheer her. Deciding she'd had enough of being miserable, she stalked down to reception, booked a city bus tour for the next morning, and a half-day trip to a country villa, "guaranteed to have you wanting more" for the afternoon.

But as she wandered in the darkening evening, the streets seemed to taunt her at every corner. Laughing couples, happy groups of teenagers, even unsteady old folk were in pairs. Paris had waited too long for her. Here she was, alone in the most romantic of cities.

From a corner bistro, she ordered Moselle, finishing it in three mouthfuls. Another glass of Moselle followed. She purchased a bottle of the same wine to take back to her sad and lonely room. When she'd shaken the last drop out of the bottle into her mouth, Katisse curled around a pillow and let slow tears trickle until she fell asleep.

The phone woke her. The bus company wanted to know if she intended to join them. Even the French could do sarcasm! Apologising profusely, she told them not to make a refund. She held the phone away from her throbbing head as he explained there would be no refund, *madam*. And did she intend to arrive in time to go and see the wonderful countryside of France? Katisse closed her eyes, told him no, sorry, so sorry, not at all well today. He commiserated and apologised for being abrupt, saying he had people waiting, and maybe you come another day, we will sort out, maybe give a discount because of no refund. She said no she was going home, keep the money, sorry I didn't get to see your beautiful country, maybe another time.

The hotel re-arranged her flight home, booked a car for the next morning, and suggested a spa treatment for her suffering body.

After vomiting up caramel-coloured mouthfuls and excess Moselle, she showered, dressed in slacks and a blouse, and headed to the spa on the ground floor. Sleeping through the foot massage but fully aware of every pummel as the attendant massaged her back, Katisse promised she'd never touch alcohol again. Transferring to the hairdressers, she felt almost human as the last squirt of hairspray made a misty halo.

Many hours later—many painful introspective hours—as the plane crossed the Indian Ocean, Katisse considered her future. It seemed she didn't crave as much solitude as she once thought.

The flight and the two days in Paris left her drained of energy and enthusiasm. She wandered through Perth, stood outside *La Joie*, cautiously watched the staff attending to clients, and had to duck behind the wall when Rachel came from a cubicle straight towards the window display.

Back home, sitting too long over newspapers and magazines, she knew she was wasting her days—and nights. Several major events covered the social pages, with some of her previous *La Joie* clients featuring.

An advertisement for an evening combining a book launch and a fundraiser for Telethon caught her eye. Brooke and James Waterman were sponsoring and hosting the Friday night cocktail party.

Breathing deeply before dialling the advertised number, she hoped James wouldn't answer.

'Pearson Agency.'

With a silent sigh of relief, Katisse asked about the event. Maureen explained the event was planned through the agency, but Mrs Waterman was the coordinator and would be happy to answer any offers of help.

'Does James get involved?' Katisse asked.

'Mr Waterman co-sponsors the event but his involvement is minimal. Is it Mr Waterman you wish to speak with?'

Katisse couldn't remember James mentioning a Maureen, so she hoped her name meant nothing to this receptionist. 'No. I've known Brooke for a while, old friends, you know... and she suggested I could be useful.'

'Good. There is always room for another helper. Can I get Mrs Waterman to ring you?'

'She isn't available?'

Maureen explained, 'We handle the calls. Direct them to the right source. I can pass on your details and your offer. What did you say your name was?'

'Katisse.' She didn't wait to be asked but spelled it out immediately.

'And your surname?'

'Ah, let's see. She probably will know me as Katisse Blanchard.'

'Thanks, Ms Blanchard. I'm sure she doesn't know many ladies named Katisse.'

Katisse's dresses filled her bed; evening tops covered both padded chairs. Sixteen pairs of high heels lined up below the window ready for inspection. If she was going back into society, she'd need to organise her outfits, dispose of some, match accessories, maybe go shopping to fill the gaps. Her hands were full of empty coat hangers when the phone rang. She dropped the hangers, stepped over them, and scurried out of the bedroom.

Once greetings had been exchanged, Brooke asked if she had another worker bee for her next event.

'I'm not sure how I could help, but I've got two hands. I could man the raffle table.'

Brooke laughed. 'It's a bit more upmarket than that.'

'Okay. I'm up for anything. Well, *almost* anything.'

'When the message came through, I immediately thought of the small number of people we have in the kitchen. No one wants to be in the back room, so actual volunteers are few. But they're important. Can't have the hors d'oeuvres running out.'

'I can do that.'

'I'm sure you can.' Brooke chuckled softly, then added, 'I was teasing. Your talents could be put to much better use, and I have another idea. What about convincing the guests to part with their money? I've experienced first-hand your expertise in this area. I mean, it might be a while ago, but I'm sure you haven't lost your touch.'

Katisse thought of the subtle ways she'd implemented at *La Joie's* auction nights. 'Sure. I'm an old hand.' She remembered the expensive clothing items she and Ashleigh had convinced Brooke to bid on. She hadn't forgotten the numerous bags James had been holding the night he'd first flirted with her. Her lip moved slightly as she held back a smile. 'Yep, I can do that.'

'Good. Not everyone has that talent. Now, I'll send the guest list over to you. You'll probably know most, by name at least. There'll be some walk-ins, always are, people who think they are so important that tickets don't apply to them. I'll give you a ring next week. We can go over any questions you have. You might like to come in and see the venue beforehand. And Katisse, I think you and I could be the next big thing to hit the circuit.'

'Holy sh—' Katisse paused. 'I mean, do you really think I can help?'

'Absolutely. And Katisse, James said hi.'

Katisse hoped Brooke hadn't heard her suck in an urgent breath. 'Say "hi" back.'

The venue looked stark without the baubles detailed in Brooke's extensive file.

'There'll be white tablecloths, orange flowers, yellow serviettes, water, wine, liqueur glasses for each guest.' Pointing towards a trestle table at the top of the room, she said, 'Jarred Lyon will display his books up there. We only have to supply a cloth; he'll bring the rest.'

'THE Jarred Lyon?'

'None other. Do you know him?'

'Only by reputation.' Katisse grimaced. 'Tried one of his books. A bit gruesome for me. All that James Bond over-the-top sex and murder.'

'He's a bit over the top too. He's at least seventy, but I can assure you his hormones must be only twenty-five. His patter is totally old school, but he'll charm everyone. And we're getting a commission for every book sold.'

'A bit incompatible to a children's charity, isn't it?'

Brooke pulled her clipboard closer to her chest. 'We know that. But Jarred offered. At least people have heard of him. And, children won't be at the function. Maybe next time we can attract a children's author. There are some good ones in WA—so I'm told. But a bird in the hand, etcetera.'

'I see, but it's a shame. Maybe I can do some research. You know, for next time.'

'That'd be wonderful. In the meantime, what do you think of the set-up?'

'Why orange? It isn't a usual colour for the tables.'

After discussing the need to be "unusual", the two women went through the guest list highlighting which ones were soft-hearted enough to react to children's illnesses, who would succumb to hard sell, and who would only donate once their so-called friends made a move. They both knew motivation to out-donate even their closest friends could be used to a charity's advantage.

Chapter 31

A fortnight later, as she waited for a taxi to arrive and take her to the Pagoda Ballroom, Katisse checked the evening's agenda. Nerves surfaced as she added a light spray of perfume. The mirror revealed a perfect dress: understated but classy enough for even the most discerning eye. It never hurt to have a peek of cleavage.

Brooke was in a heated discussion with the caterer when Katisse entered the ballroom. She headed for the display table, turned a book over, and read the blurb. A hand softly touched her arm. 'Lovely.'

Katisse turned.

Jarrad Lyon's smile increased as he looked her up and down. 'Can I sign one for the lovely lady?'

Katisse pretended to look for another female.

His grin widened showing a mouthful of perfect teeth. 'Now, now.'

'Maybe later. I've work to do.'

'I'll hold you to that.' He held out his hand. 'Jarrad Lyon.'

'I figured. Katisse. I'm on duty tonight.'

'I figured.' He took the book from her hand. 'Well, Brooke certainly knows how to pick them. I certainly hope you're not going to hide away in the kitchen.'

Katisse laughed. 'I certainly hope I didn't go to all this trouble to be in the kitchen.' She moved out of reach as he went to touch her arm again.

'Come by and help me sell my books. The men won't be able to resist.'

A voice behind them said, 'They certainly will find it hard.'

Katisse knew the speaker without having to turn. Her lungs shrunk. She had to take in three breaths before she knew they would work automatically.

'Ah, James, my boy, you know this lovely lady then?' Jarrad slapped James Waterman on the shoulder.

James's eyes flicked from Jarrad's face to Katisse's, holding her gaze longer than necessary. 'I've had the privilege.'

'Hello, James. How are you?' Katisse managed to say. He leaned in to peck her on the cheek. She stepped back, held out her hand. 'A tux suits you.'

Katisse could see Jarrad questioning her response to James but fortunately, he politely refrained from voicing his questions. 'Ah, well there, James, maybe you can talk this lovely lady into helping me sell my books.'

For a moment, Katisse thought James would ignore the older man. She opened her mouth to speak but James beat her to it. 'She could sell anything, but my wife has already optioned her.' He nodded at Jarrad. 'Come, Katisse, let's find Brooke.' He placed his hand on her elbow and led her away from the surprised author.

They'd crossed the room before Katisse spoke. 'What are you

doing? I'm quite capable of—'

'You're quite capable of anything but I just wanted you to myself for two seconds.' He released her arm and faced her. 'Just two seconds to tell you how beautiful you look.'

She wasn't quick enough to say anything before he smiled and walked away.

'Katisse! Hey! Katisse!'

Shaking her internal thoughts free of James, Katisse answered Brooke, 'Something you want me to do.'

'Yes, just check that the MC has the program. He might have a voice like silk, but he has a mind like a sieve. And Katisse...'

'Yes?'

'You look great. Just hope the women can stand the competition.' Brooke smirked. 'Your cue will be when they serve coffee. I'm hoping people will leave their tables and mingle. In the meantime, enjoy yourself. I've put you with us. Table One. James will have someone to keep him amused while I try to keep the whole thing on track.' With a quick nod towards the room, she added, 'What do you think? It's not bad, is it?'

Katisse was mid-sentence of approval when Brooke moved away.

Bloody hell, keep James amused. How did one do that? Without... she let the thought drift away and headed for a last-minute powder-room stop.

Jarrad Lyon sold sixty-five books and bragged about the success. He flirted with most purchasers as they waited for a signature—women and men. One young dandy hovered for a while but when Jarrad's charm oozed over a platinum blond with a short skirt, the young man slipped away hoping no one had noticed his momentary infatuation.

Katisse noticed many people's momentary infatuations during an evening where everyone was on their best behaviour but ready for a business advantage, a social interaction that might lead to a beneficial invitation, or something more than just an infatuation. An evening's fundraising where much was raised and, if you had the backing, anything became possible.

Brooke's deodorant worked as hard as she did. There was a good chance she'd scurried a mini marathon as she sweet-talked the volunteers and cajoled the paid staff. Her aim to ensure the evening would raise copious amounts of money surpassed the need to pander to fussy matrons who asked for a calorie count of the chocolate mousse.

Sipping a cup of coffee instead of a glass of water pretending to be champagne, Katisse enjoyed the sensation of heat hitting her throat. She watched Brooke usher the winners of the raffle towards the door.

Katisse knew her efforts had contributed towards the evening being a financial success. She'd worked the room, tittering at silly throw-away lines of guests, pretending to understand the politics involved in the local mayoral elections and ignoring obligatory-sounding flattery—all the time encouraging money out of wallets and off credit cards.

Nodding graciously to the last of the guests while wanting to desperately kick off the too-high-heeled shoes and slump into a soft chair, Katisse wriggled her toes and sighed inaudibly.

With only the cleaning staff remaining to work their seemingly instantaneous miracles, Katisse swapped her empty cup for an offered glass of champagne. She downed it in three swigs—celebrating she hadn't lost the knack of schmoozing wealthy businessmen, or the touch of supposed empathy as young millionaire housewives told of fussy gardeners and arrogant tutors. The promised donations on her clipboard proved that.

'Fabulous. Just fabulous,' Brooke said. 'I knew you'd be... fabulous.'

Katisse raised her glass. 'Glad I could help.'

'I can't remember anyone else, you know, being able to get the rich and not-so-famous to part with their money.' Brooke topped up Katisse's glass and offered more champagne to her husband.

James tipped his glass and waited as it filled. Looking across at Katisse, he spoke softly, 'Yes, quite a talent you have.'

Brooke turned, spoke to her husband, 'Now, James—'

'No,' he said, 'I mean it.' He raised his left eyebrow as he nodded at Katisse. 'Quite a talent.'

Katisse's poker face remained as she said, 'Thanks, James. A girl does what she needs to do.'

James stepped back but as he turned to go, Brooke grabbed his arm. 'Be a dear, take the empty bottle, would you? I want to talk to Katisse.'

'About what?' James's eyebrow sank, turned into a deep frown.

'Never you mind.' Brooke chuckled. 'Maybe I'll get some pointers. See how to get a *husband* to part with his money.'

James glanced between his wife and ex-lover. 'Umm, okay.' He took the champagne bottle, stepped away, glancing back several times as he headed for the kitchen.

'That was fun,' Brooke said.

Throughout the interaction between husband and wife, Katisse stayed silent. Any wrong reaction might have unwanted repercussions. She rolled the champagne around her mouth, swallowing it slowly before speaking.

'Fun?'

'James is so easy to tease. I mean, he simply doesn't know how to say no. I'm sure you remember how much money, *his* money, I used to spend at *La Joie*.'

'Sure.' Katisse took the opportunity to send the conversation in another direction. 'Is your dress from there?'

'This? No. I bought this...' Brooke fingered the lapel of the aqua jacket. 'I don't remember. Anyway, enough of James's money. I just wanted to confirm the time for next week's lunch. I can pick you up, if you like. I'm looking forward to being waited on for a change. I don't even have to do the seating plan. Maureen has it all in hand.'

'Looking forward to it. But I think I might wear joggers. My feet are killing me.'

Brooke insisted the lunch event would be a chance to relax, not having to be concerned about the colour of serviettes or what to do with unexpected guests—Maureen and the other staff at Pearson Agency were the ones paid by the sponsor to worry about every small detail this time.

The following Thursday, Katisse looked longingly at her sneakers but relented and slipped her feet into high heels. 'If men wore these...' She checked her back view in the floor-length mirror. 'If they did, then I'm damn sure they'd suddenly be outlawed.'

Lunch went according to Maureen's plan and Katisse enjoyed the light-hearted chatter—somewhere between gossip and serious state-of-the-nation information—with people she knew by reputation or previous casual interaction.

She caught up with Brooke over coffee and cheese on the balcony.

'Wasn't it great,' Brooke whispered. 'I didn't get one complaint.'

'So far,' Katisse replied, nodding towards a socialite well-known for her insistence for over-the-top personal promotion.

'Well, *she* can just complain to someone else today.'

'Ah, um...' A man in an exquisitely tailored suit tapped Brooke on the arm. 'I have a complaint.'

Katisse sensed Brooke sigh but ever the diplomat, she said, 'Yes? How can I help?'

He looked towards Katisse, then said to Brooke, 'I've yet to be introduced to this young lady.' He held his gaze on Katisse, waiting for someone to speak.

Every one of Katisse's molecules stood to attention. She couldn't look away from his brown eyes. 'I like the young bit,' she said, holding out her hand. 'Katisse. And you are?'

Feeling superfluous, Brooke's head swivelled between the two. 'Ah, Kat... This is—'

'Please to *finally* meet you, Katisse. Lewis Fielder.'

Katisse slipped her hand into his. 'Hi.'

Lewis swapped her right hand to his left and eased her to his side. She moved closer.

'Finally?' she asked.

Brooke shook her head, unable to comprehend the obvious electricity flashing between two people who had just met.

'Would you like...' Lewis rubbed his thumb over Katisse's hand.

'Yes, please.'

'I think I'll...' Brooke coughed lightly, 'fly to the moon, shall I?'

Lewis and Katisse nodded. 'Sure,' they said.

Katisse took her hand from Lewis's. 'You said "finally". Why finally?'

'Can I tell you over coffee?'

'No, I've drunk too much already.' She paused. 'Coffee, I mean.'

'Wine?'

'Can we just sit?'

Brooke followed them from the balcony, across the now-empty event space, and through to the restaurant preparing for an afternoon invasion. 'I'm going,' she said to Katisse. 'Will you ring me?'

Katisse sat on the chair Lewis had pulled out for her. 'Sure,' she said without looking up.

'Good. And Lewis, thanks for everything,' Brooke scowled, not entirely sure why being excluded came with such indignance on her behalf.

Lewis nodded, spoke to Brooke, seemingly reluctant to take his eyes off Katisse in case she disappeared. 'My pleasure. Happy to help.'

After Brooke left and Lewis ordered two green teas, he leaned back in his chair and smiled. 'You know, there's something compelling about you.'

'Really? Compelling? Is that good?'

'Absolutely.' He crossed his arms. 'I was distracted during lunch. Had to ask for people to repeat themselves. I was three tables away, but I couldn't take my eyes off you.'

Katisse fiddled with the linen serviette. 'Have we met before?'

'I don't believe so.'

'I feel this... it's a bit stupid... I mean... if we haven't met before.' She leaned forward. 'I've never had this feeling before. Like I already know you. I was sure... Well, I just thought we must have met.'

'That's why I said "finally". I'm not a young man anymore.' He chuckled. 'Met a whole lot of people over the years.' He lifted his tie, released it, and let it drop. 'And yet, when I saw you I thought, ah, there she is... finally.'

Comfortable in the silence, they drank the tea, enjoyed the view, talked little. Long after the teapot had given up its last drop, they left the restaurant and strolled along the riverside, pointing out the obvious, stating clichés—simply absorbing each other. When the sun slipped behind Kings Park and turned the river a deeper shade of watery blue, he called a taxi for her, then became a statue as he watched the vehicle pull away.

KATISSE'S DIARY

1993

2 July: So easy being with Lewis.

3 July: Don't want to share him with anyone.

18 August: Forever. This time, it's forever. I just know it.

Chapter 32

Three weeks later, after she took her second morning coffee from the machine, Brooke rang Katisse. 'You were going to ring me.'

'Mm, sorry about that.'

'And?'

'And what?'

Brooke grunted. 'We have two events next week. Surely you haven't forgotten?'

'Oh yes, two. Okay. I'll check my diary. What were they again?'

'Come on, Katisse. Maureen emailed you. *I've* emailed you.' Brooke paused. 'It's not like you. Is something wrong?'

'No.' Katisse paused. 'Would you have time for coffee? There's a lot to tell you.'

'I don't like the sound of that. Just tell me now.'

Katisse's impromptu smile flowed down the line. 'It's all good. Well, from this end. I... Look, I'd rather... please. Coffee?'

'It'll have to be in the city. I have a lunch meeting.'

Brooke had her laptop open, fingers clacking over the keys when Katisse spotted her. Katisse checked her watch, pleased to be a few minutes early even after having difficulty saying goodbye to Lewis.

When she approached the table, Brooke nodded acknowledgment and continued typing. Watching Brooke's flying fingers, Katisse ordered coffee and waited.

'So?' Brooke closed her laptop and pushed it sideways. 'This had better be quick. I'm frantic.' She raised her eyebrows in question. 'And I hope you're ready to go through the details for this Society Picnic. We've got nine days.'

Katisse watched Brooke study her face, searching for a clue to the anticipated bad news. Katisse knew her face showed a rare radiance.

Brooke rolled her eyes. 'Are you still seeing Lewis Fielder?'

Katisse jiggled a stationary dance. 'You could say that.'

'Is that why you've been unreachable.' Brooke chuckled. 'My, my. Clever Katisse.'

'Why'd you say that?'

'Quite a catch. He's loaded.'

Katisse opened her mouth but a complete sentence wouldn't come. 'What? You think I... What? No, he's...' She gathered the swirling thoughts. 'No. Well, I don't think so. And, anyway, it's nothing to do with money. I can't...' She folded her arms. 'Never felt like this. Ever.'

'Surely you're not saying it's the "real thing".

'I don't know.' Katisse stirred her coffee unnecessarily. 'We met, what—only weeks ago. Since then, we've seen each other most days. Sometimes, we don't talk much but we have to be together. I can't... I can't see life being worthwhile without him.'

Brooke ran her finger over the lid of her laptop. 'Do you know how old he is?'

'I don't care.'

'I reckon he'll be at least twenty years older than you.'

'I'll admit to seventeen.'

'He's an *old* man.'

Katisse closed her eyes for a few seconds. 'I don't care. I have to be with him.'

'A very *wealthy* old man.'

'He has a fabulous home, but I don't think he's any wealthier than you.'

Brooke crossed her arms. 'You don't know who Mr Lewis Fielder *is?*'

'I know a fair bit about him. But I reckon you're about to tell me more.'

'You know Lewis Pharmaceuticals.' She paused for effect. 'That's his family company.'

Katisse considered this information. 'Didn't connect him to them. Are you sure?'

'Of course I'm sure. Lewis is his mother's maiden name. The money came from her family. And that's where he gets his first name from.' Brooke smirked. 'Surely you didn't think he was a factory worker.'

'No, I didn't. I think we've talked about everything else except money. And anyway, the Fielder name didn't ring any bells.' Katisse steepled her hands, elbows on the table. 'I wouldn't care if he was a factory worker. I have to be with him.'

Tapping Katisse on the arm, Brooke said, 'I hope it lasts.

Marriage is tricky. Are you going to move in with him?'

'I might as well.' Katisse laughed. 'Haven't slept in my own bed for a while.'

'And while you're soaking up this new-found love, is there any time to fulfil your commitments?'

Katisse beckoned to the waiter. 'I'll pay,' she told him before turning back to Brooke. 'I'll not let you down.'

'Be in Maureen's office tomorrow morning. Eight-thirty. With your notebook. This picnic is going to be far from a picnic. You should see the lists of demands. God! Why do we do this?'

'Because your heart is even bigger than James's bank account.' Katisse stood and held out her arms towards Brooke. 'Give me a hug.'

Brooke's eyes widened.

'Yeah,' Katisse said, 'these days, I don't even recognise myself.'

Katisse heard her phone ping, picked it up, and read the message from Lewis:

***I'm home. Are you coming here?**

Or should I pick you up?*

She was on the balcony trying to organise her feelings.

He's an old man. A very wealthy old man. Brooke's words ran continually through Katisse's thoughts. However, as she paced the short length from one end of the small space to the other, she knew the aura of the man overrode *old* and *wealthy* but debated the pros and cons anyway.

She grimaced at the thought of people surmising she had seduced him because he *was* the Lewis Fielder of Lewis Pharmaceuticals. *People will*, she thought. Katisse knew there was a basis for this assumption among "society". After all, hadn't her previous lovers all been wealthy? *Damn it!*

Her phone pinged again:

***Do you still want to go to Cottesloe for dinner?**

Or, we can eat here if you like.*

She replied:

***Cottesloe would be lovely. I promised to share a sunset**

with you. Why not tonight?

Can you pick me up? I'll be ready anytime from six.*

They bought fish and chips and sat on the grass facing the vast Indian Ocean. Lewis had a thermos of tea and Katisse had grabbed a packet of Tim Tams from her underused pantry after she'd let Lewis in.

'So much nicer than fine dining,' he said, choosing a salty chip from the white paper wrapper.

'Perfect,' she said. 'This fish is, yeah, perfect.'

The sun sunk slowly behind Rottnest Island leaving a generous glow, enabling them to amble across the sand while seeing enough to dodge the lace-like edges of the waves.

Katisse squeezed Lewis's hand. 'I found out today that you own Lewis Pharmaceuticals.'

He turned and faced her. 'You didn't know?'

'No.'

'Oh, and does it matter?'

'A little. You didn't...'

'I didn't lie, did I? I mean, we didn't discuss—'

'No,' she said sharply. 'No, I didn't mean that. It's just that...'

He dropped her hand. 'I thought you felt like I do. Katisse, my dear, I can't see life being worth any amount of money without you.'

Katisse touched his cheek. 'Lewis, your money doesn't matter to me. I have enough of my own. Not zillions, but I certainly don't have to ring Social Services any time soon. It's... well, don't you see. People will think I...' She slipped her hand onto his arm. 'I wonder if we could run away. Not have to worry about anyone else.'

'I'm too old to run anywhere.' He smiled at her. 'But if I could, I'd run anywhere with you.'

'Would you really?'

'Yes.' He gripped her hand. 'But it's your decision... young lady. You might not want to be hampered with an old fool... forever.'

She pulled away from him, stepping towards the ocean, standing silently while he wished he hadn't put those thoughts into her head.

He came up behind her and ran his hand across her hip; she swivelled around. With tears dribbling down her cheeks, she said, 'Oh, Lewis. Forever sounds so very nice.'

Wiping the tears from her face, he stared into her eyes. 'What are you saying?'

'I have a question. Are you offering me "forever"?'

He pursed his lips, trying for a serious face. 'I'll have to speak to my lawyer, get the definition of forever, but...' He pulled her into his chest. She clung on, not caring that her tears increased as he whispered, 'I promise, it'll be as long as my "forever" lasts.'

Raconteur

Within the week, Katisse had placed her condominium on the market, donated her furniture to a safety house, and moved in with Lewis.

After spending an hour flicking through the pages of her diaries, reading snippets, recalling embarrassing exploits, she told Lewis they could be thrown out with the other paperwork being shredded.

He disagreed.

Katisse then offered the diaries to Lewis, wanting him to know all about her wayward life so there were no secrets between them. He didn't care about anything but their future—he said he had past misdemeanours of his own, and a hidden past just made her more interesting.

She theorised that if that was the case, the diaries should be burned. He insisted on keeping them. She relented when he offered to place them in a shoebox and relegate them to a high shelf in the enormous dressing room.

He offered to buy her another diary for a fresh start.

She declared she no longer needed to write in a diary as she didn't know how to explain such happiness.

Their intimate wedding ceremony had only forty-five guests. Maureen and Brooke organised an elaborate affair that outshone all society events Lewis Pharmaceuticals had ever sponsored.

Any time the newly married couple spent apart was tolerated, and then only because the outside world demanded their attention.

Society pages revealed many versions of the wedding and the assumed seduction of an older man by a gold digger. They read every version, chuckling at the inane, amused at the insanity of the press.

Several years later, Lewis retired from active business, and Katisse retired from schmoosing businessmen for charity. They continued to attend fundraising ventures—their name on the guestlist often enough to ensure success.

Fish and chips on the beach at Cottesloe became a regular sunset meal. However, old habits and ingrained desires ensured fine dining featured occasionally.

As the years flew by and their wedded bliss lasting, Lewis grew less nimble. Katisse took a drawing class and spent hours by his side, creating delightfully naive artwork of flowers and foliage.

At the age of eighty-seven, Lewis succumbed within three months of a diagnosis. Cancer taking away Katisse's "forever".

Her lonely days ticked over. She ceased drawing and turned to reading, becoming an avid supporter of local authors.

She funded several book launches, championed debut writers who presented stories echoing real-life struggles.

Afternoon soirees, where wealthy women came to be seen, were her forte. Her ceiling-high bookcase showed her generosity to local authors despite many of the signed books remaining pristine.

Then as her body sagged into senior years, she struggled to see a purpose of doing more than surviving each day.

KATISSE'S DIARY

2017

18 October: Today I'm going to a nursing home. End of life stage. End of my fun.

29 October: Stuck here. This isn't quite what I imagined.

18 November: Stupid chest. I think of Mum wheezing her life away—it will get me too.

2 December: Well, it's been quite the journey, as everyone says these days! Journey! Bloody hell—fast train, I reckon.

3 December: Guess there's no sense in continuing. Only boring everyday things happen.

4 December: Maybe I can stir things up. Let's see. Come on, old girl. Stir, stir, STIR.

Chapter 33

'I want my diary.' Katisse pushed away the carer's hands. 'Not now, leave my hair alone. Get my last diary. I might want to write in it.'

'Hang on just a moment.' Andrea ran the comb over the back of the old woman's hair. 'Let's get you settled. Then I'll get your book.'

'Thank you.' Katisse pursed her lips, wriggled further back into the chair, crossed her arms, and watched the young carer put away the brush and lipstick. 'You're so young. What are you doing this weekend?'

Andrea chuckled. 'Flying to Paris.'

'Really? Oh, my goodness. Can I come with you?'

Katisse's memory had the habit of misbehaving. She would stomp her walking stick and curse between broken sentences of frustration. Then she'd laugh and demand those listening ignore her ramblings.

Leaning down and meeting Katisse's eyes, Andrea said, 'Mrs Fielder, I'm not going to Paris. It's your line. Remember. How many times have you growled at me for not saying something like that?'

'Mm, okay then, my dear. Get me my diary, and you can go and pack your bag. Maybe you should fly to Prague. How about that? Yes, let's say Prague in future. It's a wonderful place, full of history, captivating, delightful—'

Andrea interrupted, 'I bet you haven't even been there.'

Katisse nodded slowly, spoke softly. 'No, I'm an old fraud.'

With her diary on her knee, Katisse watched Andrea run a cloth over the bathroom basin. Then flicking open the diary, Katisse called out, 'I can't find my pen.'

'There's fifty pens on the table.'

'Yes, but where's the one I used last time?'

Coming from the bathroom, Andrea said, 'Honestly, Mrs Fielder, you'd think I'm your servant.' She grinned broadly. 'You should call the butler. Or the housemaid.'

They fell into a friendly patter of make-believe most days. Andrea worried that Mrs Fielder might confuse the truth and the fantasy, but what did a bit of harmless chatter, which often ended in laughter, matter when your days were numbered.

The embellishment of situations had started a few days after Katisse Fielder's admission six months ago. The seventy-five-year-old had fallen for the fifth time at home and having no family, Government Services deemed it necessary for her to be admitted to Caldale Retreat—an upmarket home for the wealthy. Katisse had complained vigorously, telling the authorities she could afford as much home help as "they" deemed necessary. Demanding her home be kept in readiness for her return, she agreed to a temporary stay. However, when the luxury of continuous attention altered her opinion, she insisted on being moved from the austere single-bed unit near the ground floor common area to the three-room regency-style unit overlooking the hot tub and exotic garden.

'More me,' she said. 'More like my New York apartment.'

She'd been in this expensive suite for two months and, with a cheeky mixture of imagination and realism, kept the staff on their toes.

A young carer, intrigued by the newest resident, had accepted Mrs Fielder's eccentric behaviour, which other staff found annoying and often time-demanding, as a diversion from mundane chores and uninspiring residents.

'She's a liar,' Gretel said. 'It's impossible to know if all that crap is true or not.'

'What does it matter,' Ann countered.

'Huh, Paris, Rome, New York. Meeting the Pope, Princess Anne. I mean, she's always lived locally. I've seen her file.' Gretel humphed. 'Air and graces, that one. She's just another old lady who thinks because she's loaded, she's more important than us.'

'Pays your wages,' Ann said. 'And as I said, what does it matter?'

'Well, she's got you doing it too.'

Ann folded her arms. 'Reckon my life is bloody boring. Hearing about a trip to the boulevards of Paris or shopping in New York brightens my day. Even if she hasn't been there, it sounds real enough. It's better than dribbly chins and boring bingo.'

As a break from the monotony of drug-affected residents, Ann enjoyed Mrs Fielder's teasing manner.

In the first few days, they'd got through the formality of the ghastly weather, the Eagles win over Collingwood, when Mrs Fielder asked, 'What are your plans for the weekend?'

'Nothing much.' Ann shrugged. 'Working Saturday until late. Sunday? Probably, sleep in, wash my hair, read a book.'

'What, a young thing like you? You should be dancing with a duke or sipping wine with a celebrity.'

'Yeah, right!'

'Listen, my dear. Shake up your life. Imagine something exciting. Talk about the high life.'

Ann hesitated. 'I'll never do that stuff. Why lie about it?'

Katisse waved towards the window. 'Out there... everyone lies. White lies. Little lies. Let me tell you, lies help us fit in, they also can help us stand out. People don't want the ordinary. They want grandeur, excitement—even if it's someone else's.' She took several laboured breaths before continuing, 'Then there's the folk who turn fiction into fact and convince everyone listening to believe it too. And when those lies are too obvious, it makes the hearer of those fabrications feel superior.' She chuckled. 'What about politicians? And the magazine covers! If we believe everything they sprout, my goodness...'

'Yeah, but—'

'No buts about it, girl. I'm not talking about hurting anyone. Who knows, or cares, if you're washing your hair or going to the French Grand National? Certainly not any shop assistant or, for that matter, one of the other staff in this place.'

Running her hand over the dust-free surface of the bedside cabinet, Ann let the thought linger. 'I'm Annie, just ordinary. No one would believe me anyway.'

Katisse cleared her throat, accepted the tissue from the young carer. 'Want to know a secret?'

Ann folded her arms across her chest, stepped towards Mrs

Fielder, nodded, 'Go on.'

'Well, I was born Kate.'

'Kate? I thought…' Ann looked at the name on the door. 'Where did… then… Katisse?'

'Oh, Katisse is my legal name. I had it changed. Then back to Blanchard after being Mrs Macintyre for a minute moment in Scottish history. After the joy of Lewis, I'm happily Mrs Fielder. But, you see, deep down, I'm still "Just Kate". Deed poll can't erase everything.'

Katisse's eyes closed for so long Ann thought the elderly woman had fallen asleep, but she opened her eyes, widened them, and whispered, 'I'm a stupid old woman.'

Ann, about to contradict, shook her head, 'I don't agree, but I don't think there's anything wrong with the name Kate.'

'A bit common, but no, it's not offensive. But I *never* wanted to be "Just Kate".'

'There's a story in there somewhere,' Ann said.

'So many stories. And if you hang around,' Katisse paused, 'or if *I* hang around long enough, I'll tell you a few. Might even reveal something about the Katisse ruse.'

After the two women silently considered the uncertainty of life for a few moments, Ann said, 'Andrea. I'm Andrea. I'm not really Ann.'

'What? Andrea? Why the hell, then, are you stuck with a common name like Ann!'

Despite rules, Ann perched on the edge of a visitor's chair. 'Long story.' She looked down at her feet. 'Well, probably not that long, just ancient. Gran reckoned Andrea sounded foreign. She only called me Annie. Then the rest of the family did.' Her eyes wandered around the room as she continued, 'I felt it suited. Andrea was this exotic creature. I felt like Ordinary Annie.'

Recovering from a burst of coughing and subsequent tears from the pain in her lungs, Katisse whispered, 'You're no ordinary person. I've seen enough in my life to know who is and who isn't.' She thrust her arthritic finger towards Ann. 'Andrea. I like it. Surely someone had the sense to call you such a lovely name.'

'My cousin did. Almost. He said it like, On-drey.'

'Mm, better than Annie.'

'A stupid boyfriend—ex-boyfriend—called me Andy all the time. I hated it. He didn't care.'

'Hence the "ex" bit?'

'Yep. Do you know, he's such an idiot, he didn't even catch on that the chaps at work thought Andy was a bloke!'

'Good riddance. What about your parents?'

'They called me Ann mostly and sometimes Annie-Get-Your-Gun you know, when they wanted me. "Annie get your gun and come here". That sort of thing.' She stood, pulled her ponytail tighter in the hairband. 'Of course, it was Andrea Bettina when I was in trouble. And I'll be in serious trouble if I don't get a move on.'

'Okay, but tell me something, how do you feel with all those names?'

'Got used to it.'

'Yes, but I mean, do you feel different when you're Andrea than when you're Ordinary Annie?'

Ann closed her eyes for a split second, reached for the door handle, then turned back to Katisse. 'It would be wonderful to be Andrea all the time. Not Ordinary Annie. You probably can't understand that, but yeah, it would be nice.'

Katisse waved her finger at Ann again, squinting as she growled, 'Now see here. Get that damn name badge changed. I don't want to see you again unless you have. I won't talk to Ann ever again.' She paused. 'I mean it, Andrea.'

True to her word, Katisse refused to talk to Ann for the five weeks it took for, firstly Ann and then the powers that be, to accept the change. The old woman grunted, nodded, pointed—spoke to the other carers but continued to remain otherwise mute when Ann was around.

The day Ann wore her new name badge, Katisse cheered, clapped her hands so hard it started another coughing fit.

'Well, well, it's about time,' she managed to say. 'Now, Andrea must walk taller, smile more. And I hope to God that you do something decent with your hair when you go out. And lipstick. Why don't you wear lipstick? You never know if a fabulous young doctor will come by.'

Andrea laughed. 'Honestly, Mrs Fielder, you're the limit.'

Katisse pointed at Andrea. 'Don't you dare tell me you don't feel wonderful getting rid of Ordinary Annie! I mean—'

'It's okay, I guess.' Andrea smirked. 'I only did it so you'd talk to me. I still haven't heard all those stories you insist are true. Or the ones you created.'

'One day. One day.'

'Yeah, right.'

'You'd need to have more than half a minute. I have some beauties.'

'What if I come by on my day off?'

'Superb. I expect to see you... when?'

Andrea hesitated before knocking on Mrs Fielder's open door. It wasn't banned, but the hierarchy certainly disapproved of any socialising with the residents. Andrea figured she should be able to spend her personal time however she wanted. As she enjoyed the challenging interaction and wanted to hear Mrs Fielder's stories in full, Andrea ignored Gretel's warning.

'You'll get close, and then it'll all end in tears. You know she's going to die.'

'Not tomorrow, not next week. So, why not? I enjoy her company.'

'You're insane. Why not come to the Sunday session? Lots of us are—'

'Nup. I've already told her I'm coming today.'

Only three steps inside the room, Andrea's breath caught with surprise as Katisse yelled, 'Turn the radio up.' Katisse waved her hand towards Andrea. 'Come on. Before it finishes.'

Andrea placed the takeaway morning tea down and flipped the dial. 'I don't believe it. I would've thought you'd be the last person to listen to a church service.'

'Hush. It's my favourite hymn.'

"Onward Christian Soldiers" filled the room. Katisse's voice crackled along with the first chorus but whimpered to a hum on the last line.

'Well, turn the thing off. Pass me my coffee.' Katisse tugged at the knee rug, then growled her request, 'Turn it off. The condescending preacher will now just be telling me how to get into heaven.'

Andrea chuckled as she placed a coffee and muffin from The Pink Cafe on a tray and balanced it on the old woman's knee. 'And you don't want to go to heaven?'

'Couldn't stand it. Sitting on clouds. Harps! No way, all the action will be in that other place. Not that I believe in all that rubbish.'

'Why listen to Sunday Service if you don't share their faith?'

'It's the singing. I believe in the singing. They have the music first. Always good. Then they can save the souls of others.'

While they sipped the cooling coffee, Katisse's wheezing interrupted the quietness of the morning.

'Good muffin,' Andrea said.

'Don't think I can face mine today. Maybe tomorrow.'

'It'll be stale.'

Katisse slapped away the muffin. It tumbled from the tray to the floor. 'Don't care. Don't care.'

Andrea stood, placed her morning tea on a cabinet near the window, and stepped towards Katisse. 'Come on. You don't mean that.' She picked the chocolate muffin from the floor, tossed it successfully into the bin. 'What about some music? Something more cheerful than hymns about marching.'

'Don't care. Don't care.'

Andrea knelt in front of Katisse, took the cup and put it on the floor. Then, gently taking Katisse's hands, said, 'Please. Tell me another one of your stories. Should I get your diary? Please, Mrs Fielder. Smile for me. I want to hear more about dancing at midnight with a prince. What about Artie? Did he remarry? When did any of your famous friends get on the cover of a magazine? Tell me about Paris. Come on. Please, Mrs Fielder.'

Katisse squeezed Andrea's hands.

'What's so special about that hymn?' Andrea asked.

'Get a chair. I can't stand you begging.'

Katisse's Diary

2017

9 December: Andrea has been transferred. Bugger the bosses. Don't they know I need her?

12 December: This new person isn't Andrea. I want her.

18 December: Andrea came to see me. Life is good again.

19 December: I'll leave my diaries to Andrea. Yes. That's what I'll do.

23 December: Not long to go. Perhaps I won't reach New Year. I feel it. I wonder if I can remember what is truth and where lay the lies?

Truth. Hah. Bugger truth. I hope Andrea can write her own story.

Bugger. Shit. Bugger. Shit. I wonder what they'll say at my funeral.

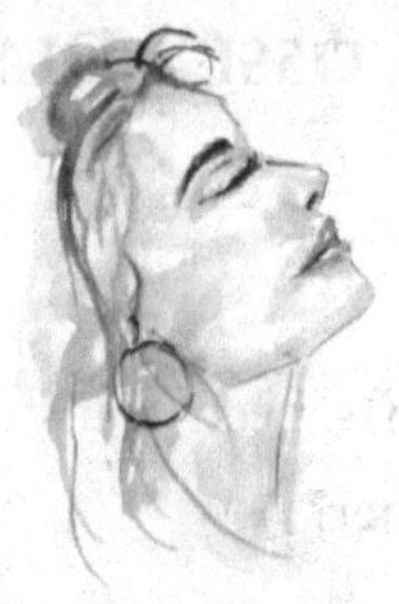

Chapter 34

Andrea's roster had changed again and she rarely saw Katisse in working hours but had grown used to Katisse's quick mood changes over the weeks of regular Sunday visits. She'd become fond of the old woman and intrigued with exploits of unreliable truths.

Katisse admonished Andrea for spending time with an "old bag of bones" instead of "meeting dukes and dandies".

Each visit entailed morning tea from a local café, a courteous inquiry on each other's health before Andrea flicked open one of Katisse's diaries, read the brief notes, and encouraged Katisse to expand. Only interjecting with exclamations of disbelief or questions for more details, the stories mesmerised Andrea. Usually, lunchtime arrived before either woman tired of the interaction.

'The hymn,' Katisse said. 'Nothing exciting there. So very long ago.' She paused, smiled at her memory of a child's first church service where only the song remained. 'There must be something better than that. Let's see. Get the grey diary.'

Six mismatched red diaries lay neatly in the drawer of the carved sideboard. Katisse had always insisted the solitary grey one wasn't to be read by anyone. Andrea had selected it several times, tempted to peek at the secrets while Katisse was in the toilet, but couldn't break a promise.

'The grey one.' Andrea tucked the red one back into place. 'You sure?'

'I said, the *grey* one.' Katisse's raised voice emphasised her insistence.

'Okay. The grey one it is.'

Flicking through the pages, it was obvious most pages were blank. Andrea pulled a chair close to Katisse, opened the diary to the first page, and read, *Today I'm going to a nursing home. Won't be much fun. End of life. End of my fun.* Andrea looked up. 'I doubt that. I'm sure you've had your moments, even in here.'

'Put the bloody book away.'

Andrea looked up in surprise. 'What?'

'I said... well, you heard me. That one is just like its cover. Grey. Not appealing.'

With the diary closed, Andrea waved it at Katisse. 'It's unfinished. Don't you write in it anymore?'

'Not much. The grey depresses me. I didn't want it. That woman, the one who shops for us "poor old dears" refused to take it back. I told her, but no.' Katisse dropped the book on the floor. 'Awful colour.'

Andrea picked up the grey diary, flicked it open, and scanned the ineligible scrawl. 'Would you like me to re-write it?'

Without answering, Katisse grabbed the little book and attempted to put it in the box with the other ones. She stopped, struggling with the action, tossed it towards Andrea.

'Take it. And the rest. You can have all my diaries.' Katisse watched for a reaction. 'You're to have them. Today. Take them today. Don't want those people who pack up my things to get their hands on them. You. Take. Them. Today. I insist. I don't want to see them ever again, you hear.'

'Me?' Andrea placed the grey diary reverently back in the box with the red ones. 'No. I couldn't.' She ran a finger across the spine of the five books. 'Really? Me? Why me?'

'Come. Sit. But bring the grey one again.'

Andrea did as bid and held the diary towards Katisse.

'No, I want you to read something. It's probably... well, the last of the decent writing. Before... before the scribble. Before these damn hands wouldn't cooperate. Read it. Silently.'

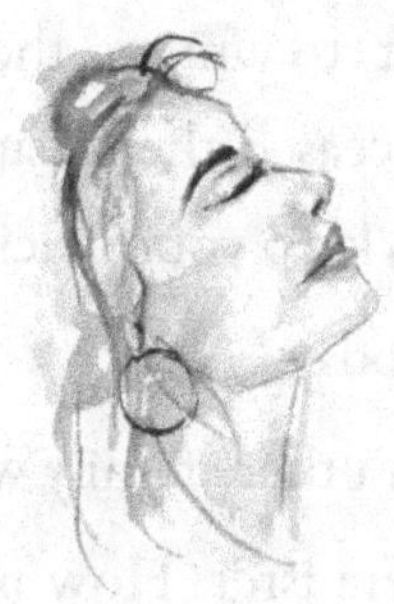

Chapter 35

Laughter and tears fought for prominence—a short giggle won. 'Mrs Fielder, honestly! Your funeral? Come on, I don't believe that.'

'Don't give me that rubbish. You and I both know I've seen my last Christmas. These bloody lungs, they'll be...' her lips twisted in a cheeky grin, 'the death of me.'

'But you're not that old. I mean not like Mrs Chapman, she's ninety-six.'

'I won't get there. Now, don't fuss. My mum didn't last long either. Not by today's standards. She was terribly overweight, never walked if she didn't have to. She'd catch the bus one stop if it meant not wearing out her shoe leather.' Katisse sighed, remembered Syd saying the same thing. A deep breath caught, causing another bout of coughing. She refused the glass of water Andrea offered and wiped the phlegm from her chin. 'It's genetic. This thing that troubles our lungs. It wouldn't have mattered if Mum was as skinny as me. Once she lay in that damn hospital, the curtain came down. It'll be the same for me.' Katisse wriggled into a more upright position. 'That's why I want you to take my diaries. Time is ticking, and—'

'You've got years left to annoy the staff.' Seeing Katisse's moistening eyes, Andrea ceased the teasing and offered her hand. 'Do you really want me to keep your precious diaries?'

'You must take them today.'

'I'm honoured. But isn't there family who—?'

'You bloody know there isn't. How many of the buggers have visited? Total of none! There's certainly no one who would do more than laugh at me.'

'Surely not.'

'Take them. Please... My diaries shouldn't be with anyone else. They wouldn't understand them.'

'Okay, I'll take them. But I have a question. And I need you to answer it honestly.'

'Holy hell, I'm not sure I'm much good at that.'

Andrea pursed her lips, waited.

'What's the question?'

Picking up a random diary, she waved it at Mrs Fielder. 'Is there anything you regret? Something that *isn't* in your diaries. Something you wish you hadn't lied about?'

Katisse attempted to grab the diary but with a yelp of pain, fell back in the chair. Andrea jumped up, dropped the diary. 'Sorry, sorry.'

After flapping away the apology, Katisse spoke softly, 'I don't do regret. It's a waste of time. However, yes, I can see that my life was a little selfish... at times.' She waved away Andrea's attempts at futile disagreement. 'But why shouldn't it be? You only get one shot at it.' She paused, shrugged. 'I like to think I didn't actually hurt anyone. That's the difference, isn't it? Not to have hurt anyone.'

Andrea frowned. 'Maybe.'

'James was a willing participant.' Katisse smirked. 'You can be assured of that. Yes. And Artie, well, marriage was a big mistake. But the man was one sexy bloke. Then, the white lies in between it all. People can be so gullible. You asked about regrets. No regrets about any of it. My ability to "enhance" spiced up my life. I reckon it *was* my life.'

Nodding slowly, she considered her words. 'We're forever being bombarded with media saying, "poor thing, had an awful childhood", blaming the circumstances of birth, unhappy family or financial situation. I can see that it might alter one's perspective. I think it did mine. But to *blame* it! No. I don't blame my childhood. I bloody *claim* it.'

Andrea reached for Katisse's hand again, stroked the skin of the arthritic fingers. 'That's good. That's good. But are you sure there isn't even one tiny thing you wished you could change?'

Pulling her hand free, Katisse said, 'I wish I hadn't had to lie to Fiona. We were good friends. I shouldn't have... That's the one thing that comes close to regret.'

'Fiona? Your friend from typing school? The posh one?'

'The very one. Such a nice girl. Perhaps we would have drifted apart anyway. People do as their lives change, and they move on.'

'And your regret is because...'

'Don't pry.' Katisse wiped away the hint of moisture from the corner of her eye.

They suffered the silence, glancing at each other, Andrea's expression demanding a proper answer. Katisse frowning at the thought of revealing her last secret.

'Come on,' Andrea said, 'last one. I promise I won't ask for anything else.'

'I might not believe that. Not if I start.'

'Then you'll have to start *and* finish.'

Without preamble, Katisse said, 'I took advantage, and then I lied.'

'Advantage? What advantage?'

'The advantage of money. You can simply not know the real advantage of money unless you have it. I always wanted money for what it could buy: real estate, clothes, dinner at the best of restaurants, pretty baubles of the expensive type. My desire for money consumed me. Then, I found out what money can really buy. Power! Power is the ultimate purchase. And that, my dear, is what I quickly learned. And what *his* money bought... was *me*. Then *I* had the power.' Katisse bowed her head, drifted off to memories she would never share. Looking up, she continued, 'Believe me, I paid for that power. In the end, it all became a bit too tricky. Then there was no other way but to tell many lies. You see, there were so many secrets. If I hadn't lied... many lives would have been shattered... I couldn't ruin their fairy-tale life. I had to lie.'

'And you still reckon on not telling me? After those tasty morsels! You can't leave me hanging. I've heard all the others. This one can't be any worse.'

After a sigh that induced another burst of coughing, Katisse waited until her breath became easier. 'Huh! It is.'

Katisse fingered the diary, avoiding Andrea's intense stare and questioning eyebrows. After demanding a glass of water but not drinking any, Katisse grumbled out her acquiescence. 'Might as well go to my grave having revealed it all.'

'Come on, it'll be ages before we'll be digging that grave.'

'I'm not at all sure about that. Before I tell you, you must remember that all this happened long ago. I was very young and… well, bordering on naivety, definitely stupidity.' She nodded with recollection. 'Let me tell you about him. All charm and confidence that one. Bloody full of self-importance under all that Mr Nice Guy. "Experience is valuable," he said. "A lovely young woman like you needs experience," he said. Ah! Fell for that propaganda, didn't I.'

Pointing to the box holding the diaries, Katisse said, 'The red one. Lying flat. Underneath. Sort of hidden.' She smiled. 'And today, I know for sure that you haven't peeked. If you had, you wouldn't be asking so many questions.'

KATE'S DIARY

1969

17 June: All that money. Mine! Mine! Mine! But I will have to put out.

19 June: So that's what sex is when it's done properly. Good God, he could certainly show Peter a thing or... ten!

5 July: Mum is a bit hard to trick. Fortunately, the diamonds look like cheap stuff. She thinks it's a bit sus that I'm late home so often. But hey, she'll soon shut up when I show her the handbag that Mrs Noble (hah!) didn't want. I nearly gave it to Mum. Maybe I should buy her one.

10 August: Seems he has a bottomless pit of money. My advantage. Lovely stuff, money. Bit of a pity I have to bank it. Even have to hide the lingerie he insists I wear. Again, Mum! Regulation ones on the washing line—lacy ones done in the bathroom when she's at work. Good thing they dry quickly. Well, there's nothing of them.

13 August: Who would have thought a little pill would do the trick. See, money can buy anything—even doctors. Another lesson.

25 October: Getting a little tedious. Not the sex. Nup! But the slinking into hotels, avoiding him when there are others around, and the lies—tremendous scenarios—I've had to be totally creative. Even Stan wouldn't believe some of them.

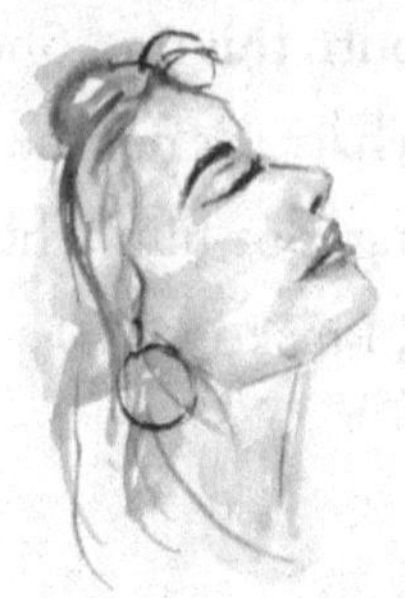

Chapter 36
1969

Kate slipped into the front passenger's seat, running her hand around the edge of the leather seat beneath her legs as Mr Noble started the Merc. She said, 'It's a gorgeous car. I could ride in it forever.'

'Mm, I suppose it is.' His eyes flicked over Kate's face as he turned to sight the exit. 'Not many people comment on it.'

'Sorry.'

'No, no. Don't be.'

Mr Noble eased the car out of the drive and into the street. Kate crossed her arms over her chest, then uncrossed them and fiddled with her watch before sighing softly and crossing her arms again.

'You're a very perceptive young lady. I've forgotten how lovely the car is.'

'I didn't mean—'

With a chuckle, Mr Noble interrupted, 'My first car was a heap of rust on four wheels. Couldn't even open the boot. My mate fixed the driver's window so I didn't get my face blasted all the time.' The car eased through the gears. 'Does your mother have a car?'

'Um…'

'I guess not. Otherwise, I probably wouldn't get the pleasure of driving you.'

A sharp twitch in her chest made Kate frown. 'Nup. Not at the moment. She's between cars.'

Mr Noble nodded slowly. 'I see. So, you wouldn't be averse to me driving you home?'

'I don't mind. It's nice to be seen getting out of this here Merc. Pity no one I know will be at the station.'

Clearing his throat, Mr Noble broke the silence. 'No, Kate, I meant I could drive you all the way home.'

Her eyes widened, without moving she glanced sideways at his profile, then back at the road ahead. 'Why would you do that?'

'It's simple. I have a car. Want to treat a lovely young lady. After all, you did say you'd like to ride in it *forever.*' He patted her knee. 'And while Beaconsfield won't take forever, it'll be further than the station.'

Kate battled between the excitement of being in a car which few could afford, and the fear of cross-examination by Nora when she turned up at home in a car which few could afford. Then, she realised, Mr Noble might expect to be asked in. 'Nup,' she said.

'Kate? Why not?'

'It's not for the likes of me. I mean, I'd give anything to have one. Even a second-hand one. But my street isn't the place for it. Please, just drop me at the station.'

'Okay, okay. If you're sure I can't tempt you. It's a shame as I'd enjoy your company for a little longer. Each time you visit, you're either in the kitchen with my wife, or upstairs with Fiona. I mean, you're an interesting young lady, we should talk more often.'

'Sorry if I was rude anytime. I just didn't think you'd want to talk to us. I mean, you know...' She took in his expensive shoes, his tailored trousers and shirt, and embarrassed by comparison, pulled at the sleeve of her chain-store jacket. 'I might start saving for a Merc, I mean, second-hand, maybe... No, as nice as it is, just drop me for the train.'

'So, you like nice things. Why not? Work hard and the world's your oyster. You're just the one to get what you desire. I can see that.' He patted her knee again, this time his hand lingered. 'Are you sure I can't tempt you to make me your chauffeur for the afternoon?'

Oh boy, I could be so tempted, Kate thought as the car pulled up. She opened the door, got out, but leaned back in to thank him for the lift. 'Tell Fi I'll ring her.'

'Don't make it too long. We love having you stay over. And Kate, enough of this Mr Noble, it's Gene.'

Kate nodded at him. 'Yeah, ta, bye.'

She watched the car pull away and could see his eyes flicking from the rearview mirror to the road. Her chest repeated the twitching sensation and she almost forgot to buy a ticket.

As the train pulled out of the station, Kate sighed repeatedly. She rehashed Mr Noble's conversation. There was something of a strangeness to it. She whispered, "tempt you" three times. What sort of temptation did *he* have in mind? If it had been Peter saying that she'd expect his hands would be wandering inside her clothes, tempting her resolve, tempting her desires. But Mr Noble... Gene? It hardly seemed likely the temptation of just riding from Cottesloe to Beaconsfield in a Mercedes Benz was what he had in mind.

Somewhere in her body nerves fluttered and her face flushed. 'Frigging too old,' she said as she alighted the train, keen to board the bus and get home.

The next time Kate stayed overnight at Fiona's, they spent most of the time either at the beach or in Fi's bedroom.

Not quite sure of the reason for a mixture of apprehension and excitement, after a meal of roast chicken and lively conversation about a protest against dog beaches, she followed her friend into the kitchen, pleased to find only Mrs Noble there stacking the dishes.

Their chatter stopped when Mr Noble entered. 'Ah, what do we have here? Three lovely ladies. My, my.' He stepped towards his wife but his smile broadened as he turned and sighted Kate.

'Kate, you should wear your hair down more often.' Mr Noble ran his hand around his wife's waist and nodded at Kate.

'Now, now, Gene. No flirting with the teenagers.' Mrs Noble held out a mug of coffee to her husband.

Kate didn't know where to look.

'Mum!' Fiona said. 'Dad's just being nice. We spent two hours doing our hair for dinner. Glad *someone* noticed.'

'See, Coral.' He took the mug. 'We have to teach young ladies how to accept a compliment. What would the world be if we couldn't accept niceties with dignity?'

'You're an old softy, Gene Noble. Now, are you able to run Kate to the station? I have things to do for tomorrow.'

Kate stopped wiping the bench, glanced between Mr and Mrs Noble. 'I can get the bus to the train.'

'You are certainly not catching the bus at this hour. It'll be dark before you get home. I'll happily take you. The work I brought home is almost finished. It'll wait until I get back.'

Kate shook her head but no one took any notice. 'Bus,' she said.

'No, Mr Noble's right.' Mrs Noble held out the sugar bowl, indicated his coffee. 'You'll have time to finish that, if you're quick, Kate has to get her things together. Off you go, girls. And Kate, don't forget to take that cardigan I've tired of.'

'I won't,' Kate said, already heading for the door. 'I've never had a designer anything.'

'And Fi, get your dad to stop in at the shop and get some milk. I need some for breakfast.'

'Mum! Dad is old enough and ugly enough to remember himself. And, anyway, I can't go with him. Andrew said he'd call.'

Kate's next breath caught. 'Ring him later.'

'Nup, I'll probably call him. That way, I can talk longer. Not sit around waiting. You know what he's like.' She linked arms with Kate. 'Anyway, Dad would rather not listen to our girly gossip. You can badger him some more about the dog's beach.'

A pocket of silence had them all watching each other. Mr Noble, the first to move and speak, said, 'Well then, that's it. Come on Kate, get your bag.'

'Gene,' Mrs Noble said, 'why don't you drive Kate all the way home? It's late, and it's cold, and who knows what lurks in dark corners.'

Kate imagined homeless men, women tottering on high heels. 'That's okay, Mrs Noble. I'm used to it. Got my kung fu ammunition ready.' She clenched her fist and pretended to box.

Fiona chuckled. 'Kung Fu! Next you'll be saying you've been to boxing lessons.'

'Well, would you believe...' Kate playfully stabbed at Fiona's arm.

'Now see here, Kate. You must let us look after you. Can't have anything wicked happening. It won't take Mr Noble long. Straight there and back and Gene, you'll still have time to bury yourself in those blasted figures before bedtime.

'Well said, my dear. Come, Kate. Let's get the Merc out.'

After promising Fiona she would visit again next weekend, Kate followed Mr Noble to the car.

When they approached the railway station turn-off, Kate spoke. 'Just drop me at the crosswalk. The train's due in about five minutes.'

'Don't you like my company?'

'Sure. Just... I'd hate to overstay my welcome. And... I'm not used to men showing me too much attention.'

Mr Noble nodded, ignored her request, and pulled the car into a parking spot opposite the train station. 'Kate, don't get out. Please. It'd be as easy to drive you home. Mrs Noble said so.'

The air closed in on Kate, her heart raced. She didn't have much experience with men... even with *young* men... but she was sure the tension circling in the small space demanded resolution.

Her left hand gripped the edge of the seat as she turned towards him. She remained motionless as he placed his hand on her shoulder and moved it to the back of her neck, pulling her slightly towards him. She let go of the seat and turned her head. His delicate kiss invited a response.

Kate pulled back, touched her lip. 'I think I'll catch the train,' she whispered.

'Kate, please. I've been wanting to do that for such a long time.'

'And what would Mrs Noble say about that?'

Unsure if the movement of his mouth was a grimace or a smirk, Kate stared into his eyes. 'And Fiona? How can I face her now?'

With his right hand, he caressed her arm. 'You're so beautiful. I could give you so much.'

'And what would you expect in return?'

Seemingly caught off guard by her direct approach, he took a while to reply. 'Kate, Katie... Nothing. Only that we can be together.'

'What? Together! What does that mean? No, I think I'll catch the train.' She grabbed her bag from the floor and opened the door. 'Don't forget the milk.'

Mr Noble ran his hand over his chin as he watched her hurry across the road to the station.

She knew he wouldn't be worried—she had too much to lose by a loosened tongue.

Her diary had only a few of her chaotic thoughts as she processed the encounter. Flashes of expensive jewellery, exotic perfumes, and wonderful clothes filtered through the warning signs going off in her head. One question she repeated silently, *why? Why would a man of his age want to be "together" with me?* Her grin widened, she nodded, approving her next question. 'Why not?'

She tucked the diary back into its hidey spot and stood in front of the mirror. She examined her hairstyle, considered her profile, then twirled as she laughed loudly.

Nora tapped on the door. 'What's going on in there?'

Kate stopped twirling. 'Nothing, Mum. Just...'

Opening the door a smidgeon, Nora asked if she could come in but entered immediately.

'Your hair looks nice. I guess Fiona did it?'

'You like it?'

'It makes you look older. I'm not sure that's a good thing. All the boys will be after you.'

Ignoring the compliment, avoiding the inference, Kate said, 'Mum, look at this cardi.' Kate eased it from the top of her overnight bag. 'It's Edgeworth.'

Taking the cardigan, Nora fingered the soft blue angora. Her frown deepened as she asked, 'Never heard of Edgeworth. A posh brand, is it? And how did you afford such an expensive thing? I hope you're not getting airs and graces by mixing with the likes of the Nobles. Nothing good comes from stepping out of your spot in life.'

Kate snatched the cardigan back. 'It was Mrs Noble's. She gave it to me. Because she knows I can't afford it. She said she didn't wear it. I think she felt sorry for me.' Kate fiddled with the buttons. 'I'm not too proud about how I get nice things, but, one day...' She turned her back on her mother, picked up her bag and tipped the contents onto the bed. 'One day, I won't have to wear these cheap things. One day.'

'Now look here—'

'No, Mum, you look. Look at me. I've luckily got your decent looks and my father's height, but the rest is *me*. And I'm going to make the most of it. I don't care about my current "spot in life". I'm going to get a different spot. You just wait and see.'

Nora sighed. 'I just hope you don't get hurt in the process.' She stepped towards her daughter, held open her arms for an infrequent hug. 'Be careful, Kate.'

A tear threatened as they hugged. Kate moved from the hug before saying, 'Sure. If you can't be good, be careful.' She chuckled. 'I intend to *be* both.'

Some weeks later, when Kate was in the Noble's kitchen about to pour a glass of water, she jumped when Mr Noble walked up behind her and placed his hand on her shoulder. 'Kate,' he murmured.

She faced him. 'Don't,' she whispered.

He took an envelope from his jacket pocket, offered it to Kate.

'What's that?'

'Incentive.'

Five crisp notes peeked out at her. She took the envelope and glared at him. 'Incentive? You'll have to have a better reason than that.'

'Take it, we'll talk later. In the meantime, I'm sure you can buy something pretty to wear,' he said and walked away.

Images of "pretty" dresses from the boutiques she'd entered with Fiona flashed through her mind as she stood at the kitchen bench staring at the envelope.

'Kate,' Fiona called from the hallway. 'Come on, I'm ready.'

With a flick of her hand, Kate shoved the envelope into her bag and as Fiona entered, she poured a glass of water and sipped slowly.

'You okay?' asked Fiona. 'You look... as if you've seen a ghost.'

'Ghost of the future, perhaps.'

'Of the future? I think you mean of the past.'

'No, I don't. The past is past. I'm about to invent my future.'

With Fiona frowning and Kate smirking, Mrs Noble stood at the doorway, eyes flicking from one teenager to the other. 'Something up?'

'Kate's just being Kate.'

Mrs Noble dangled the car keys in front of them. 'I'm sure I don't want to know, but I'm ready if you are. Let's get you to the train.'

Incentive. Incentive. Incentive. The train seemed to clack out the word as it headed towards Fremantle.

Kate knew what it meant. She just wanted to organise her emotions enough to make the most of this new challenge—*or should that be, opportunity.*

Through Fiona's friendship, she had learned the joys of vast amounts of money, how to manipulate men—well, fathers at least, and Kate knew she was a fast learner. She tucked the incentive money into the bottom of her wardrobe; she might be young, but life was not about to pass her by any time soon.

Kate initiated an invitation to the Noble's home for the following weekend. She had rung from the corner phone box, which was *unusually* working and had all its glass intact. She told Fiona she had argued with her mum and *simply had to* get away from home.

'Yeah, sure. Mum's going to her cousins, but Dad will be home. He won't mind. He seems to have a thing for you.'

Kate's pulse pounded in her neck. 'Don't think so. I certainly haven't noticed.'

'He doesn't usually appear from behind his desk when my other friends come around.'

'Your imagination.'

'Not sure. He's a bit of a flirt, my dad.' She laughed. 'So, you'd better watch out.'

'Am I invited then, or not?'

'Course. Bring your bathers, we can go to the beach. Will you stay over?'

'Possibly. You don't mind?'

Fiona sighed. 'Mum wants me to go to Aunt Maisie's with her. Bor-ring! If you come it'll be perfect. I'll get Dad to pick you up. Can you ring when you get to Cottesloe station? That phone box is usually okay.'

A smile built as Kate thought of the money stashed away. Now she was ready to earn it.

The short silent trip from the station to the Noble's home proved electric. Polite greetings preceded surreptitious glances, tilts of shoulders, eyebrow raises, and many half smiles. Fiona prattled on, oblivious to it all.

Gene carried Kate's bag to the bedroom and hesitated at the door, watching Kate as she removed her shoes.

Fiona shooed her reluctant father away, demanded Kate listen to the latest gossip about a new bloke in her father's office who had shoulder-length hair.

After a morning swim, a sandwich for lunch, and a couple of hours lounging in the sun by the pool, Fiona insisted she'd had enough of hanging around home, and as there was *nothing* in the pantry worth eating, they should *beg* her father to take them to dinner—seeing her mother wouldn't be home to cook the meal.

'He'll take us somewhere nice. Maybe we can talk him into the Parmelia. Have you been there?'

'Me? Yeah, right.'

'I thought Peter might've taken you.'

'We've not been out for a while. I think he needs a more... I'm too outspoken for him. I see him with a dutiful wife, slipping out children every second year.'

'What's wrong with that?'

Kate blew a raspberry. 'Holy hell, Fi. Do you honestly want that sort of life? I certainly don't.'

'Yeah, well, let's forget about our future and go talk to *Daddy*.' She wrapped a towel over her bikini, fluffed up her hair, and strutted across the patio. 'Come on, get your arse off that sun lounge. He won't say no to you.'

Mr Noble wasn't impressed at being interrupted but smiled when Kate followed his daughter into his study.

'Young ladies. What can I do for you?' His eyes remained on Kate.

'We were hoping you would take us out for dinner. Somewhere nice.'

He raised his eyebrows, put down his pen. 'Did you now? And where is *somewhere nice*?'

'The Parmelia.' Fiona approached her father, fiddled with his ear. 'Please. Pretty please.'

Kate was waiting at the doorway, expecting '*Please, Daddy*' to be next. However, Mr Noble stood, put his arm around his daughter's shoulder, having not taken his eyes from Kate, and said, 'Can I assume Kate will come with us.' He glanced at Fiona. 'Yes? No?'

'Of course she will. Won't you, Kate.'

'Maybe.'

Fiona glared at Kate.

Kate smiled sweetly, first at Fiona then, with a slight nod which Fiona missed, at Mr Noble. 'Teasing,' she said. 'It'll be educational.'

Mr Noble pointed to the door. 'You two, go and make yourselves beautiful. I'll make a booking.'

When they reached Fiona's bedroom, Kate flopped down on one bed—now considered hers—and Fiona sat on the edge of the other bed. 'Sometimes, I don't understand you. How is going to dinner ed-u-cational?'

Rolling across the bed so she faced Fiona, Kate hesitated. Mr Noble—she couldn't think of him as Gene—not yet—would have got the message. Tonight was indeed going to be educational.

'Never been to such a posh place. A *young woman* certainly needs to know what's what to get on in the world. Starting with the Parmelia.'

As they drove to Mill Street in Perth, Fiona chatted about the last time they'd been to the Parmelia, comparing it to the many other restaurants where they'd dined due to her mother's regular insistence.

Kate sat in the back examining the side of Mr Noble's head. Here was a man who not only used his financial worth but knew his good looks as well. His immaculate grooming and elegant suit impressed Kate.

'Everything okay in the back, Kate.' His eyes caught hers via the rearview mirror.

Before Kate could reply, Fiona swivelled around and said, 'Anything educational to observe from there.'

Catching herself before she poked her tongue at Fiona, Kate smiled. 'All comfortable back here. Learning to like this.'

'Good.' Mr Noble remained silent the rest of the trip, although his eyes continued to dart to the mirror and Kate's face.

Throughout the evening, Kate watched Fiona's familiarity with the elegant and expensive dinner, copying etiquette, relying on Mr Noble's choices. The staff reacted immediately to requests, and the meal couldn't be faulted.

This I could get used to, Kate repeatedly thought.

On arriving home, Mrs Noble didn't hide her disappointment. Dinner at Aunt Maisie's never came close to the elegance of the Parmelia.

The next morning as Kate followed Fiona down the stairs, the raised voices reached them easily.

'I know damn well what it was all about. You're so obvious.'

'Now see here, my dear, it was Fiona who asked to go out. Surely a treat now and again—'

'No, Gene. If I thought the treat was for our daughter... that'd be one thing. You'd better be careful, one more time and you'll be treating me big time.'

Fiona stopped so abruptly that Kate bumped into her. 'Let's go back,' Fiona said. 'We can get breakfast later.'

Every word had reached the two young women, but neither mentioned the conversation as they re-entered the bedroom. They stood awkwardly at the window, feigning interest in a teenager on a skateboard negotiating the curb.

'Sorry about that,' Fiona finally said. 'Happens sometimes. Parents! What can you do?'

'Think I should go. Might be better.'

Fiona grabbed her friend's arm. 'No, don't. If you do, they'll know we heard them.'

'They didn't know we were there. I'll just say I've remembered I promised to help Mum at the shop.'

Fiona laughed. 'I don't think they'll believe you.'

'I can be convincing when I want to be.'

'I reckon you can. But why don't we just go for a walk to the beach? Mum will cool off soon enough.'

When they returned, Mrs Noble was all smiles, Mr Noble having gone to find some important file he'd left at the office.

After consuming a late breakfast, Kate *suddenly* remembered her promise to help her mum at the laundromat. It was just as she predicted—Mrs Noble believed her and happily drove her to the station to catch an early train. Fiona, on the other hand, refused to be anything but polite, rolling her eyes and smirking behind her hand as Kate rabbited on during the short drive about wiping down surfaces and folding discarded laundry.

Some weeks later, Kate couldn't refuse Mr Noble's chauffeuring offer after Mrs Noble had to drive Fiona to an after-hours clinic to have a cut to her hand attended to. She hadn't taken enough care when dicing carrots and sliced her forefinger. Mrs Noble ignored the blood-soaked carrots as she wrapped her daughter's finger and shouted for her husband. Fiona whinged with pain. Mr Noble hurried from his study. Kate stood frozen to the spot, unable to find anything worthwhile to add.

Once Mrs Noble and Fiona had left, Kate retreated to the bedroom with a glass of orange juice. She stood by the window, watching the rush of wind create havoc with the trees.

The door opened, and Mr Noble knocked softly as he said, 'May I come in?'

Kate turned. 'Your house, Mr Noble.'

'Are you okay? Bit of a shock for us all.' His cologne entered with him. 'And for God's sake, it's Gene.' His eyes flicked over her. 'Mr Noble is my rather elderly father.'

She took in his casual steps and noticed the smile in his eyes didn't match the seriousness of his words as he said, 'Fiona will be fine. It's you I'm worried about.'

'Me?'

'You seem so... I guess I can only explain it as "lost"—lost between your life and the one you want.'

Kate chuckled nervously. 'Lost? No, I'm never lost. I know exactly where I'm going.'

He stepped closer. 'And that, my dear, is where I can help. I can help you get there quicker.'

The room seemed smaller. She didn't know why her heart raced. Didn't quite know what to say or seemingly even how to speak.

'Katie,' he whispered. 'You need to understand how beautiful you are.' He reached out and took her hand.

'Don't, Gene.' She pulled her hand away, but her eyes remained glued to his.

'No, you're right. I have no claim. But...'

His fingers touched her face. She looked away; his fingers fell to her shoulder and lingered in the space between her neck and the collar of her blouse. Then, he stepped back.

'I could show you so much. A young woman, a *beautiful* young woman, needs to know so much. Kate,' his voice became husky and deep, 'I could...' He reached out and placed his hands on her waist. She stiffened as he drew her closer. 'It's all about experience, knowledge.'

She let his kisses travel from her neck to her cheek and smother her mouth.

His urgent kisses exhausted her resistance.

The swiftness of his movements as he unzipped her slacks and lowered her panties, left her motionless. His eyes never left her face as he dropped his trousers and eased his erection between her legs. She draped her hands over his shoulders, clutching at his shirt as he climaxed.

He lingered briefly, buckling his belt, while she stood by the bathroom door fumbling with her clothes, not knowing the etiquette of the moment. He retreated quickly, only hesitating at the door long enough to say he'd drive her to the station.

She let the hot water scold her back as she drifted between the pleasure and error of the encounter. A grin followed chastisement but she grimaced at the thought of facing Mrs Noble and Fiona.

Standing in the foyer, staring at the chandelier, the marble stairs, and past the glass-fronted door to where the Merc sat in the driveway, Kate knew exactly what was what. One didn't *run to Mummy* with tales of seduction. Who would believe her? No, this knowledge, this experience, was something valuable, and she'd be the winner—eventually.

During the trip to the station—no offer of being driving all the way to Beaconsfield this time—Gene voiced careful platitudes. He touched Kate's knee several times between the silence.

'I'm sure we don't need to tell—'

'I'm sure *we* don't,' she said. 'I'll keep your secret.'

'Kate, Katie. There's a good girl.' He pulled into a parking bay. 'Now, if you need anything, just let me know.' He pulled his wallet from his pocket.

'Please, Mr... Gene... you will insult me completely. Honestly, not more money.'

'I just wanted to thank you. I can hardly offer you dinner and dancing. Please, take it. Buy yourself something. I like to see you in something lovely.'

With one hand on the door, Kate tossed up between *something lovely* and self-respect. Without a second consideration, she said,

'Well, since you insist, Gene. Maybe I will. Just a *little* something.' She couldn't even recognise her simpering voice. It reminded her of Fiona saying, '*Please* Daddy'. *Quick lesson learned*, she thought as she took the folded notes. Avoiding her desire to count the bulging fold, she slipped it into her purse, leaned over, kissed him on the cheek, grabbed her overnight bag from the floor, and opened the door.

Feeling a little guilty about the abrupt exit, she stopped at the station entrance, turned around, and waved. She noticed Gene hadn't started the engine but sat rubbing his chin, his shoulders hunched.

Ringing the next day to inquire about her friend's injury, Kate hoped Gene wouldn't answer the phone. Her luck stood, and Fiona was all giggles as she related the tale of stitches, medication and cute doctors. She begged Kate to visit during the week, but Kate insisted she needed to keep looking for employment.

When Fiona turned her attention to the weekend, Kate said she'd have to stay home as her cousin Veronica was visiting, and she was obliged to spend time with her as Nora was working.

Running out of excuses, Kate said she'd come the following weekend, 'perhaps just Saturday', but wouldn't stay over. The begging continued, the excuses continued, until Fiona demanded to know why *her best friend* suddenly didn't want to visit.

'It's like this, Fi. I feel like I've worn out my welcome.'

'Fiddlesticks. Mum loves you. She's even made coconut slice for you. And Dad keeps asking when you're coming around.' Fiona paused for effect. 'You're my best friend. Or supposed to be.'

'Well, maybe we can see each other, you know, at the beach or in town.'

'And how are you going to get to the beach. You might as well come here.'

After silence, Kate said, 'I can't, Fiona. I just can't. It's not right. Taking advantage and all.'

'You're not! And I demand to know the real reason. Kate, please. Kate—'

'Sorry, Fi. Really, I am. Look, I'll ring soon. Meet you—'

'Don't bother. Just don't bloody bother.'

The phone went dead. Kate walked from the phone box, tears building, but a bigger twitch built in her stomach, bigger than she'd previously thought impossible. She shook her head as she put the key in the door lock. 'Bloody hell!'

Raconteur

Kate didn't tell Andrea about the other times spent at Gene Noble's whim. He had the habit of coming home unexpectedly, most times when Fiona had excitedly announced that Kate was visiting midweek. He'd slip her envelopes of money with instructions on when and where she should meet him.

A resourceful man and, despite the inconvenience of no telephone, he found ways to intercept her movements—insisting she join him at exclusive hotels in the city where secrets were kept, as a matter of course, by smiling receptionists and hovering waiters.

She obliged, quickly understanding just how money could buy anything—even prescriptions for contraception for a young woman who wasn't your wife.

Kate's bank balance increased significantly, as any extravagant spending would have seen Nora issuing an inquisition. Gene would have given her everything—well, anything that wouldn't rock his proverbial family yacht.

The affair dwindled despite his generosity. She got tired of the clandestine meetings and his time demands, and she certainly didn't want a forever with this man. After a tiresome disagreement, she declared her "education" enough to go on with.

She knew she had the upper hand, and with barely more than a twinge of guilt, she insisted the affair was over.

After more contrived arguments with Fiona, the final slam of the phone had announced their friendship over.

Chapter 37

Andrea hadn't moved more than her face muscles as she listened to Katisse's explanation of the diary entries. She'd gasped, raised her eyebrows, and shook her head, sometimes in unison, unable to reconcile this story with the women she'd come to love.

Katisse shrank as she delivered the tale of her regret. 'That man,' she said several times before folding her arms and declaring the story had been told and now it was time to forget it.

'But surely he shouldn't—'

'No, I was as much to blame.'

'No way!' Andrea stood. 'No frigging way. A married man? Taking advantage!'

Wriggling up straighter, Katisse said firmly, 'You're completely wrong. I knew, at least thought I did, what I was doing. And how quickly I grew up after that.' She fiddled with her rings, a grin emerging. 'I totally used him but had a lot to learn. It came in very handy over the years.' She smirked. 'I certainly jumped a few lessons with him in charge. Very nice lessons they were, too!' Katisse nodded slowly, memories dancing behind her closed eyes.

'I still think he was totally out of place. Why didn't you say something to—'

'What?' Katisse's eyes opened wide. 'What? Disrupt a family? Spoil my source of income? As I said, I used him. Got what I wanted.'

'But... your friend? Fiona?'

'Well, that was awkward. I did visit Fi a couple more times. We smoothed over our arguments but it wasn't quite the same. I had to be careful with everything I said. This made our get-togethers a bit stilted. And she couldn't quite overcome an affected attitude to money when I was around. Didn't quite pull off the attempted middle-class status she was going for, supposedly to make me feel more at ease.

'Eventually, Gene rarely surfaced midweek. I don't think Mrs Noble twigged. She seemed as upset about my lack of visits as Fiona.' Katisse sighed. 'A real nice woman. She deserved a better husband.' A smirk snuck across Katisse's face. 'But, hey, perhaps she was living the perfect married lie, knowing exactly how her bread was buttered—definitely with the bonus of jam and cream.'

'You reckon she knew and didn't care?'

'Not necessarily that she didn't care, but the argument we heard seems to say she knew something, but not *my* dalliance.'

Andrea chuckled. 'Dalliance! Don't hear that word these days. And what about your mum, do you think she knew about it?'

'Nora? She had no idea. She was more worried about me getting home to make dinner, so she didn't have to do it.'

'That's unkind.'

Katisse humphed. 'You're right. I do think I could have done more for her. But she could be so damn annoying. We never did see eye to eye. Certainly not very often. And talking of her thoughts about my visits to the Noble's home, she did wonder how I could afford labelled clothes. Always quizzed me. Saying I was getting too big for my boots.' She chuckled softly, avoiding another bout of coughing. 'Mrs Noble didn't know how often her cast-offs came home with me.'

'You're incorrigible. You mean you bought clothes with his money and used his wife as an excuse.'

'You'd better believe it.'

Katisse's shoulder suddenly sagged. 'But Fi. I honestly am sorry I had to lie to Fi. She *was* my best friend. But how could I blow the perfect father image to bits? I mean, that's what would have happened. No, I couldn't have done it.' She straightened her back, looked Andrea in the eye. 'Regret? No, after thinking it through, the answer to your question is a definite "no". I did what I had to do.'

Andrea packed the diaries into the shoebox and kissed Katisse's cheek. 'See you next Sunday. Now you behave. No booking tickets to Paris... or Prague, for that matter.'

Katisse died two days later. Andrea stood in Mrs Fielder's room and cried, unable to believe such a strong-willed person could be gone. 'No more stories,' she repeatedly whispered.

At Katisse Fielder's funeral, more nursing home staff gathered than family or friends. Three distant relatives appeared, argued over the few pieces of furniture, and shed a few obligatory tears as they listened to a glowing eulogy prepared by an uninformed celebrant.

Indignation, followed by a threat of legal action, extended the settlement of the will, but Katisse Fielder's lawyer held a water-tight document.

Andrea Simpson was granted fifty thousand dollars with the legally worded instruction stating the funds were to be invested and the profit spent only on travel.

Pearson Agency gratefully accepted a lodgement of funds on behalf of several charities, with Katisse's generous bequest topping up the millions she had previously schmoozed from unsuspecting businessmen over many years.

La Fin

In the passing years, Andrea followed Katisse's example. She flew to Paris and Prague. She happily danced at midnight with the prince of her heart. And after reading Katisse's diaries again, she spread a trickle of ineffectual lies. Andrea remembered the details of the cryptic diary entries, laughed at hidden adventures, and held back tears as loss resurfaced.

She understood that somewhere between the truth and the lies was a life well lived.

YOU'D BETTER BELIEVE IT!

Being a writer can be a lonely slog—except for the myriad of characters muddling the brain, demanding attention and recognition!

A begging storyline often distracts from interaction with other people, but a writer needs a *network*.

I've been extraordinarily fortunate to find those with a similar mindset in Gosnells Writers Circle and Writefree Women's Writing Group. Since 2008, they've encouraged, inspired and often, just been there when needed. Thank goodness. Otherwise, the journey from my first novel to *Diary of Lies* would have been a lot less enjoyable and considerably more error-prone.

Family ensures a grounding amongst all the creativity. Their understanding of my writing indulgence is beyond evaluation. Hugs.

And friends. The ones who are generous in camaraderie without counting days of absence. The ones who bring joy and laughs. I am lucky to have many.

I'm proud to be a Dragonfly. *Diary of Lies* is the second publication with Dragonfly Publishing, and I thank Lisa Wolstenholme and Rebekah Sheedy for their expertise and professionalism, all given within the embrace of affinity.

With a *Diary of Lies* reference—I love that Graeme is my *forever*.

My appreciation and thanks to each and every one of you. Without your support, this whole writing adventure may still be in draft form.

And that's the truth.

ABOUT THE AUTHOR

PERTH-BASED Barbara Gurney is a fiction writer and poet.

Her novels are diverse in their storyline, but all have a connection to people and places, to desires and self-growth.

She tackles everyday characters who see beyond reality or, in her newest novel, *Diary of Lies*, a main character who creates her own reality.

The idea for *Diary of Lies* came from considering a response to the question, "What are you doing tomorrow?" Our answers are invariably truth-based. But what if we embellished: "Having dinner with the Premier" or "Jetting off to Hawaii?"

Who cares? No one, really. That is the assumption—until they get out of hand.

Having fifteen publications on her shelf, and many awards on file, she's pleasantly gratified at the success of her writing.

She becomes a writing, painting hermit during the Western Australian heat, but is generally open to coffee and cake on any given day!

OTHER WORKS

Fiction

2013: Road to Hanging Rock

2017: The Promise

2018: Ribbons of Love

2019: Lessons of the Universe with Imogene Constantine

2020: Dusty Heart

2021: Doors of Prague

2022: The House on Redhill Corner

Poetry Collections

2012: Footprints of a Stranger

2015: Life's Shadows

2020: Seeking Self

2023: Brushstrokes of the Mind

Short Story Collections

2018: Purple and Other Hues

2020: The Green Book of Short Stories

2020: The Blue Book of Short Stories

www.ingramcontent.com/pod-product-compliance
Lightning Source LLC
Chambersburg PA
CBHW010256100726
47904CB00011B/2623